Kate Mathieson is an Australian author whose memoir *Ways to Come Home* was published in September 2017 through Ventura Press/Simon & Schuster. It was a finalist for the Finch Memoir 2017.

In a past life, she interviewed 90s celebrities for *Dolly* magazine. This is her first novel.

@katemathiesonauthor

Just As You Are

KATE MATHIESON

OneMoreChapter

One More Chapter
a division of HarperCollins*Publishers*
The News Building
1 London Bridge Street
London SE1 9GF

www.harpercollins.co.uk

This paperback edition 2020

First published in Great Britain in ebook format by
HarperCollins*Publishers* 2020

Copyright © Kate Mathieson 2020

Kate Mathieson asserts the moral right to
be identified as the author of this work

A catalogue record for this book
is available from the British Library

ISBN: 978-0-00-832845-0

This novel is entirely a work of fiction.
The names, characters and incidents portrayed in it are
the work of the author's imagination. Any resemblance to
actual persons, living or dead, events or localities is
entirely coincidental.

Set in Birka by Palimpsest Book Production Ltd, Falkirk
Stirlingshire

Printed and bound in Great Britain by
CPI Group (UK) Ltd, Croydon CR0 4YY

All rights reserved. No part of this publication may be
reproduced, stored in a retrieval system, or transmitted,
in any form or by any means, electronic, mechanical,
photocopying, recording or otherwise, without the prior
permission of the publishers.

To every girl in the world – be fabulous.
Do the things. All the things.
And always wear cute knickers – just in case.

DUNDEE CITY COUNCIL

LOCATION

MOBILE

ACCESSION NUMBER

CO1 031 520+

SUPPLIER	PRICE
ASIC	£8·99
CLASS No.	DATE
82391	10 11 20

Chapter 1

O n the first morning of February, I woke up drooling on
a stranger's arm.

'Oh God, sorry.' I said, horrified, trying to wipe off the
small patch of my saliva from the strangers' navy-blue jumper.
Shit, it looked like cashmere. Hoping I'd got it all, I looked
up at the man whose arm miraculously tasted like mint
toothpaste and wood shavings.

His steely blue eyes were staring at me, a hint of shock
glimmering across their surface. His skin was smooth and
tanned. His hair was short, slightly wavy and styled to the
right, a light blonde like white chocolate. He was well built,
like a fit, broad Swede who biked everywhere and sailed
yachts. He was wearing brown boat shoes, beige linen pants,
and a thin, navy-blue wool jumper which I had just salivated
on. Everything about him screamed 'expensive'. Including the
large titanium watch on his tanned, left wrist. He would have
been about thirty-five, maybe a little older.

I wiped my mouth quickly, eliminating any traces of sleep
saliva from my face. *What was Thor doing in economy?* And
how had I not noticed him when I'd sat? But then I remem-

bered, I'd taken a valium because I'm not a great flyer and I'd fallen asleep as soon as I sat in the middle seat. And here he was now that I'd woken up, perched on the aisle like a glowing angel.

Thank you, thank you, thank you. I'd been praying the universe would find me someone. MY PERSON. And here was this Scandinavian Norse God, deposited next to me on a jumbo jet. Of all the seats, in all the planes. Here we were.

We both looked down to where I'd been lying on his arm just moments before. Small little saliva marks had dried on his sleeve, like salt did on your clothes after being at the beach. He took a tissue, pulled a face and tried to wipe away my mouth imprint.

'I should at least have waited until you bought me a drink first,' I joked awkwardly, readjusting so I was back in my seat.

He looked at me strangely. 'The drinks are free.' His voice was low, gravelly, and had a slight Northern European lilt.

'Shall we have one then?' I said hopefully. I would never usually be so presumptuous, to ask a *gorgeous* man, to have a drink with me after I'd drooled on his arm, but it seems the valium had reduced my filter to zero.

'It's 4 a.m.' He said curtly, reacting exactly how I would too, had some stranger left their tongue lolling about on me.

'Well yes in Australia, it's 4 a.m., but somewhere else in the world it's happy hour.'

He paused for a second, before finally saying 'I suppose.'

Oh God, isn't this how lifelong romances begin? Yes, we met on a plane. Your mum drooled on me, but she was adorable. I couldn't help but love her. Yes, your dad was a tricky one at first, but after being single for so long, I thought why not, and suggested a drink – how could he resist?

With a flutter of excitement, I flicked my light on and hoped the attendant would arrive quickly, before he changed his mind.

A slightly irate, and brusque flight attendant arrived at my seat, with a curt, 'Yes?'

'Bloody Mary please.' I said and looked over at Norse God, hoping she'd think we were together, a couple, a *thing*.

'Water and a whisky.' He smiled and it was glorious. Glorious teeth. Beautiful lips. It seemed to melt her too because she almost skipped away saying she'd be 'Back in a jiffy.'

'So, what do you do?' Norse God asked.

'Well I ... um ... I'm travelling.'

'I gathered that, considering you're on a plane.' He stared at me, up and down. I was hoping my long, dark blonde hair wasn't the humid mess it had been in Thailand, even in the airport – humidity did bad things to my hair. I instantly regretted the, *lets wear something comfy on the flight* idea and hoped he didn't mind my oversized black jumper, white singlet top and black stretchy leggings.

'I meant, what do you do for, uh ... income?'

Perhaps he was struggling with the thin cabin air, or he'd taken a valium too, because I thought, *did he just ask what I did for money?*

'Gentleman first.' I smiled at him, thinking I couldn't tell him I'd most recently been working at Los Tacos in London, where the Mexican/Spanish fusion of fast food meant the kitchen deep fried everything before it went out; enchiladas, burritos, tacos, you name it – they were cooked, or worse microwaved, and then dipped in a vat of bubbling oil until they were crunchy. It was like serving a heart attack on a plate, but people gathered, usually very drunk people, for a plate of golden crispiness, stuffed with low-grade minced beef.

I shuddered remembering all the double shifts I'd had to do, just to be able to cover my rent and save for my next shoestring trip to Europe. I'd eaten pot noodles for breakfast, and free heart-attack tacos for lunch and dinner. Oh, the glorious life of a backpacker. Before that, I'd been a little more successful, working for a few years as a glorified filing and coffee girl, aka PR Assistant, but when the company hit a downturn, I was made redundant. And I needed another job pronto. But no one was willing to hire someone whose visa was almost up – hence why I ended up at deep fried Los Tacos hell.

'I'm a buyer for clothing companies. Spend a lot of time in Asia, India, but now on the way back to meet some friends for a holiday in Fiji, before I'm off to New York.'

Yep. I definitely couldn't tell him about what I'd really been doing for work.

I jumped in before he could ask about me again. 'Family? You have kids?'

A wife? I asked silently.

'No kids. Single.' He shrugged.

'Oh?' My stomach flipped. Maybe this *was* happening. 'Me too.'

'So, you didn't say what you did? Or where you're off to?' He said.

'I'm heading back home to Sydney, via Fiji, after travelling for quite a while.'

'How long?'

'Seven years.'

'Wow. Where did you go?'

When I first left Australia, all those years ago, I went all 'Girl Meets World', being single and independent, trekking around Argentina, Chile, Peru and Bolivia. In Panama, I got a job at a bar, and there was an Irishman I liked – but I think I liked his accent more than I actually liked him, and despite some flirting, nothing ever happened. I did a whirlwind tour of the USA, shoestring style, before being persuaded by friends to join them at their swanky new villa in Bali.

Bali was hot and humid, full of post-career, corporate hipsters obsessed with yoga classes and shots of turmeric juice. At my yoga class, or the local market where I sold jewellery and bags, everyone smelt like sweat and none of this laid a good ground for romance. The closest thing to a crush was a drunken kiss with an English backpacker, who thought my name was Alyssa for the first hour. He was quite good-looking and funny, until he decided to have five vodka shots in a row, and passed out on the sand.

The only other thing of note happened during a full-body massage from Wayan, a local healing man. My towel slipped off accidentally as I was turning on the table, exposing one pale boob to the elements. He rushed out of the room, blocking his eyes, saying, 'Sorry, Miss Emma, sorry,' as if he'd tugged the towel himself and now had to deal with the nightmare consequences of this action. This was not the idea I had in my head when I read in *Cosmopolitan* magazine – that no matter how you look when you're naked, men aren't going to complain. Nope, they're just going to rush from the room screaming.

After two years in Ubud, I flew to the UK, where I travelled around Wales and Scotland, and learnt I had a love for whisky and was especially fond of haggis.

I was adamant that I didn't want to live in London. London was just a larger, busier, more historical version of Sydney. And I needed something entirely *different*. Although my friends urged me not to, I moved to a small riverside town by the border of Wales, where everyone lived in quaint little cottages, and it rained a lot. I rented a granny flat from a lovely family who had a veggie patch in the backyard – my dream – but the winter seemed to go on forever and froze all the seeds, so nothing ever grew. I spent days drinking tea, and painting the misty, rainy moors – and I wasn't bad. In fact, I thought my paintings turned out really well, and even considered selling them at the local markets, but in the end, I totally chickened out.

That life was glorious. No men though, unless you count balding fifty-something businessmen at the counter in Boots, who raised their eyebrows at me as if they were looking for a bit on the side. Erm, no, thanks. (Embarrassingly I later realised this eyebrow raising was probably due to the fact that I'd been queuing from the wrong side of the counter, accidentally jumping in front of people. Apparently, the English hate queue jumpers but are far too polite to actually say something.)

After a few months by the river, my bank balance had dwindled – living in the UK is a *lot* more expensive than Bali. And even though I tried my best, I couldn't get a job. Turned out the town only wanted engineers and concreters, and I can't even pour a drink without spilling it, let alone a concrete slab.

Down to my last few hundred dollars, I took the train to the city. London. Where everything was grey. In a small windowless office, I was interviewed by a senior manager for a public relations role. I'd worked in marketing in Australia as an assistant before I'd left, so I'd seen a lot of PR and events, but not actually *done* much more than send emails and organise people's calendars and travel.

When they offered me the job on the spot, I said, 'Absolutely!'

I moved to London and into a house of ten people. Ten. And it still cost more than half of my salary for a teeny room, with a single bed and a tiny window. There was even a queue to get into our damp small shower every morning (thankfully, I had learnt queue etiquette by then, because that kind of behaviour in a house of ten people would probably get you stabbed at night).

I smiled at Thor. 'I started off in South America, travelled for a while through the US, and Bali, then flew to England and, of course, around Europe. I loved it – the food, the people, the mountains, especially the smell of pine forest in the middle of Winter in Austria, the Alps are *so* beautiful.'

'That's a lot of travelling.' He paused and lowered his voice. 'Isn't it horrible being cramped back here in economy? It was a last-minute flight for me, and business class was full. You too? And how did you save up enough to stay in hotels for seven years? You must have some job.' He leaned in excitedly, as if I was about to tell him I was heir to a throne.

Yep, Thor seems to be all about the dollars, I thought. Well, this love affair will be short lived then. I looked at him and said in a small voice. 'I didn't live in hotels. I lived in a house in London with ten other people. I worked at a Mexican fast food restaurant, and I spent most of my travels staying in hostels, because I was backpacking.'

He laughed as if I'd told the funniest joke, throwing his head back and slapping his knee. When he saw I wasn't joining him, he stopped abruptly. His lips turned down slightly in disgust.

'Backpacking.' He said, like someone would say 'Urine Drinker'. 'Aren't you too old for that?'

He sat back, grabbed the inflight magazine, opened it and pretended he was deeply absorbed in an article entitled 'Top Beauty Spas in Copenhagen'. *No wonder he's single,* I thought. He was most definitely *not* my person.

When the flight attendant arrived with our drinks, she must have sensed the tension. Couple's fight. Instead of being the soft understanding type, she was the other. The Swooper. Diving onto my once-potential-boyfriend like an eagle spotting fresh prey. She plonked down my Bloody Mary without a look, and then handed Norse God his whisky, so her hands met his.

8

'Sir let me help you with anything else you need. More pillows? Blankets?'

I drank my Bloody Mary quickly and loudly, so the sound of straw slurping interrupted any potential romantic spark. In my mind I was saving her, because if backpacking didn't please him, I'm sure flight attendant-ing wouldn't either. But she didn't pick up on that because she looked at me painfully. He stared through both of us, as if we didn't exist. He downed his drink, passed her the glass, curled up away from me and towards the aisle, and went to sleep.

For the last two hours of the flight I watched *Bridget Jones's Baby* again, so I could remember that maybe it did work out for thirty and forty-something singletons, and when I cried and got puffy, I told The Swooper I had allergies, and asked if she couldn't bring me an aspirin and another Bloody Mary.

I finished eating my delicious minty watermelon and took a last sip of milky coffee. The sound of the sea in the distance, crashing waves, and then the roll of the tide on the sand, was like a lullaby. I felt the sun beat down upon my skin, the rays making my muscles melt, thinking, *I'll just close my eyes for a bit.*

When I woke up the sun was almost behind the hill. I'd spent the entire afternoon sleeping? Oh, well, that was the beauty with holidays, it really didn't matter. Suddenly, I realised I'd spent the whole day on the balcony day bed, in the sun. Oh, God – my skin! I rushed to the mirror, expecting to see lobster red, but thankfully I'd put on a thick layer of sunscreen before drifting off, and instead I'd gone a slight brown with only a hint of small red around the chest. At least I no longer looked like a goth.

The Fijian air was warm and humid, even at night, and I sweated just pulling on a maxi dress and throwing my long, wavy, dark blonde hair, which was now huge and frizzy – as big as a planet and twice the size of my head – into a loose, messy bun.

The pathway below my room gave way to a lush fern garden, beneath a strand of palm trees. A short sand walk took me to a soft white sand beach. The sea was calm and frothy, small waves washed up on the shore, but otherwise it remained flat and glassy. I kicked off my shoes and walked into the water, feeling the waves wash with warmth over my bare feet. I looked up at the sky and put my arms up and shouted, 'YEAA!' This was the sense of freedom I loved, the newness, the variety, places that were beautiful and where I could marvel at the world. There was so much sky out here. So many places to breathe.

Further out, someone was fishing off a dock. I thought about raising my hand in greeting but then thought better of it. What local wants a strange sky-yelling tourist waving at them as if they were long-lost BFFs?

Thinking of BFFs, I was stunned to realise I'd left the UK without even telling Maggie or Tansy, my best friends in Sydney, that I was coming home. They had no idea that right now I was standing under a full moon in Fiji. This wouldn't have happened before when we were single and free, nope, the whole gang would have been together, probably downing Pina Coladas or doing shots of something terribly girly, like Malibu.

But now there were kids, lots of kids, and my friends were mothers – busy, tired, distracted. Before I'd left, they'd all been married and had baby bumps, and little ones running around. The truth was, we'd all lived in the same city, but emotionally it was as if the Grand Canyon had opened up between us and our lives had all fallen away from each other.

Would it always feel this distant? I felt a bit like crying, and you can't cry on a holiday. It's simply not allowed. In true London fashion I knew what I needed to buck up – a stiff drink.

The sun had set and the night sky was scattered with stars. I headed to the open-air beach bar for the complimentary welcome drinks. A swarm of people – mostly couples, some with kids – were standing about chatting and meeting each other. The women had on long dresses and strappy gold sandals, the men had beige shorts and polo T-shirts, with jumpers slung around their shoulders. I started to laugh because they all looked a bit like each other, and then I felt sad again, because if my friends were away with their families they'd look like this too, which made me miss them even more.

Right, Emma, I told myself, *get a grip.* I thought my floral maxi dress might be making me weepy, the way it was all floaty, so I went back to the room to change into my shorter, black wrap dress and applied some red lipstick and two coats of extra-curl mascara. Although I would never have a thigh gap, or wear size eight jeans, at least I'd won the genetic lottery of eyelashes: mine were super long and everyone always commented on how they framed my sea-green eyes. My friend

Tansy had once said my eyes were so beautifully large that I must have been a cow in a previous life. I wasn't sure how to take that, because really it sounded quite awful, but she assured me it was a very good thing and with her smaller, dark eyes she was incredibly jealous.

Back at the beach club, I marched straight up to the bar and ordered two whiskys. Neat and straight up. I downed the first one and it felt like fire in my mouth. I love that feeling. So, I downed the second one. Dutch courage. I didn't know a soul here. Was I expected to just go up and start chatting to random couples with kids? And what do you say? Hello, how's your tan line? Your hair in this humidity? Which one is your husband?

Husband. I'd almost had one of those, I thought. But then, I shook my head, and thought *No, Emma, now is simply not the time to think about that.*

Anyway, I didn't want to focus on the past. I wanted to figure out my life. Plan for the future. As soon as I landed in Sydney, everyone would be asking me – what now? What next? And I wanted to tell them, I'm staying. I'm settling down. I'm doing what you've always wanted me to do. Tansy had always joked that I'd had wings for feet, because I'd been struck by the travel bug ever since my first trip at nineteen, to Lake Tekapo, a creamy spearmint glacial lake in the middle of New Zealand's South Island. It had been a beautiful, pictur-esque small village, with snow-capped mountains dotted all around it, and the most wonderful spring lupines with cherry pink and smashed violet blossums. I still remember holding a warm coffee, and eating a freshly baked cheese scone, sitting in front of that lake just after dawn as the sky turned a firey red, the biggest grin on my face. It was so peaceful, and it made me feel like there was nowhere to be, and nothing to do – like I had all the time in the world.

From then on, I travelled whenever I got the chance – Fiji, New Zealand, Vanuatu, Japan. It was mountains that tempted me, or large sandy beaches, places I could enjoy the peace. I liked silence. Places I could get out my makeshift easel and paint, or just take a white pad and sketch the landscape in charcoal, or pencil, or pen – whatever I had with me. It was like my own little meditation and zen, just me and nature.

Who knows how I'd recently ended up in busy, bustling London. Sometimes, on the weekends, I'd take the train to France, to the countryside just for the day, so I didn't have to hear the sounds of the tube, the midnight sirens wailing down the street. I wanted to stay every time, but London called me back – cities offered jobs, opportunities, they were the places you could earn as much money as possible, and 'make it'. I'd move to a small country town in a second if I could. I'd tried before in Wales, but I didn't have any skills or trades, and no one in a small town seemed to want to hire someone who wanted to work in marketing or public relations – there was just no need. So I'd moved back to London, and realised maybe I did belong in a city after all.

Sure, I'd never wanted to settle down before I'd left, but now I was older. I was in my thirties. My *mid*-thirties. Things were going to be different. Maybe I could be like Tansy and Maggie now too. With a husband and a few kids. Yes, me! Why couldn't I? Hadn't I spent the whole of last year telling myself it was time to stop living out of a suitcase? To get a job that didn't revolve around refried beans. To finally settle down. Not to mention that I wanted to find someone that I really liked, to date, to live with. To *marry*.

Before I could chicken out, I asked the bartender for a piece of paper and a pen and wrote down my new future, aka The Plan:

1. Get a job
2. Get a house
3. Get a partner. Marry him.

There, simple. That was what I would do.

Chapter 2

I ordered another whisky to celebrate The Plan and was about to slide onto the bar stool, in case I got too tipsy downing another Scotch, when I dropped my room key on the sand. I stepped back to try and look for it, at the exact time someone was stepping forward, because I felt my body slam into something hard – like a wall of cement. I tried to right myself, but my shoe went one way, and my foot went another and, before I knew it, I was on the ground in a heap, my knee-length dress hiked around my upper thighs.

'Sorry, are you OK?' A hand appeared in front of my face. It was a rather nice hand, square and large and quite like you'd imagine a tradie's hand to be, but without the rough bits or anything covered in grime or paint.

When I looked up, a very good-looking man with his good-looking hands was standing above me. 'I'm Nick,' he said in a broad Australian accent. He had kind chocolate brown eyes that crinkled when he smiled. He was admittedly gorgeous, with blond hair, a dark sandy colour, and tanned olive skin. He was about six foot, with broad shoulders. He was wearing dark blue shorts, a fitted blue plaid shirt and white slip-on sneakers. The cool kind.

'And I'm better when I'm dressed,' I said, grabbing on to Nick's hand and letting him pull me up. He looked away like a gentleman whilst I straightened my dress and brushed the sand off. I could feel the heat of the blood, still in my cheeks. Had I shown my bum to the world? To Mr Gorgeous? My knickers?

'That was some tumble.' Nick stared at me.

'Yes, I'm training for the Worlds. Floor is my best. I was about to do a back flip, but you got in my way.'

'Funny that, I thought you were looking for something in the sand. A room key perhaps?' He opened his palm and there was my white room key.

'How did you—?' My heart was beating so loudly, as if it were trying to escape my chest. At any moment, this gorgeous guy would make an excuse to leave. To go back to his girl-friend. Or wife. I bet he had a lovely, pretty woman, beautiful and slim with blonde hair, who went to the gym more than three times a week. She was probably an Instagram influencer or model, because they mostly were nowadays.

'Stealth.' He smiled. 'Is that whisky?' He pointed to my glass.

'Single malt.'

'I'm impressed.'

'Are you?' I could feel him staring at me.

'A girl that drinks whisky? Absolutely.' I tried to hide my smile. Was this gorgeous man *flirting* with me? Stuff like this didn't ever happen to me. Broiled chicken cheaters happened to me. Vanilla guys who were into computers happened to me. Hot men on islands did *not* happen to me.

Nick smiled at me, and his eyes crinkled in the most adorable way. I opened my mouth to say, *Well, have a good night,* expecting he was just being pleasant because he was on holidays, and his wife was probably eyeing me up and wondering why her wonderful husband was talking to the awkward girl at the bar who'd just fallen in the sand. But then I stopped myself. There are times in your life when there is a moment. A moment that presents itself as a possibility. The universe had conspired to plant this man right in front of me. Bumping into me. Literally. And it had to be for a reason.

Ask him to have a drink with you.

This was one of those moments when the man in front of you is gorgeous, and maybe he's not living in a granny flat with his parents, or a workaholic with a heart problem, and it's not a weird blind date, and he might be taken, or not, but still, you think – *just go for it.*

Ask him to have a drink with you, I thought again. I mean, it's just a drink. Why not? Why the bloody hell not!?

I took a deep breath, smiled and said, 'Well, I was about to have a shot too. Are you up for it?' I held my breath and waited for him to respond.

'I am,' Nick said, laughing. 'But none of that girly shit.'

My heart did a little cha-cha. 'You mean, no Cocksucking Cowboy?'

'Slippery Nipple,' he chimed in.

'Jam Donut?' I teased.

Nick held up his hand. 'OK, that's the only one I'll let you consider. Because it tastes like—'

'Gummy snakes!' I interrupted.

'Exactly!' He laughed and nodded at the bartender. 'Two Jam Donuts, please,' Nick ordered. The bartender had no idea what that was, so in the end we got two shots of Baileys with a dash of chambord. We cheers-ed and tossed them back quickly.

'Ugh, that was sweet.' I shuddered.

Nick ordered two whisky chasers, and paid for both rounds. A true gentleman.

'So, what are you up to tonight?' he asked. 'Did you watch the game?'

'Game? No.' I almost snorted. 'I hate sports.' I thought it best to be honest, and not pretend I was really into cricket or rugby, and then have to listen to him prattle on about his team for the next thirty minutes.

'All of them?' Nick asked.

'Well, except that Japanese show of people falling into the water whilst trying to balance on slippery apparatus.'

'Oh, *Kamikaze*! I love that too.' Nick grinned.

'Were you here watching ...' I put down my whisky to use air quotes '... the game?'

'No.' Nick leaned in. 'Don't tell anyone, but I kinda don't like sports either.'

'What?' I feigned shock and horror. 'How un-Australian!'

'It's true. I think I was dropped on my head as a child.'

'Your head does look a little lopsided.' I grinned.

Nick laughed. 'So, what brings you to Fiji's top sports bar, then?'

'This is a sports bar? I thought it was welcome drinks.'

'It's both.' Nick smiled. 'But mostly a place where guys get to hang out all day, every day.'

I nodded. 'Ahh, a man-cave. A male den. A place to grunt away from the ladies.'

'Yes, we're on our best behaviour right now,' Nick teased. 'How's our English sound to you? Can you understand us? I've been really practising losing my grunt accent.'

'Hmmm.' I squinted at him, feeling my heart beat faster. He was cute and funny, and had great banter, and he didn't seem to have anywhere to go. He was staying longer than a man who was here with his girlfriend or wife would stay. And in an instant, I knew – I *kinda liked* him. There was something so likeable about him, something so easy, something I felt I could trust.

'Better keep trying,' I teased.

'So, what brings you to Fiji, to the land of snorkelling and sun? Kids? Husband?' Nick asked casually.

'None of the above. I'm just here for the weekend and I thought I'd try my luck at winning big on the turtle races. Mumma needs some new shoes.'

Nick looked down at my black Havaiana thongs on my feet and said, 'Yeah, I wasn't going to say anything, but—'

'Hey!' I slapped him playfully on the arm. 'Don't get me started on your shirt.'

'My shirt? What's wrong with my shirt?'

'Um, I could lay it out and have a picnic on it.'

'Wow. Are you asking me to take my shirt off? You move fast. I don't even know your name.'

I laughed and blushed. 'Emma.'

'So, Emma, besides trying to update your wardrobe at the local ocean bar, what brings you to this island?'

'Just a few days in the sunshine.'

'Same as us,' Nick said.

'Us?' I looked around. 'Seeing imaginary friends now, are you?'

He chuckled. 'The boys, Brett and Mark, headed back to the villa. I've got a timeshare unit down by the beach so we fly over from Sydney as much as we can, especially since the summer is almost over.'

'And Fiji is so warm, thank goodness, warm enough to swim.'

'You going swimming later, then?' Nick asked.

'Maybe.' I laughed. My head was saying *yes, yes, YES*, but I was trying to play it cool.

'Well, this bar closes soon,' Nick said. 'Did you aim to be so fashionably late?'

'Are you saying I'm fashionable now?' I teased.

Nick laughed. 'Not quite. We can talk more about your clothing choices later, as it may take some time.'

Just then the lights flicked on and off. Welcome drinks were over.

'Shall we?' Nick said, pulling out my chair for me.

I followed him down a side pathway through a row of huts and bures. Down at the beach the entire place was quiet, except for the small whoosh of waves lapping at the shore. Everyone else was tucked in their beds. The moon was full and round. A white streak of moonlight flashed across the water. The tide had gone out, and the waves were soft and round, gliding without any mermaid froth.

Nick grabbed my hand and pulled me until my feet hit sand. Soft, cold sand. He seemed to hold my hand for a beat, but then let me go.

'How good a swimmer are you?' He looked at me.

'I'd beat you in an eggbeater contest.' I could feel the warmth of the whisky flushing through my veins. It made me feel like being reckless on my last few nights of freedom.

'You're on!' Nick said, unbuttoning his shirt.

'I'll have you know,' I said, pulling my hair from its bun, 'I'm an avid aqua aerobics-er. Is that a word?'

He looked at me curiously. 'Aren't you a bit young for that?'

'Ageist.' I threw my sandal at him.

He laughed and ducked. 'Oh, man, do you wear one of those cap things?'

'Those caps are kinda cool, I'll have you know. Possibly ironic. Maybe even hipster?'

'Yes, possibly cool for the mid-seventies age range. Thankfully you are cap-free tonight. Just so you know, I bet you look better without it.' He winked.

He took his shirt off, revealing a taut chest, tanned and smooth with not an inch of hair. Yikes! He looked even hotter than I imagined. There were curves of muscle around everything. His shoulders were like boulders. His chest broad and smooth, and his stomach muscles, without an inch of fat, were etched deep. He had the defined diagonal hip muscles of swimmers and runners. I could see every pair of muscles that made him up. I tried not to look, but kept stealing glances.

'Emma, are you OK?'

'Huh? Yes, yes, I'm good.' I'd stopped undressing, and was standing there, my mouth open. My eyes wandered all over him as I took off my other sandal.

Nick was now taking off his shorts and his boxers. Wait. What? His BOXERS?

'Wait, what is happening here?' I said, trying to suppress my laughter.

Suddenly Nick was standing in front of me and, oh, my God. He was naked.

I burst out laughing. 'Why are you naked?'

'Why not? Aren't we swimming?' Nick said, not making a move to cover himself up. This guy had confidence.

'I want to tell you something,' he said.

'That we're naked?' I laughed.

'Yes, Emma.' He smiled.

'Are you a nudist?' I couldn't stop laughing.

'No, Emma. Actually, I want to tell you something else,' he started.

'I'm sorry'. I could hardly breathe I was laughing so much. 'Can we have a serious conversation while you're naked?'

'Can we?'

'I'm really not sure.' I tried to stop laughing and compose myself. 'Wait, is this the way you get girls back to your villa?' I said, trying not to look there. His package.

'It's not about sex, Emma,' Nick said.

Oops. It wasn't? Because I was still sneaking mini-glances at his nether regions.

'It's about just being comfortable with who you are.'

Clearly this boy was *very* comfortable.

'You can go in with your underwear on,' he offered.

'Now where's the fun in that?' I laughed. I would never see this guy again, it was Fiji, why the hell not. I took my dress off. And stood in my black lace bra and lacy bottoms. At least someone was seeing my French lingerie! Hurrah! I hadn't bought them for nothing. I shimmied off my pants. And unclasped my bra.

Naked. I was bloody naked! I gave a quick glance around to make sure no millennial was hiding in the bushes, filming us – I'd be on YouTube in no time, going viral. Doing it for size fourteen women everywhere.

I felt totally exposed. But surprisingly good. Also, I wanted to sneak a little glance at him down there. But that felt wrong. And weird. And he was looking at my eyes. And not at any other places on me.

He was staring at me intently. I held my breath. I thought he was about to lean in and kiss me. I started to close my eyes, thinking, *yes, please kiss me*, but he said, 'I want to tell you …' he paused '… first one in is the winner!' and started sprinting towards the ocean.

'Not fair!' I gave it all my might, running as hard as I could. Running made my boobs jiggle, and then I wondered how my stomach looked so I snuck a glance to see. It looked OK. A bit soft. And white. But OK.

Nick was athletic as well as muscular, and he got there yards ahead of me, diving into the cool ocean. I splashed into the sea after him. The water was warm and soothing, and felt amazing. I waded out to my thighs and dived in. I closed my eyes, and felt the water rush over me. It felt strange to be in the salty sea, without any clothes. And rather great too.

When I emerged, Nick was a few metres away, gliding over the small waves.

'So what do you win?' I asked, swimming closer to him.

'That's up to you. Loser gets to decide.'

I splashed him with a huge wave of water. He was surprised and made a few choking noises. 'OK, nice, death by drowning to the winner.'

'Well, it wasn't a fair race. You had a head start.'

'You want another challenge?'

I laughed. 'I do.'

'Wow, I think it's too early for "I do's", Emma. Now you're practising for our wedding. You do move fast.'

I sloshed more water his way, then turned onto my back, kicking as hard as I could so all the water would go in his direction.

When I stopped, I expected him to complain again. But he'd disappeared.

'Nick?' I turned to my right, to my left. I couldn't see him at all. The sea flattened out.

'Nick?' I called out, spinning around. He hadn't come up to the surface yet. I hesitated. I swam a little further out, to where I couldn't stand, but it was as black as black further out, and scared me.

'Nick!?' I counted to five. Now I was getting worried.

Something tugged at my leg. I'd heard about this, that most shark attacks happen at night and close to the shore. I thought I'd dreamt it at first, but there it was again. Tug. I gave a loud squeal, convinced it was a shark that had taken Nick and was now coming from me, then swam as fast as I could back to where I could stand, in the water reaching my hips, my heart beating out of my chest. Where was Nick?

Something tugged again at my leg. I yelled out, 'Help!'

Suddenly the shark emerged from the water laughing, stood and splashed me. 'God, Emma, you'll wake the entire hotel of people trying to sleep.'

'What ... the ...? You ...' I was so mad, I tried to push him away, but he grabbed each of my wrists in his hand. He had nice hands, and now they were pulling my hands towards his chest.

'Were you going to try and hit me with your tiny, ineffectual fists?' He had a twinkle in his eye.

'Not ineffectual. As you may likely find out.' I could barely speak. I wanted to look away, but I couldn't. My body seemed to crave his; it was all I could do not to grab him and kiss him. I'd never wanted someone to touch me, to kiss me so much. I could hear the blood pulsating in my ears.

Suddenly he reached out and pulled me into him. Our bodies pressed together. I felt his warm skin against mine, his breath hot on my neck, and a delightful buzz spread out across my chest. My mind ticked over. He was a stranger. And this was a naked hug. Was that weird? Should it be? Oh, God, was he getting excited? Um, down *there*? Before I could think of anything else, he'd put his hand on my right cheek.

'Emma,' he said in a soft, serious voice.

'Nick,' I whispered, staring into his chocolate melt eyes.

The entire beach disappeared from sight. It was just him and me.

He leaned forward, smelling of warm whisky, and ocean water; his lips found mine. I closed my eyes. He gently kissed me, no tongue, but I felt breathless. My body shuddered.

'Emma.'

'Yes?'

'You're shivering.'

'Well, I'm cold.' And this situation is making my body quiver in ways it never has.

'Let's get you back.'

'But I—' I wanted to stay out there and kiss him all night.

'We can go swimming again later.' He stepped back.

'OK,' I said, and was glad he kept holding my hand, feeling the warmth tingle up and down my arm.

'Can you wait here a second?' he asked. 'Just stand in the shallows.'

'A naked girl by herself at the beach? You better be quick.' I turned to face the ocean, so no one could catch a glimpse.

He dashed off before I had a second to watch his body. I couldn't believe this was happening. My last travel hurrah, and I was going to return with this story. What a story. My friends would never believe me.

In a few minutes he was back with two fluffy towels, one already around him, and a jumper for me.

'Oh, and this.' He held up a bag of chips and a bottle of whisky. 'I nicked it from Brett's stash.'

He held the towel around me, and then handed me my

black dress, underwear and his jumper – which smelt like the ocean, and felt so warm. He took a sip of whisky and handed it to me. The liquid warmed up in seconds.

'C'mon,' he said. Dragging a few logs together, he started to make a fire. It was crackling in no time, and he laid out the towels for us to sit on.

'Well, this is quite nice,' I murmured, sitting down in front of the fire. 'I didn't realise it got this cool in the evenings in Fiji – isn't it meant to be summer here all year round?'

'Sometimes it gets cool, which is nice, because then you can cuddle up by a beach fire.' He sat next to me, near enough to touch me. I could see the flames and reflection dancing on his face, in his eyes.

'So, what's your story, Emma?' he asked.

I felt my body leaning slightly towards his. 'Well, I'm a retired aqua aerobics World star, who's bringing pink petal caps to the masses. And you?'

'I'm a retired picnic rug, who got tired of people walking all over me.'

'That's terrible!' We both laughed.

He paused. 'Now, truthfully?'

'Well, I've been travelling around the world for seven years, working here and there, and now here I am in Fiji.'

He gave a low whistle. 'Wow. Seven years. I'm impressed. I think I'm heading back to London for work. Maybe via France. And Austria. Don't tell me you've been there too?'

'Why, yes, I have,' I said and realised he was leaning close to me too. A burst of warmth and excitement spread across my chest. I wanted him to kiss me, and I didn't even know what I was saying. I felt tongue-tied and nervous, and when I do that – I talk.

'In fact, it sounds like you need travel advice, and, wouldn't you know it, besides specialising in petal caps, I am a great travel guide and know lots of random facts about all kinds of things.'

'Like?'

'Like it would take one million two hundred thousand mosquitoes, each sucking once, to completely drain the average human of blood.'

'Morbid, but interesting.' He chuckled.

When we stopped talking, there was only the sound of the breeze through the palm trees.

'How great would it be to do this, and travel, for the rest of our lives?' I said.

'Depends how you travel,' he pointed out.

'Good point. How about hiking in the wild, the mountains, waking up to fresh air and trees every morning, then a few nice hotels thrown in so you can remember what it's like to wear a bathrobe, rather than a scratchy towel the size of a postage stamp?'

He laughed. 'Yep, I know all about those towels. I spent some time on a boat travelling around Antarctica.'

'Antarctica! What were you doing there?'

'This sounds cheesy – but I took some time to volunteer with seals and penguins.'

'Yep, you're right, sounds very "I'm a dolphin trainer" to me,' I said, trying not to laugh.

'Do dolphin trainers even exist?' he teased.

'In every woman's fantasy they do.' I winked.

'Oh, we're sharing fantasies now!' He laughed. 'You do move fast.'

I playfully swatted his leg. 'Well, right now, my fantasy would be to live by the ocean, perhaps in a palm tree.'

'I hope you'll wear clothes,' he teased. 'Could get sore.'

I suddenly became aware that I'd been completely naked before – it was strange to think that I hadn't felt that awkward, that embarrassed, in fact I hadn't really given it a thought.

'I'm not the crazy idiot that decided to take off my clothes.'

'Aren't you?' he asked with a smile.

'Well.' I nodded. 'Perhaps I'll call it peer pressure from a picnic rug.'

'I'm not sure anyone would believe an inanimate object made you take off your clothes.' Nick laughed then took a swig of whisky. There was a moment of comfortable silence between us, before he looked over at me with his gorgeous chocolate eyes. 'So, if you could, would you stay in Fiji for a while, then?'

'Why not? Sun, sand ...' I paused. Was it sex? God, was that the perfect trilogy?

'And?' he teased.

I waved my hand as if I were shooing away a fly. 'You know the answer to that.' Then I changed the subject. 'So, what's every man's idea of a woman's fantasy job?'

'Well, personally speaking, I go a bit crazy for someone trekking up a mountain or taking photos in a double barrel wave.'

'I've trekked through a jungle in the Amazon. Does that count?' I asked coyly.

'It sure does.' He leaned in, putting his hand lightly on the small of my back. My stomach did a small flip as he asked, 'Can I get you another whisky? Water?'

I couldn't breathe for a second because he'd got too close, and now I could only smell the wonderful scent of his after-shave. Up close, I noticed he hadn't shaved in a day or two and I wondered what his stubble would feel like. His perfect jaw line, his full lips.

'I ... I'll just have a water,' I stammered. 'Actually, no, I'll have a whisky.'

'Both?' He dug around in the bag in front of him. 'I don't want to get in trouble for looking like I'm trying to get you drunk.'

'Are you?' I teased, still thinking about his lips.

'No.' He shook his head. 'Yes? But more no. I mean – how can I answer that?'

He handed me the bottle of whisky. I took a sip and let the warmth flush around my body. He pointed at the stars.

'That's Sirius there; look closely, can you see it flashing? It's one of the nearest stars to us, but if you are patient you'll see it has flashes of green and blue.'

'Now, Mr Penguin Trainer, you're just showing off,' I said, my head tilted to the sky, trying not to look at him.

'Am I?' He was staring at me, instead of the stars.

He took a deep breath and looked back at the stars. 'Where are you headed next?'

'Who knows?' I shrugged, trying not to think about kissing

him. 'Alaska,' I said dreamily, thinking about my list of places to travel next. 'Or the Galapagos Islands.'

'I hear Alaska's beautiful, but expensive.'

'Kinda like Antarctica.'

'Will you be volunteering with penguins?'

'Maybe wolves.' I smiled. 'But they're not as high on the totem pole as dolphin trainers or penguin volunteers.'

'I've heard. Sadly, wolves are down near otter trainers or snake collectors.'

'Well, I'm going there determined to bring the sexy back to wolves. Correction, sexy wolves back.'

He chuckled. 'You're bringing sexy wolves back. Where? In your suitcase?'

I laughed. 'No, I meant ... it was ... a Justin Timberlake reference.'

'Yes, I got that. I'm not *that* much older than you.'

'Really?' I teased. 'Could have fooled me. Since you've got a lot more grey hairs than I do.'

'Hey!' He leaned away from me and covered his hair. 'The truth doesn't always need to be pointed out.'

I giggled and reached to point them out, but he ducked away. 'And what do you have planned next, Mr Penguin Trainer?'

'Well, me and my grey hairs may decide to step up on the career ladder, and earn lots and lots of money. Or just quit and travel. Or live somewhere near the beach. Or the country.'

'That sounds wonderful,' I said, thinking of my perfect place. 'A little white country cottage?'

'With a veggie garden,' he added.

'An apple orchard and a bunch of chickens.'

'Definitely chickens. Some dogs too.'

'A chocolate Labrador!'

He laughed. 'How good would that life be?'

I sighed and took another sip of whisky. 'I'd give up anything for some space and wildness out of the city. But how would I make money?'

'How do you make it now?'

'Oh, you know, bits and pieces.' I thought back to my Mexican burrito days. Do *not* talk about them, they're as sexy as mentioning that you wear granny panties three days in a row. 'But I really like to paint and draw.'

I couldn't believe I'd just said that. I'd always wanted to be an artist. But I'd never actually sold a painting; in fact, showing my paintings to people made me feel awkward and unsure, like I was handing them my baby, and asking was it ugly? For that reason, I hardly showed anyone my paintings Right now, in my backpack was a rolled-up wad of landscapes – the turquoise seas of Cyprus, a piece of Dubrovnik coastline, an old door I couldn't stop looking at in Venice. They'd probably end up shoved to the back of my wardrobe. I hadn't divulged my secret passion to anyone.

So, I couldn't believe I was telling Nick this fact about me. I was used to meeting travellers, and going out with them for the night, sharing silly stuff, but this felt different, it felt much more personal.

'I'd like to see one.'

'Maybe one day.' I smiled at him, and was surprised to realise I meant it.

Nick took the whisky bottle, which was dug in the sand, and took a swig. 'I've been focused a lot on work these last few years. Working really long nights. It's the same thing day in and day out. Deadlines. And appointments. And bills to pay. Being single, sometimes I'm not sure when to leave the office. Nothing to go home to, you know?'

I nodded. I did know that feeling.

'Maybe you don't, because you're always travelling, being a free spirit, you probably have no idea what it's like for us nine to fivers.'

I was about to let him know that I knew all too well, when he leaned in closer to me, and I could feel the warmth of his body. The smell of whisky and ocean salt on his lips. I forgot all my words. He paused for a second. 'Do you ever get lonely, travelling by yourself?'

I swallowed as he leaned in closer, inches from my face.

'Maybe,' I said, then admitted, 'sometimes I think that's part of the reason I keep moving around the world so much.'

He looked into my eyes, and traced his finger along my cheek. The sound of the waves against the sand was a soft lull, like someone whispering. He leaned towards me and brushed a piece of hair back from my face. My stomach flipped. I could smell sea salt on him, and mint aftershave; his lips were close. He kissed me softly and I melted slightly. His lips were soft on mine as he held my face in one hand. I lost all track of time and the night. An hour could have passed. Or a second.

Finally, he broke away. 'Wow.'

'A lot, wow.' I felt light-headed and dizzy.

'Do you want to go home and warm up?' he said, looking into my eyes, then he held up his hand. 'And before you ask, this is not how I get girls back to my villa. This is how I hopefully get *you* back to my villa.'

I nodded quickly. He put out the fire, grabbed towels and my hand and led me across the soft white sand. His villa was about fifty metres further down the beach. A white stucco town house, with white tiles inside, an open-plan kitchen, a long, carpeted corridor, and a small plunge pool at the back in a green-grass courtyard.

'You own this?' I think my mouth was hanging open.

'Part own it. It's a timeshare.' Nick threw the bags down on his blue striped couch. 'C'mon, let's get warm.'

He disappeared down the hall to the right. I peered in the doorway just in time to see him stepping naked into the shower, and letting out a sigh.

'It's hot! And feels so good,' he called out, leaving the shower door open.

'Um, both of us?' I asked from the hallway.

'Sure, why not?' Nick shrugged. 'Don't you want to warm up?'

Despite the rivers of alcohol pumping around my body, I was still shivering and cold. I caught a glance of myself in the bathroom mirror; my bottom lip looked almost blue.

'OK, then.' I took a deep breath, peeled off my dress and underwear and quickly stepped carefully into the shower. Nick guided my shoulders and moved me until I was in the middle of the water. My ice-cold feet and hands started to tingle as the blood rushed back into them. I paused at this point, aware of him being naked, standing behind me. I imagined him getting closer, whispering in my ear, and it shot a tingle down my back.He squeezed a line of body wash across my shoulders and started to massage it deeply into my neck, my shoulders, my arms, down my back. Warm water. Suds. He turned me to face him. Fire curled around my belly, and I wanted him to kiss me.

As if sensing my thoughts, he leaned down and brushed his cheek against my lips. I could feel the tiny stubble against my skin, his square jaw. My stomach fluttered. He cupped both my cheeks with his hands and kissed me, gently. It wasn't the type of kiss where I was thinking, where should I put my hand? Which way do I tilt my head? Tongue? Or no tongue? We just came together, and my brain thought of absolutely nothing except how amazing it felt to kiss him. It felt *right*.

When we broke away from our kiss, I was so light-headed I almost needed to put my hand on the shower glass to steady myself. I closed my eyes and felt as if I were floating. When I opened them, Nick was looking at me intently.

'Are you warm?'

I laughed. 'Um yes.' Because I couldn't be warmer, but he was turning off the shower. The water stopped running, and he was stepping out and handing me a towel, and as I stepped onto the fluffy white bathmat and dried off, I thought, *oh, that's it?*

And I felt disappointed by that. Not disappointed like I'd felt with Norse God – because that had been nothing. But disappointed because I liked Nick, in a way that I probably shouldn't. I liked him more than any of the guys I'd been on awkward dating app first dates with. I liked him enough to want to see him again. I liked him in a way that made me not care about what I 'should' or 'shouldn't' do, because I knew what I wanted right in this moment – to be with him, to sleep with him, to stay here, and wake up next to him.

As if reading my mind, he waited until I had dried off, and wrapped the towel around my body. 'Do you want to stay?'

I nodded.

He led me down the white-tiled hallway to his bedroom. Without saying a word, he leaned down and lifted me up – effortlessly – his muscles flexing, he slid me onto the bed. I'd always dreamed of an amazing man, a sexy, wild version of me, a beach hut somewhere, but *nothing like this.*

Was this happening? My stomach fluttered and I grabbed the back of his neck and pulled his face towards me. He kissed me again, passionately. 'I like it when you do that,' he said.

He traced his lips over my lips, then my cheek, following the line of my neck down the right side, leaving soft kisses that gave me goosebumps, then licking in long strokes, and finally tiny bites. He tugged gently on my hair, then a little stronger, pulling my head back, and exposing my neck to his kisses.

He moved his hands to cup my breasts. I arched my back, and he sucked my right nipple in his mouth. I moaned with intensity, all other thoughts immediately leaving my head.

'I thought you'd be the noisy type.' He licked between my breasts and looked up at me.

'Do you like noisy?' I asked coyly, letting my fingers float across his perfect chest and abs, honed to perfection, smooth and taut.

'God,' he moaned, 'I love it.'

I'd always dreamed of a summer fling, but nothing like *this*.

I curled my legs around his back, locking my ankles, pulling him closer to me. Without thinking, I leaned forward, licked his neck, then whispered in his ear, 'I want you.'

His hot breath was on my chin, on my neck, as he ground into me. Our bodies rocked against each other. He grabbed onto my thighs where he was holding me, so hard, that he left fingerprints. I scratched my fingernails down his back. The pain and pleasure pushed us both over the edge in a large shudder. He groaned and fell into me, gently placing me back on the bed, kissing my lips gently.

We stayed there for a minute, not moving.

'I did not know this was going to happen,' I said, panting from the effort.

'Why are you panting? I did all the work!' He laughed.

I swatted his arm. 'I was doing a lot of hip action there too, buddy. It takes yoga classes to get that flexible.'

He leaned back and looked into my eyes. 'That was amazing.'

'Sleep time?' I asked, suddenly exhausted and wanting to feel his warm body pressed against me all night.

'Sleep time,' he said, kissing me gently on the tip of my nose. 'My bed is king size. It's comfy, I promise.'

He tossed me a T-shirt and shorts from the top of the

wicker basket. 'I only wore them earlier today for ten minutes – they're clean.'

When I put them on, they smelled of him slightly, his minty aftershave. I collapsed onto the bed and yawned again, almost slipping instantly into sleep.

Nick crawled on the bed next to me, one arm around me, tucking my hair away from my face. I wanted him to kiss me, but before I could do anything, I fell asleep feeling his soft warm breath tickling my skin and listening to the sounds of the ocean in the distance.

Chapter 3

'Good morning, sleepy,' Nick said, standing there, his perfect body in perfect boxers, smiling, an orange juice in his hand. 'Do you want coffee?'

I nodded limply, because everything seemed to hurt my head.

'Hangovers,' he'd said, 'are the version of adult nightmares that you can't wake up from.'

We laughed and delicately tried to eat toast and sip water. Then we spent an hour laying next to each other, our arms and legs touching, intertwined, chatting about places we wanted to visit, and places we'd loved, and our favourite books, and music – all the things that you loved discovering about another person. And there was no doubt about it, Nick was a nerd, a poetry nerd at that. He liked Yeats, but mostly E.E. Cummings. I knew that he liked his coffee extra black, extra shot. That he visited him mum every second Saturday. That he would move to Canada if he could, to the west coast.

Finally, I knew I had to get up and go back to my hotel, to shower, and sleep, and feel human again. I mused about how to say goodbye without making it uncomfortable or strange.

Of course, I wanted to see him again, but I had no idea if he felt the same way. For a moment I stood awkwardly in my black dress, my shoes in my hand, looking around his room. Did we swap numbers, or email addresses, or *something*? Or maybe we just kissed ... and said goodbye like mature adults and went on with our lives.

'How about a seafood lunch later?' Nick said casually, pulling on a T-shirt after a quick shower. 'I'm flying back tonight, but I could see you before three o'clock.' He paused. 'Only if you want?'

'Sure,' I replied excitedly. *He wants to see me again.*

'My number is 04—'

'Wait. My phone is out of battery and there's no way I'll remember that.' I laughed but then it hurt my head a little, so I stopped. 'Ouch.'

'Poor you. OK here's my number.' He said quickly scribbling it on a piece of paper and handing it to me. 'Text me where and when, and I'll be there.'

'Great,' I said and pocketed it, giving him a long hug before slipping out the front door.

Outside, I walked quickly back across the sandy beach where just hours ago I'd been naked. The sun was up and blinding already at this early hour, there was no breeze, and the humidity sat heavy in the air. I was sweating in seconds as I trudged through the sand, step by step. I wandered down a road and then left along a small beach cove. Where was my hotel? And, where was I? Feeling confused and disorientated, I'd turned down a few streets and walked for a while, before realising they were dead ends. Was I even going the right way?

After the longest, hottest walk I'd found I'd taken a wrong turn, and had to backtrack twenty long, hot minutes before I arrived at the hotel, feeling like a limp dishrag.

Slipping into my deliciously cool room, I showered and took a quick power nap. When I got up, I'd looked at the crumpled piece of paper on my bed with Nick's phone number. I read the numbers aloud 0402 773 944. Before I could second guess myself, I texted him *Hey you, hope your head is feeling better. My hotel apparently does a great seafood lunch. Freshwaters, at 1pm?* And then I'd put his number in my purse, and called down to reception to book a table near the pool for two.

Excited, I jumped in the shower again and spent an hour getting ready. I put on my sea-green maxi dress and sandals and I styled my hair straight and then spent a lot of extra time giving it beach waves. By the time I was finished it was just past 1 p.m., so I grabbed my phone and purse and took the lift to Freshwaters. The waiter seated me at one of the best tables right next to the pool, and the sun was shining so brightly, I had to wear sunglasses. I ordered two glasses of sauvignon blanc, because I knew he liked really crisp, dry white wines. I laughed, then, because I already knew what he liked and didn't like. I picked up the menu and planned what we'd eat for lunch. We'd start with the calamari rings – fried to perfection – then grilled Yasawa lobster to share. I'd have the panko fried mussels, because for some reason he doesn't like mussels, and he could have the Fiji crab, as long as he promised to save me a bite, or two. Or maybe we'd just splurge and order two of them to be sure.

I grinned. It felt strangely like I was waiting for a boyfriend. Not a boyfriend, *my* boyfriend. And I *liked* it.

I checked my phone, but he hadn't responded. *He's coming though,* I reassured myself, *he seemed excited to see me again.* I ate a bit of the complimentary sourdough bread, my teeth sinking into the warm crust, and invented a list of reasons he was ten minutes late. He's trying to find the place. He decided to walk and took a wrong turn. He's not sure what shirt to wear.

The poor waiter kept on trying to take my order, as the restaurant filled up, and I kept on saying *could you wait a bit longer please.* I swallowed a sip of wine and watched all the other happy couples ordering platters of seafood. I quickly sent him a text. *Hey there, are we still on for lunch?* I checked my phone – yes it had signal, yes international roaming was switched on.

I tried texting Tansy – *I'm in Fiji! Tell me if you get this, possible issues with phone.* And I'd sent a quick photo of the sun, the pool, the palm trees. And she'd written straight back – *AMAZING! Can't wait to see you xxx.*

After another five minutes, I looked at the second glass of wine I'd ordered, and I realized it was possible he wasn't late. A strange, queasy feeling churned in my stomach. Had he stood me up?

But there had to be a reason. He had fallen asleep, yes that was it. We'd been up most of the night. Or maybe he was packing and the time had gotten away from him. Because he had been so lovely last night, he was a *good* guy, wasn't he? As the waiter closed in on me, his notepad ready for my entrée order, I picked up my phone, closed my eyes and thought, *just do it*. I found his number, saved under 'Naked Nick', and pressed 'call'. I put the phone to my ear and felt like I was going to faint. What if he answered and didn't want to talk to me? What if it was someone else's number?

I waited for the ring tone, but there was nothing. All I could hear was a beep beep beep and a robotic voice saying 'this number is not connected. Please check the number and dial again'.

I checked the number, and then looked at the piece of paper he'd written it on. Had I got the number wrong? I tried it again, this time punching in the numbers, one by one. But it was the same robotic voiced response.

Oh God. I felt a flame of embarrassment wash over me. He'd given me a wrong number, and I was sat here, at bloody Freshwaters, dressed up like a ham at Christmas, and completely by myself like an absolute idiot. I turned around, suddenly paranoid, as if I was about to catch him hiding in the bushes laughing at me. But the only people in the bushes were kids jumping into the pool, and all around me people looking at each other in a lovey-dovey couple way.

He wasn't coming.

I felt like I was going to cry, but I couldn't cry by myself at a table in a frou-frou restaurant. I tried to keep a shred of dignity, but I could feel the tears brimming and the lump in my throat, as I called the waiter over, apologized, told him my friend wasn't coming and asked him to charge the wine to my room.

Thank God for large sunglasses. On the way back to my

room, I could feel the hot tears at my eyes. He'd given me a fake number. He'd lied. What else had he lied about? Everything? If he wasn't into me, he was a great actor, and that had been as Oscar-worthy performance.

Suddenly I wasn't the bright, self-confident girl I had convinced myself I was after all these years away. I was me, seven years ago, standing in a white dress at the end of the aisle and someone was whispering to me those three haunting words.

He's not coming.

Chapter 4

Murray and I met in university. I was doing a bunch of classes including anthropology, art and psychology, trying to figure out what I really wanted to do. He was a straight-A economics and computer studies student. Our paths would never have crossed had I not needed a tutor. I was taking Psychology 101 and needed desperate help with computer statistics. A friend suggested Murray would help me out, so I texted him immediately.

When we met over coffee to discuss tutoring, he was so geeky I knew he was going to make the perfect coach. He dressed in too-loose jeans. He was slightly pudgy. He walked self-consciously. He didn't look at anyone directly when he first met them because he was too shy.

I felt totally relaxed in his company. I didn't bother wearing make-up and I said what I thought. After a few months of weekly catch-ups, we became more like friends, and started meeting for coffee before tutoring, going to the movies afterwards, which turned into dinner, which turned into long drives down to the beach, where we talked about everything. He'd never had a girlfriend before, and so I was surprised when he kissed me at first. Besides, it was comfortable and good. We fitted together so easily. And we made each other really quite happy. I was the energy and fire, and he was the solid anchor – that seemed to balance us.

He was practical and calm, he taught me the best ways to save, about interest rates and how to accumulate Flybuys points (until then I'd had *no* idea what that even was). I got him dancing for the first time. We took a trip to New Zealand, and went on a fast speedboat. Although the entire time he kept saying how risky it was, afterwards he was as exhilarated as a little kid on Christmas morning.

Two years later, he proposed at the top of Centre Point Tower after a dinner of oysters and Champagne. It was terribly clichéd, but he looked so sweet in a dinner jacket, on one knee, that I said yes. Part of me was excited, and part of me was terrified. I knew I loved him, but ...

But. It's a horrible word to use, especially when you're talking about someone you should be happy with, for ever after.

But. We had completely different ideas for our future. I talked about doing a worldwide trip then buying a small place near the woods with a large veggie patch within walking distance to the cute local store.

Murray was focusing on getting his first role in an international tech company, and climbing the ladder. He talked about things like security, and stocks, and mortgages, and planning where we'd go when he got long-service leave after twelve years.

I dreamt about a cottage with an apple orchard. An apple

orchard! Who doesn't want one of those? And maybe renting a place in Tuscany for a year, or the French countryside, or living like locals on a sleepy Greek island. He dreamt about a nice suburban house, on the Sydney busline. *Ugh,* I thought, *who wants one of those?*

I wanted to do up an old van or bus, put a bed in it, and travel around New Zealand. He wanted a 4WD for all the kids we were supposed to be having, except I didn't even know if I wanted kids. Ever.

I couldn't see the life he wanted becoming mine. And neither could he see the life I pictured becoming his. His felt too fixed to me, too vanilla. And mine felt unstable to him, too spontaneous. We pushed back the wedding date. Twice.

Finally, we talked about saving enough to buy our suburban house *and* the country cottage, and, even though that felt big, we said in small voices, *we can do this.* We booked a wedding date, in the early spring, and this time we committed to it.

A few nights before the wedding, Murray turned over in bed and held me really close and kept saying, 'It's OK, it's OK.' I didn't know if it was him or me he was comforting, but for the first time I felt a distance between us. My best friend, Tansy, already married, told me it was just cold feet. Perfectly normal. Everyone went through it.

The night before our wedding, I was packing the final parts of my over-priced wedding underwear, preparing to stay at Maggie's house. Before I left, Murray held up his three-piece tux to show me. We didn't believe in fate jinxing us – but maybe we should have. He was so proud that he'd lost weight to fit into it. He asked what I thought, and I said he'd look amazing. He was looking at me strangely, and he kept asking, 'What's wrong, Em? What's wrong?'

I said nothing. That I was fine. Excited. But then I felt wetness run down my cheek. I was crying. But they were tears of happiness, weren't they?

I told myself it was nothing. I kissed him on the cheek and said, 'Tears of happiness.'

The next day was our wedding day. I was standing in a small makeshift marquee next to a colourful spring garden. Dressed in white. My hair in soft waves, half pinned up, a crown of flowers. Soft blush make-up. A long lace dress, a sea-green sash around my waist to match my eyes. I held a bunch of wild pink roses, tied with string. We'd chosen soft pink peonies, bunched, at the end of each row. The aisle had no carpet, and instead was just flushed with white petals.

The sun was out, and it was a gorgeous spring day. The celebrant was waiting at the end of the garden, peering at her watch and trying not to make it look obvious. Murray was late. People in the congregation were waving their programmes in front of their faces, like fans. My mum was pacing, muttering under her breath, 'Where is he? Where is he?'

I stuck my head out of the marquee. The string quartet had finished 'Pachelbel's Canon in D' and they glanced across at me. I made a circling motion with my hand, a *play it again* sign. They nodded, and picked up their instruments. The guests started looking around because it was very obvious that something wasn't right, or, really, that someone hadn't turned up yet. I bet everyone thought it would be me. Because it was never Murray. Murray was never late.

'Give me my phone,' I'd said to someone. 'Where is my phone? I'll call him. He's in traffic, maybe there are roadworks down on the M2. Or the M4.' I was babbling about roads, and traffic lights, and where they were doing roadworks, and someone had my phone in their hands, and I was reaching for it, and still talking about the M7 or M2, and trying to figure out what road he would be taking to get here.

Then someone was whispering, 'He's not coming.' *He's not coming.*

Someone got me in a car. Someone took my dress off. Someone covered me in a blanket because I was shaking. Someone made sure I ate something. Someone put me in the shower. Lay with me through the night, while I tried to sleep. Someone kept bringing me tissues, and a million hands patted me on the back. For the first few days everything was a blur.

When I finally got out of bed, Tansy helped me throw that awful bad-juju dress in the garbage bin. Mum helped me get money back on the honeymoon to Europe. I couldn't have done any of those things myself. Maggie wanted to know if she could clock him. Amy said she'd slash his tyres. God, I love my friends. They were all I had, when my world fell apart for a while.

He texted me. *I'm sorry.*

And a few days later I managed to respond. *OK.*

He texted me. *I hope you're OK, and that you find what you really want.*

I didn't know how to take that. Was he right? I thought I knew what I wanted, but then ... maybe I didn't. For days I thought about his text and what it meant. Murray was someone who was born knowing exactly what he wanted. In all likelihood, his head probably popped out of the birth canal and, before the rest of his body was out, he was saying, 'I want a white-picket-fenced house in the city, on the busline and a stable job for life! Pronto, people!' I mean, he was genius-level smart, so it's completely possible that he could talk on entry to this world.

Deep down, I felt guilty that I couldn't be the wife he wanted me to be. Why didn't I want to settle down and have kids and live in a nice house? Who *wouldn't* want that? I thought maybe there was something fundamentally wrong with me. I remember Murray had once shown me pictures of great houses we could buy in a newly developed suburb that were only forty minutes from the city in peak hour. He'd had a look of excitement in his eyes. For me it felt as exciting as a root canal.

A few days later, Murray texted again, asking if we could meet. I read his text over and over for days. In the end, I didn't respond. I couldn't. I just couldn't hear what he had to say.

All I knew was I had to leave – immediately. I felt a strange mix of self-loathing and guilt and anger, at Murray, but also at myself. I was unsure why I didn't seem to want to fall into domestic bliss like everyone around me. Plus, everywhere reminded me of Murray, and I couldn't be around the places we used to visit. Where we had coffee. Held hands. Got engaged. Planned a future. I had to get out of Australia, and not look back.

I arrived, relaxed and sun-kissed, at Sydney airport after sunset, where Mum and Dad were anxiously waiting. Mum gave me an extra-hard hug.

'Hi Mum, it's good to see you.'

Before she could utter a word, I raised my hand and said, 'No, I didn't meet anyone. But I took a cooking class and can make a mean lemony fish. Plus, I wove this basket.'

I held up a slightly wonky reed basket that the customs guys had ummmed about before finally letting me keep it.

'I wasn't going to ask that,' Mum said.

I shared a look with Dad.

'I *wasn't*,' Mum insisted.

Dad said, 'Lorna,' in a warning tone, then turned to me. 'Hey, sweetie.' We hugged.

'Yes Lorna, listen to your husband.' I said smiling gratefully at Dad. I'd taken to calling her Lorna when I was fifteen just to annoy her. When I'm irritated, it comes back out – like now, since I was feeling a bit weary that I hadn't even stepped out of the airport, and already the Relationship Rant was beginning.

'I mean, but *did* you meet anyone? Perhaps any kind of special someone?' my mum asked, leading both of us out of the airport, marching ahead. 'I think we're parked over here, Ted.'

I thought about Nick for a second. 'No one special, Mum.'

To make matters worse, she didn't get the hint, and I had her smiling at me over the parking machine, suggesting it was time to start dating.

'I can't just start it, Mum. It's not a car engine, or a board game.'

'Well, try that on-the-line meeting thing perhaps?'

'Online dating?' I screwed up my nose. 'No, thanks. It just doesn't seem natural. Organic. Who picks out a date from a series of photos like one would pick a jumper out of a catalogue?'

'Well, I got this top on-the-line,' Mum said, pointing to her silky pink T-shirt. I had meant to ask where she got it and tell her not to go shopping there again. It looked strange, almost like PVC, too shiny and a little too tight, too.

'Online,' I corrected her again, stuffing the money in the ticket machine.

'Just give it a go,' she said, nodding. 'You never know.' She paused while my dad heaved my backpack into the boot of the car in the parking lot. 'Ted, don't put it in that way!' Dad leaned in, and turned the backpack the other way. Mum nodded and slammed the boot.

'Now, Ted, take the trolley back to the trolley bay. Why are you just staring into space like that?' She waved her hand in front of his face. Then turned to look at me. 'Did you know Bec has a new baby?'

'Yeah, I saw. But how do you know that?'

She waved her hand as if I'd asked something silly. 'Facebook, dear.'

'But they're not your friends on Facebook. Are they?'

'No, but they're your friends. I think they call it face-stalking.'

'Have you liked one of their photos by accident?' Oh, God, I felt mortified. How could I explain that? 'Oh, sorry, guys, that was just my grandkid-wanting mother wanting me to have a life like yours. Please excuse her.'

'No, of course not! Dear, give me some credit.' She paused. 'At least, I don't think so.'

'Mum, please don't do that again.'

'Doesn't everyone in this day and age?' she said casually, getting into the car.

She talked non-stop as Dad drove us out of the airport and pulled onto the highway for the hour's trip home to Sydney's North Shore. For the entire journey I managed to get in about twenty words, and the rest of the time I heard about the Chus (our neighbours) putting in a pool, whether or not the Sinclairs (other neighbours) were having marital problems, and something about a grey cat that kept finding its way into our yard and mewing for food at the back door.

When I got home, it was 11 p.m., too late to do anything but fall straight into my old, comfy bed.

The next morning Mum dragged me out of bed to go to the pool.

'I'm still jet-lagged,' I mumbled into Mr Bear.

'You'll love it, Emma, it's good for your physique.' She looked at the empty bowl on my dresser, and raised her eyebrows. 'Ice cream? In bed?'

'Actually, it was yoghurt.' It wasn't. It was ice cream.

Mum stripped back the covers then clapped her hands, 'Right, up you get!' When I didn't move, she reminded me, 'Betty's been asking about you ever since you left.'

'Betty?' My ears picked up. 'She's still alive?'

'Yes, Emma,' Mum sighed. 'She's only in her early seventies.'

'OK, OK, I'm coming.' I stumbled out of bed, threw my swimming costume and towel in a bag. The truth is, I love aqua aerobics, even though I'm decades younger than everyone else. Before I left for London, I went every Saturday to the local pool with Betty and the gang.

In the pool change room I changed into the old swimming costume I'd found in the bottom of my closet. It was chic black Speedo, size fourteen, with a large print on the front that read in white letters 'HAWAII'. I got the right side strap on, but the left side just wouldn't stretch. I caught sight of myself in the bright changeroom mirrors and realised something terrible: it didn't fit. Damn.

Under these horrid lights, my pale thighs appeared clotted with cellulite. But when I stepped out of the lights, the cellulite didn't disappear as I'd thought (hoped) it would. My belly, which had always been somewhat flat, had a roll and a mound of pudge, that I'd never noticed in London, being dressed in jeans and jackets most of the year. My arms were undefined, and, when I held them up, the lagging skin where my triceps should have been, moved with a three-second delay, as though it was perpetually trying to keep up.

My dark blonde hair, long and wavy in the best of conditions, was now frizzy with humidity and escaping like a prisoner from my ponytail, my green eyes looked dull and sunken into my face and, to make matters worse, my chin had broken out in a heap of whiteheads since I'd got back. I looked like a very large, hungover version of Kate Winslet.

Had I looked like this in Fiji? During my night with Nick? I felt horrified ... surely not. But it had been less than a week and so I guessed I really had looked like this.

'Oh God, it doesn't fit any more.'

'Hmmm, yes.' She was looking me up and down. 'It doesn't.'

I sat on the wooden benches feeling deflated. I stared at her trim figure; her string-bean legs were smaller than my arms. How did I even come from her?

'Well, Emma, that's why we're here. So you can exercise your way to a tight tum and bum!'

'You sound like one of those annoying motivational personal trainers,' I said glumly.

Lorna laughed. 'Funny you should say that. I'm thinking of getting my certificate.'

My mouth dropped open. 'You're going to be a personal trainer?'

'Well.' She looked at herself in the mirror and flounced her blonde shoulder-length hair. 'Why not? Ted's so busy in that damn garden, he may as well live in it. I want to do something for me.'

She fished around for fifty dollars in her purse and put it in my hand. 'Now go and get yourself a new costume from the shop upstairs.'

'Thanks, Mum.'

The class had almost started by the time I slipped into the pool wearing a new black costume and pool-regulated swimming cap. But they'd run out of the normal swimming caps, and so I'd had to buy a new petal-covered old-woman's swimming cap, in a soft baby pink. It made me think of Nick. His hands. His kisses. But that was in the *past*, Emma, I told myself. Stop thinking about Fiji!

Tina, the class instructor, was getting everyone to do eggbeater legs and arms.

'Emma!' a raspy voice called from the other petal caps.

'Betty!' I exclaimed, swimming over to her.

'How was your trip?' she said breathlessly, keeping her wrinkled face above the water. Some grey curls had escaped out of the side of her pink petal hat and were wet and plastered across her forehead.

'Great!'

'Got any goss for this old girl?'

'Well, I learnt how to do the American two-step. I celebrated the Mexican dance of the dead. And I'm very good at telling an enchilada from a burrito.'

She laughed and I could see the gold fillings in her teeth. Her robust arms and legs pumped hard, moving her thick body up and down in the water.

Tina blew her whistle, and we started running clockwise in a circle, creating a whirlpool.

'How was London?' Betty spluttered.

'Grey!' I spat out a mouthful of chlorinated water.

She laughed. 'You are a little pale.'

'And fat.' I grunted.

'Nothing like some indoor exercise for that!' She winked.

Tina blew her whistle again. We turned against the whirlpool current and went anti-clockwise. For the next hour, it took all my effort to keep my head above the surface.

I was absolutely exhausted by the end of the class; I needed to float a little on my back before my shaky legs could kick me to the edge of the pool. And even then, it took me five attempts before I could pull myself out of the water.

Chapter 5

'Why haven't you called him?' Tansy demanded.

We were sitting in Miss Marmalade, a cosy bungalow café, nestled into a corner booth, filled with plump pink cushions. Tansy, sleep-deprived, had almost fallen asleep twice in five minutes. She'd apologised – having three children meant sleep was a foreign concept. She'd also brought her toddler Brie with her, who was happily biting down on an old rabbit toy as if it tasted like chocolate.

In a few minutes, we'd managed a quick catch-up of events. Tansy had shared how it had been seven years since she'd gone to the toilet or had a shower by herself, and thank goodness for the new au pair who was looking after Toby, all of which reminded me of what my life might have been like, had I stayed and married Murray. And I'd given Tansy my highlights reel of my last seven years, finishing with Nick without adding in the not showing up to a seafood lunch bit, because I couldn't bring myself to say it aloud yet. Which had made her eyes widen. She'd muttered, 'Oh, wow, single life,' and then demanded I call him.

'Nick sounds really nice. Give me one bad thing about

him,' Tansy protested on behalf of a man she'd never met.

'He sleeps with girls on the first night,' I pointed out then added silently, *and he gives girls the wrong phone number.*

'And so did you,' Tansy challenged me.

'Exactly! It was a fling, and a really good one, but nothing more than that.' I took a bite of my sourdough toast with avocado. 'Besides, I'm not looking for a fling. I want to find someone, you know, forever.'

'Well,' Tansy said, thinking aloud. 'He seems to like everything you do: travelling, he's got banter, he's apparently gorgeous, he's got a good career—'

'Which he seemed to really hate.'

Tansy raised her eyebrows. 'You've never regretted a job?' Then kept on rattling off her list. 'He's got a timeshare in Fiji, which means he's financially stable, he's spontaneous, going for a skinny dip, but seemed attentive what with getting you drinks and towels, and being quite a gentleman. Yes, he slept with you on the first night – I'm not suggesting you marry him, but a little coffee date could be good,' Tansy said, nibbling the side of her cream cheese blueberry bagel, then she put it down and yawned. 'Speaking of coffees, where are ours?'

She looked up at the waitress in hope, who signalled they'd be out shortly.

'I think really all he wanted was to get in my trousers.' I smiled wryly. 'And he did a very good job.'

Tansy looked down at my comfy extra-large black trousers, which I'd chosen because they were the only ones in my wardrobe that still fitted. 'Well, they are nice trousers.'

We laughed. We'd always shared the same type of humour since we met at kindergarten.

'These? Did you want a catwalk? I've been to Italy, I know how they do it in Milan,' I said in a fun, teasing voice, kicking out a leg trying to look seductive, but ending up looking more like an awkward newborn fawn learning to walk.

'Well, I think you should consider him, at least for a coffee.' Tansy was as stubborn as a mule most of the time. But I loved that about her.

I shrugged.

Tansy swallowed audibly and paused, before finally saying, 'Have you talked to him since you got back?'

'Him?' Then I realised she didn't mean Nick, she meant Murray. *He's not coming.*

Tansy must have seen the look on my face, because she quickly said, 'Sorry, I shouldn't have said anything.' She looked flustered.

'It's OK.' I looked at her. 'It was a long time ago. And no, to answer your question, I haven't seen him, talked to him, thought about him. Much.'

'Facebook stalked?'

I half smiled. 'Maybe once. Years ago.'

'And?'

'He'd blocked me. But I heard through the grapevine, he's married. Kids. House in the burbs. All the trimmings.'

'Oh.'

I took a sip of water. 'It's OK, Tans, it is. I didn't want those things.'

'Didn't or don't?' she asked softly.

'Didn't.' I looked up at her. 'I mean, I still don't want a house with a massive mortgage, on the busline, and a nine to five job in an office for another forty years. But I think I do want to get a job, buy a house, and get married.'

'You think?'

'Fine, I *want*. Is that better?' I decided to tell Tansy about The Plan. It was pinned to my corkboard at home, so it was the first thing I saw when I woke up each morning. I'd even gone as far as to cut out some images that looked like the house I'd want (country cottage) and some really cheesy advertisements of couples laughing as they did things together (I think they were trying to sell mortgage insurance). It felt extremely cheesy, but vision boards were a *thing*, apparently; besides, it couldn't hurt. I confessed all this to Tansy.

When she finished laughing, she said brightly, 'Well, didn't Nick give you his number? Step three, possible tick.'

I groaned. 'Marrying us off already? Please. Anyway, the number he gave me could be a fake. It could be for the local pizza place.'

'Well, I could go for a full meat-lovers with barbecue sauce.' Tansy sighed. 'I'm all for eating my feelings at the moment. Or just eating for energy. I'm so tired I can't tell any more.' Tansy was as slim as a rake, and tall, she'd be a size ten at the most, and had beautiful long dark hair, dark cocoa eyes, and olive skin. The last thing she needed to worry about was eating too much.

I handed her the menu. 'I'm a supportive friend – if you need to eat everything on this menu, I'll pay for half. I'd pay for it all, but, you know.' I shook my wallet and a scant few coins jangled. 'I don't know if I could cover it.'

Tansy grinned ruefully. 'This friend doesn't need your money. She just wants her friend to find a partner, so she has something to do on the weekends when the rest of us are knee-high in diapers.' She scanned the menu. 'Although a little piece of lemon pie couldn't hurt, could it?'

'Get the lemon pie,' I encouraged her. 'Anyway, sometimes it's better not knowing. What if I tried to call Nick, and got Luigi's pizza palace? Sometimes ignorance is bliss.'

'What do you mean?'

I quickly told her about sitting at Freshwaters, and his disconnected number. I brushed it off a bit, but it had really hurt. She let out a long huffy breath 'What is *with* some people? God. I'm sorry that happened to you. You're right don't ever call him. Well you don't have his number to call, do you? What a dick. We shall never ever speak of him again.'

I felt a wave of gratitude wash over me, she really was the most loyal friend. 'Thanks Tansy. Anyway' I said, keen to change the subject. 'I do need to find a job though.' I opened up the newspaper on the café's table in front of us. All I could see were ads for chefs and kitchen hands, so I shut it firmly. It reminded me too much of Los Tacos, which made me shudder as the waitress delivered our coffees. 'What about public relations? Or marketing? Do you think I could do that back here?'

Tansy narrowed her eyes at me suspiciously. 'Need I remind you of how much you wanted to leave your marketing job? I believe you told me never to let you work in an office again.'

I laughed. 'I did say that, didn't I? Well, I'm older and wiser now,' I teased. 'Plus, I made great tea in the London office and didn't get too claustrophobic.'

'Hmm ...' she said, staring at me. 'Are you sure?'

'Yes.' I nodded my head. 'Ever since I realized I was leaving London months ago, I've been sending out my CV for any PR job I can find, even assistant ones, gosh, even *receptionist* roles in PR firms. But not one response.' I was feeling quite dejected about that. 'I keep getting told "you don't have *enough* experience", or "you don't have the *right* experience". All those long days working at Forster & Wolfe, as a PR Assistant, hasn't helped me at all.'

'Well, then, I've got some good news for you.' She took a long sip of coffee. 'Oh, God, caffeine, what would I do without it?' She paused and closed her eyes. 'Sorry, I just need to let this soak in. I got a total of three hours' sleep last night. I'm like an eternal zombie.' Tansy downed her coffee in three large gulps. 'Anyway, it's a favour.'

'For me, or you, or someone else?'

'For everyone possibly.' Tansy got out her phone and started scrolling. 'When I heard you were back in town, I put out some feelers, and, well, I may have mentioned you worked in PR in London.' Tansy looked up at me. 'Anyway, I talked to Jess and Mona, and they talked to Beattie, and she talked to a few other people.'

When I looked blank, Tansy said, 'Friends from my previous life, when I worked at Sony and Universal.' Aha, I twigged. Tansy used to be a senior manager in marketing and sales, which meant we'd got a lot of red-carpet premiere tickets and stacks of free DVDs. We all missed those days a bit. 'And they know someone, who knows someone else, who's looking for a PR and events person.'

I sat up straighter, and felt a tingle of excitement rush through my body. 'I could do that.'

I imagined travelling across Sydney, maybe even Australia. Putting on events, meeting clients, maybe they'd even let me draw the designs for an ad campaign, or an event invitation.

Tansy nodded. 'I know you could! Which is maybe why I told them you were really experienced.'

'How experienced?' I bit my lip.

'Well, that you'd had a lot of international experience, and had run your own events before, and been a PR superstar really.' She looked bashful. 'I think I just got carried away, because I wanted you to find a job so you actually stayed in Sydney, rather than leaving us again.' Her face looked crumpled and sad.

'Oh, Tansy! I'm here to stay now. Promise.' I gulped. 'But I have nowhere near that experience.'

Suddenly her face flushed with excitement. 'I haven't told you the best bit yet – the job is with Maker.'

My heart thumped in my chest. Maker was *the* place to work. It was a swish multi-service PR and media, events, advertising and marketing firm, with a stellar reputation. They were known as creative, funky with a cool edge, and the one of the leading companies in Australia. People were excited about working at Maker, because it meant international job offers would literally drop at your feet. After a few years you could walk out of Maker and stride into a top job in New York, or London, or Italy.

I paused. 'Is there a reason they don't want someone else, who's actually amazing? I know you talked me up, but surely there are hundreds of people more qualified and dying to work at Maker?'

'Ah,' Tansy said. 'Well, they need someone who wants to do the work, and doesn't mind, ah, how do I put this? Being paid a nominal amount.'

'You mean tiny.'

She nodded. 'I mean tiny.'

'What exactly is that, in dollar figures?'

'I'm not sure exactly, they wouldn't let on, just they didn't have the full budget to cover what they wanted, so they're looking for someone who wants to get Maker on their CV, and doesn't mind "getting dirty". I take that to mean what it normally does in corporate speak, which is doing a LOT of work, long hours with bad pay. But it will work out in the end for you.'

'It will work out in the end,' I repeated her words, thinking that if I had Maker on my CV I could get a job anywhere after that. I could be in Paris again. Or Rome. Or London. Or even better – in just a few years I could create my own PR firm in a small town, and then paint on the weekends – yes! I could do this!

'Of course, you're going to have to apply, just like everyone else. But at least they know to look out for you, and I'm sure they'll give you an interview,' Tansy said, handing me a scrap of paper with Maker's details.

'But my CV? I mean, I don't really have that experience,' I worried.

'Em, you've travelled around the world by yourself for almost a decade. I'm sure you can handle some press releases and putting on some events.'

'True, but wouldn't I be lying?'

'Who doesn't lie a little on their CV?' She shrugged. 'Isn't that a given? No one believes in the honesty and integrity of CVs.' She laughed loudly. 'Now, here comes my lemon pie!'

Right on cue, Brie dropped her dummy and started bawling as if a thousand ants had just bit her. Tansy had to abort the lemon pie mission because, instead of calming down, Brie got even louder, her red face now nearing a troubling shade of purple. Finally, Tansy picked Brie up in a wrestler-style grip, threw some money down on the counter, and waved as she stormed out – yelling, 'Another time soon!'

I think I must have had a horrified look on my face. I was sitting looking at an empty chair, and a lone little piece of lemon pie, knowing I'd have to eat it.

She was halfway down the path when she yelled back, 'And for God's sake, apply for that job!'

Chapter 6

'So how long will you be with us?' Mum asked one after-noon, shooing my feet off the couch. I was watching *Wonder Woman*, and wondering where I could get a pair of gold wrist cuffs, and how I'd learn to ride a stallion bareback. Wonder Woman would never have had to fudge her CV a little.

'On this earth?' I asked. 'I plan to be around a little longer, thanks for asking.'

'Here. Home, Emma.' Mum bustled about the living room with a duster, flicking off imaginary nano-particles of dust. 'I'm sure you'll want to get yourself started, a job, a house.'

'Mum, I've literally been home for a few days, and am so jet-lagged I was up last night until the sun was coming up, wired like I'd been drinking too much coffee.'

'Emma, you're not in your twenties any more. You need a plan. Goals.'

I did have a plan. A three-step plan. Step 1, I needed a job, and, just as I put that out into the universe, along came Maker. The idea of applying had been running through my head ever since Tansy had mentioned it a week ago. But I'd been procrastinating at the thought of having to lie on my CV to get a job. I didn't mind a slight tweak here and there – I mean, who didn't do that? Even so, changing my CV more than that, made me feel horribly guilty. But all the other jobs I'd applied for, I'd received that terrible standard email:

We regret to inform you that you have not been successful in your application for this role. We will keep your CV on file for any other relevant roles we have in the future.

Trouble was, my CV would be filed away and no one would probably ever look at it again. At last count, I'd applied for a total of 27 roles in PR, jobs more junior than I wanted, with measly little salaries, but I'd failed to even get an interview for them. Tansy had given my CV a onceover and told me honestly, 'Em, this isn't going to cut it in the Sydney market. You were probably lucky to score that London gig. Basically all you did in your last role was file and answer phones.'

'And make coffee.'

'Right.' I could hear her sigh. 'That's not PR at all.'

'I know. The things I did just to travel around Europe.'

'Well, you could apply to be an office assistant. Are you interested in that? You'd probably be snapped up in a second.'

'Not really.'

'Well, if I was you, I'd just fake it until you make it. You're capable Em, you're smart and savvy, and you said you listened to everyone in PR even if you didn't do the tasks, at least you understand what they're talking about.'

But, I wasn't so sure. Instead, I'd sent my CV to a few

recruiters, most hadn't responded, but Shirley Henderson from Blue Recruiting, had given me a quick call and suggested a graduate intern program would be perfect, if I was looking to get my foot in the door.

'In fact, we have openings for the next program at Ludrum, starting in three months!'

'Three months?' That felt so far away. My mind started to worry about paying bills and finding a new home without a job.

'Yes, and I know they'd love you Emma. You'd get to rotate around all the different teams, copywriting, social media, publicity and media.'

'OK.' I said warming a little to the idea. 'What's the salary?'

Shirley laughed. 'Oh Emma, it's not a paid position, but when you finish the program in a year, it could set you up for a role as a PR Assistant.'

There didn't seem to be many options left, and my bank balance didn't look as healthy as it had in England – everything was going out, and nothing was coming in. And Tansy had said she'd pulled a few strings to get my CV noticed, but it needed work.

For the next few days, I kept thinking, a chance to work at Maker? Tansy was right, working at Maker opened doors into any future you wanted. Finally, I decided it wouldn't hurt to just *look* at the role. I sat on my bed and flicked open the job link Tansy had given me. There it was, PR and Events Advisor, Maker. The job described multiple events, working across well-known labels and companies, and government. I scanned Maker's list of clients – many of whom were on the front of the Sunday papers, in fact on the front and centre of all papers, and every news site. They were in every sector, in every industry.

Taking a deep breath, I opened my CV, and started tweaking it a little. The Los Tacos nightmare place became LoTa, a chic Spanish PR firm, where I managed all the events (aka food ordering, waitressing and children's parties). I felt bad about this one, but it had only been five months, so it wasn't like I was pretending it was five years.

My PR Assistant coffee girl days became Creative PR Advisor and Event Coordinator (because when taking meeting notes, I'd been privy to a lot of senior executive discussions. How to 'spin' things. How to create a 'brand'. How to 'pitch'. Even if I hadn't really done that much of it myself. And towards the end they had allowed me to draft press releases, blogs and social media posts even though I wasn't sure they were actually published.)

And my Bali days became PR Executive, connecting Australians with Indonesia, building international relationships, and raising the media profile (well, I did get an IT guy to create a website where I sold jewellery. That was media-ish).

I googled PR résumés and copied over words they used to make me sound irresistible. When it was finished, I had to admit I sounded like a PR superstar. But I couldn't send it. I couldn't pretend this amazing PR woman was me. It was way too far from the truth. So, I took out the glitzy senior PR words and responsibilities. But without them, my CV seemed bland and junior. *No wonder I hadn't made it through to any interviews.*

And, I thought back to what Tansy had said earlier. Who doesn't lie a bit on their CV?

So, I put a smattering of the glitzy PR buzz words, responsibilities and achievements I'd supposedly had back in and thought, *there, I've only fudged this a bit.* Feeling nervous, and still with a pang of guilt, I took a deep breath, before sending my CV to the amazing powers that be, whispering prayers of hope. *Please, please, please.*

A week later, I got a call from Maker's recruitment team informing me I'd made it through to an interview. I was so stunned I couldn't even speak. When they asked me what time I could make it in, I breathlessly said, 'Any time,' and when they asked me to spell my last name, it took me three times to get it right, I kept fumbling over the letters 'o' and 'n' and, to make up for it, or some other odd reason, I started speaking in a really posh English accent, as if that excused everything.

When I put down the phone in astonishment, I ran around the house in my tracksuit pants doing a dancing victory lap. Thank God my mother wasn't there because I almost knocked over some ancient gold urn/vase thing from Italy that she loved so much, I was sure I'd seen her pray to it.

Maker's recruitment team emailed through all the job details. My interview was with Donna Allbright, Associate Creative Director (three PR buzz words that meant nothing – but everything) and head of the specialist events team. They sent me through a full position description for the PR and Events Advisor role, which was a whopping seven pages long.

Finally, disclosed at the bottom of the email was the salary, in measly little numbers. Tansy was right, it was tiny. Teeny tiny. I wouldn't be able to afford renting a mid-city apartment. No café lunches. No morning espressos. It would take me at least fifteen years before I even had enough to consider a deposit for a parking spot, let alone a house. In fact, I was looking at a Kmart budget. Beans on toast. Wearing the same work trousers three days a week – would people notice?

But it was worlds away from working on burrito Tuesday, and I was willing to do anything to not be covered in deep-fryer grease. *It's a stepping stone,* I kept telling myself. It means in two years I could go anywhere. Plus, I needed to get out of my family's house – I'd already had enough of High Knees Lorna, who this morning had strode into my room at the crack of dawn, and poured water on me from a glass, so I could 'get prepared' for aqua aerobics. I needed my own place, like *yesterday*.

Maker was located right in the middle of Sydney, a plush building, with black funky wallpaper and chandelier lighting. The entrance looked like a slick bachelor pad, all expensive black leather and white patent leather ottomans, the walls lined with the kind of geometric graphic print people raved about, but I thought looked like a wonky zebra. Just looking at it made me feel drunk.

There was a large TV screen that hung down over the two identical male receptionists, both with big blue eyes and light brown hair in topknot buns. The screen was flashing through headlines so fast I couldn't keep up. It was flickering like a strobe light and I felt I might have a panic attack or epileptic fit if I kept watching it.

I sat in the foyer, waiting for Donna Allbright, trying not to stick to the black leather chair. Out of habit, I started nervously scrolling on my phone. But that wasn't professional, was it? I put my phone in my old – and slightly frayed if you looked really close – faux-leather black bag and zipped it up. There wasn't one magazine or newspaper on the table to flick through. I was just about to reach back in and pull out my phone to search PR trends, when the elevator doors opened and a woman walked straight towards me.

She towered above me in stilettos so high and pointy I could never balance in them, even if I was holding onto a wall. They were black and shiny as if she'd just dipped them in a fresh coat of lacquer. Her perfect slim legs were encased in slightly pleated black wool pants, and she had on a silk top with pearl buttons. Her blonde hair was long and had an unbrushed, sex-hair look. She had barely there natural-looking make-up and the focus was drawn to her bright red lips. Her cheekbones were high and pronounced. I bet she never needed a contouring kit. Her eyebrows were immaculately perfect – full and arched. She looked French. She looked designer. She looked like everything little girls ever hoped to be when they grew up.

'Emma.' She smiled thinly as though she'd never want to admit she was in the same room as me. I stood and hoped my palms weren't sweaty. But she didn't offer her hand. She just said a quick, breathy, '*Follow*,' and led the way through the swanky foyer to the lift, which we rode for a long time in silence, into the sky.

Level 46 was a floor of colourful meeting rooms. Donna led me into a pink room – literally everything was pink.

'This is the black room.' She smiled elegantly, taking a seat in a fuchsia chaise, as if we were in her living room.

'Huh?' I stood there awkwardly like a maid who didn't know if she should sit or bow or dust something.

'Black room. You know, it's like ...' she waved her perfectly manicured hand around the blush room '... ironic.'

'Of course.' I nodded too energetically and sat on the small pink stool opposite. But the way the stool was positioned meant I couldn't quite cross my legs, so I sat with my knees open, and my body slightly forward, as if on a toilet, whilst she lay about, on the chaise, as though she were about to welcome a lover.

'Remember, this is just a casual and informal chat. That's how we like our interviews. It's much more organic. Feel free to be who you are. We take that very seriously here.' Donna paused. 'So. What are you about, Emma?'

What was I about? Suddenly all I could think about was ice cream and lying on the couch in sweats and my mum wanting me to go with her to aqua aerobics. But she wasn't asking what I did on the weekend. She was asking me to sell myself, my work ethic. I hadn't forgotten how these job interview questions were set up.

'Coffee,' I said quickly. So quickly I hadn't even begun to formulate what I even meant by that.

'Coffee?' Donna's lips turned up slightly; was it in amusement or was it a sneer?

'Yes, coffee. Firstly, I love it. Don't you? And it's, um, well, everyone drinks it. You know? In fact, people crave it. Every day. They line up at their favourite place. They'll travel long distances to get their favourite cup. And the people who haven't had it don't know they crave it yet, but they do. They will.'

'And so, you're, um, saying that you're ... coffee?' Donna looked dubious. She was looking over my shoes, my pants, my top, my bargain four-dollar necklace – could she tell they were all cheap knock-offs? Was she wondering, if I was coffee, what did that make her – vintage Cristal Champagne that cost over tenthousand dollars a bottle?

'No, I'm the person selling the coffee. Behind the coffee. I'm the one who makes you want coffee, even when you don't.' I wriggled around a bit in my seat feeling quite uncomfortable.

'So that sounds like you want to be a barista?' She did an empty little laugh.

'Well, I think coffee can be anything. You know? You could switch it out for a car. Or a lifestyle. I think creating intrigue and need is about understanding how to angle something,' I said, trying desperately to steer our chat back into the world of PR and the role I really wanted.

'Aha.' She nodded politely. I couldn't tell if that had been a win, or if I was just blathering. Because I knew the truth of it. I was blathering. 'So, you can angle anything so I want to buy it? How?' She looked around. 'Make me want something in this room. Really sell it to me.'

I felt like fainting. Sell a pink room? I thought about what a real estate agent would say. What an interior designer might mention. The carpet looked expensive. The chandelier above us almost magical. The chaise was nice. But *nice* wouldn't sell a thing. I moved my bag, which was behind me, to the side, where it leaned against my leg. I took my jacket off and folded it on top of my bag and then smiled at Donna.

I stood and asked her to step outside. I waited for her to stand too. She looked taken off guard.

'Where are we going?'

I opened the door and let her out first, wondering if my idea would work. Would I be sent from the building and told never to return? Either way, I thought this was make or break. Do or die. I'd have to wing it.

I closed the door behind us and stood there like an unsure bouncer. Except, I wasn't very mean. Donna had her eyebrows raised, and her dainty nose slightly flared, as though she'd just smelt my cheap Kmart underwear. We were both standing uncomfortably in the plush black (real black) corridor. I cleared my throat.

'So, Donna, what you don't know is that when I was in there, I left something behind my chair I think you'd really like. Did you see it? You probably didn't. I was quick. It was while we were chatting about the coffee.'

'So that coffee talk was a cover?' Her eyes squinted with the hint of a smile; she seemed interested.

'Yes.' It wasn't. It wasn't a cover at all.

'But the only way you get to go inside the, um, black room, and find what I've left for you, is if you know the password.'

'Password?' Her eyebrows rose.

'Yes, password.' I had no password. I had nothing. I was making this up as I went along.

She stood for a while, thinking. I was sweating under my arms, and into my bra, and I'm sure a little rivulet ran down my leg, which seemed to come from my general bottom area.

'Was there a clue?'

'Yes.' No. There was no clue. I had done nothing. Left no clue.

'Lifestyle?' she asked.

I shook my head and did a laugh, as if to say, *Oh, Donna, really?*

'Well, I just don't know.' She ran her hands through her hair. 'But I'm quite intrigued.'

'So, you want to know what's inside the room?' I asked.

She laughed more persuasively this time. 'Well, yes, I do.'

'And you'd want to buy your way in, to see what I'd left in there for you?'

She laughed again. 'I would!'

'Excuse me for a second.' I held up my hand to her, quickly opened the door, stepped into the queasy pink room and closed the door immediately in her face. I waited two seconds – long enough for her to think I was actually doing something – then grabbed my bag and opened the door.

'Well, Donna, it's back with me now. But if you can work out the password, give me a call, and I'll bring it back for you.'

I held out my hand to shake hers. I was leaving. I was leaving the Goddamn interview. And hopefully this little stunt would set me apart from all the other 'sell me this room' descriptions she'd had to live through.

Her mouth was slightly agape as she shook my hand.

'I'll see myself out,' I called cheerfully as I turned and walked down the corridor. 'Thanks again!'

When I turned the corner, she was still standing outside the door to that ironic black-pink room, her head slightly cocked to the side, perhaps still trying to figure it all out.

As I rode the lift back down to ground level, I knew I had either won myself a position at Maker or I had just made the absolute biggest fool of myself and would never work in PR again.

Chapter 7

After *that* interview I needed a night out. With lots of wine. I called everyone and demanded they come to the pub. They all said they would *love* to, but just *couldn't* because of kids, or burning dinners on the stove, or having piles of laundry to get through. Maggie was exhausted and on kid bathing and bedtime duty, Tansy and Brie were fighting off uncontrollable gastro (I didn't need the details) and Amy was having an argument with Brad, her fiancé, over what type of candles to have at the wedding. I wanted to text, *there's more than one type?* Then thought it would only add fuel to the fiancé fire, and deleted it.

I tried friends I hadn't spoken to in ages. I went on a Facebook binge and group emailed long-lost friends I hadn't spoken to in years, suggesting we start the night off with a round of shots – I even offered to buy us all tequila, or whisky or fluffy bunnies or whatever people's drink of choice was. No luck. Everyone was with partners, and kids, and sick kids, and broken dishwashers, or on the couch in sweats and not moving after hideously long days. I couldn't blame them. But was this what life was like now?

Since arriving back in Sydney, I'd begun to realise that when I asked any of my friends to go for a coffee, they all had to check with the husband/lover/partner/nanny /babysitter/ parents-in-law/dog/cat/dusty shelf-top before they could commit. Brunch was another story. So were drinks and dinner. I needed to schedule that in their diaries at least three months in advance, as if I were booking in to see a ridiculously popular hairdresser.

Finally, I popped open a bottle of wine and decided instead to stay in and watch *The Proposal*. Like always, it made me want Ryan Reynolds to secretly fall in love with me rather than Sandra Bullock. After the movie, and half a bottle of wine, it was only 8 p.m. and too early for bed. All my friends were busy, they had lives, and I was laying on my bed, in my pajamas, in my parents' house, and I realised – this is not what most thirty-four-year-olds are doing. For a second, I felt a pang of regret wash over me. I regretted going overseas, I regretted not marrying Murray, I regretted leaving for so long – for what? For some travel and living in a house crammed with other expats in London. I could have been back here, working on my career, stepping up the ladder, finding a husband like all my friends.

All these thoughts were running around my mind, and truthfully, I felt a bit lonely. And a bit blue. I suddenly craved to talk to someone, but the last thing I felt like doing was putting on some clothes and going out to a bar or a restaurant by myself. And before I could think better of it, I downloaded an online dating app on my phone, you know, just to *see* what it was like.

I shouldn't do this, I thought. But despite my trepidation, I found myself clicking yes, I'd like to confirm my profile. I uploaded my main photo – tanned and happy, I'm standing on the balcony of a Monaco hotel, my arms in the air, a large grin on my face. My normally light brown hair is long and highlighted blonde by the summer sun, pulled into a large messy bun. My green eyes are happy, bright. My legs look almost muscular underneath a blue sundress, rather than stocky and a bit wobbly, like they actually are. And just like that, in a few easy clicks, I was officially online.

Let the games begin.

In one hour and another half a bottle of wine, I had ten 'kisses' in my inbox. I'm not sure if this was a normal number. Should I be expecting more? This meant one man every six minutes had been 'kissing' me. And when you put it like that, I'd been quite a busy girl.

I scanned the catalogue of men within the parameters I'd set. Age thirty-three to forty. Distance under 50km. Must have a photo. And the photos were *interesting*. I was seeing quite a lot of men without shirts. A lot of girls would like this. I'm not sure if I did. I'm not repelled by the six-pack, by all means, well done to you dedicated souls out there that have a set. That means plenty of non-fat whatever and stomach crunches. Or perhaps just really lucky genes. And muscles are definitely a thumbs-up attribute on a guy. I'm definitely not going to say *well well, you have a six-pack? A* six-pack? *It's over.* But, I could only imagine our conversations would be solely about how many reps they did at the gym that morning and what they can do with tuna – tuna salad, tuna bake, tuna in omelettes, tuna in cottage cheese.

And I did feel a little strange knowing these guys waxed their chests before I even knew their real names. Speaking of names there were some interesting choices; CaringGuy, SweetGuy, LookingforLove, FunlovingMan etc. There's also the six-pack guys Hot4U, CheekyBoi, FixitMan and FunTimez. This seemed to leave little choice for the newest members who had to get a little more creative to pick a unique name. One example went something like 'xxoohxxooh' which made me feel like I was either watching Gossip Girl or overhearing a budget X-rated flick.

And suddenly these men were landing in my inbox, 'kissing' me, and then making some very unusual offers.

36yo man led with this, *I'm a guy with a tiny heart.*

Probably not your best selling point. Maybe you should be sharing this with your cardiologist instead?

40yo divorced guy emailed to tell me, *I'm naughty. Very naughty.*

De-friend. Block. Reject. Hide under my mattress.

45yo Italian guy 'kissed' me and I dutifully accepted his offer to take it to the 'next level' with an email.

Do you like ital pizza? That was his entire email to me, no hello, or goodbye or anything else.

Me: *Hey there, Yes I do like Italian pizza—actually it's one of my favourite foods. I love Italian coffee too—actually all coffee really. Especially at 7am in the morning when I'm struggling into work. Do you live or work in the city?*

Him: *You should come for ital pizza. norton st.*

Me: *I actually live on the north shore so not really out norton street way all that much. Perhaps we could grab a coffee halfway instead? Have you always lived in Australia?*

Him: *I from Aus. come to ital pizza.*

I was beginning to think I was part of an advertising campaign for Norton Street. On the other hand, he clearly thought I was from the immigration department enquiring about his living status and his strongly confirming he was from Australia – except without the use of helping verbs.

All the other men had written 'Hi'. And that was it. Nothing else, just 'Hi'. I responded 'Hi'. And they replied 'Hello'. It seemed this online dating bar was set low, very very low.

The last 'kiss' in my inbox was from SnakeGuy, who managed to write a whole six sentences, about himself and seemed coherent and intelligent. He also referenced a book I liked, and given the low bar already set, this almost swept me off my feet. *Jeez, this is what online romance looks like.*

I said that I was happy to hear from him and I'm glad he liked *Booky Wook*. Wasn't Russell Brand just the best?

SnakeGuy wrote back within minutes and asked to add me on Facebook – was this part of the dating ritual now? I cautiously accepted. And when I did, I found out he hailed from England and liked snakes. Actually loved them. According to his frequent status updates, he currently had eight snakes in his house that liked to 'roam around'.

Now, I adore animals and even extend my love to all things reptilian, but the thought of them dropping from curtains into my hair, coiling up from the inside of a toilet bowl towards my ... erm – well it makes me feel like nervously piddling on the floor.

SnakeGuy 'liked' eighteen of my photos in two minutes after we 'friended' online. He then asked me out for dinner. I replied and downgraded dinner to coffee (in case he bought a snake and I needed a quick getaway). He didn't reply. Ten minutes later he 'liked' another ten or so of my photos, then emailed *How about that coffee?*

I replied, *'Sure sounds great. When were you thinking?'*

I took the chance to open up a second bottle of wine, even though I shouldn't. I did. While I was mid-pour SnakeGuy sent me a Facebook message. Hurrah! I excitedly opened it.

He'd written: *what's your best kiss and your favourite sex position? Send me a pic of your hot self. You're gorgeous.*

Oh God. SnakeGuy. I felt deflated. He seemed to have potential and now *this.*

Even though I didn't want to remember, my brain flicked through my memories back to my best kiss – Nick. Kissing him had been so easy. Oh Nick, why did you give me the wrong number? Did you really like me? Was that the only lie you told me? Was everything else a lie too?

Ugh, men. I thought. They promised things, said things to get what they wanted. And then they didn't follow through, or they gave you wrong numbers or asked you to send *hot pics.* And worse still, they got away with it, because some of us ladies were too worried about coming off bitchy, or needy, or desperate – or any of the labels they used to make us feel unsure about things we should rightly have feelings about. And I was feeling a little off about this last email, so I thought I should actually reply to SnakeGuy. I downed my entire glass of wine, before replying.

Dear SnakeGuy, playing with snakes on the loose is a bit weird. But I can work with that. What I can't work with is you asking me out several times for the never-occurring coffee. We're not planning to get a mortgage together, just a little cup of hot brown liquid. You either do want to or you don't, and frankly after all your multiple likings of my photos and asking me my favourite sex position or to send a hot pic (please), I don't.

p.s. snakes are not cuddly. Buy a dog.

p.p.s. unfriend

Maybe I hadn't given it a proper go, but it seemed there were weirdos out there, and I didn't want them turning up in my inbox, so I deleted my dating profile and wiped the app permanently from my phone. And then poured myself another wine and decided to watch *Ten Things I Hate About You*.

Chapter 8

D onna called at the very early hour of eleven the next day. 'I'm still intrigued!' she purred down the phone.

I'm still drunk, I thought, sitting up so quickly in bed, all the blood rushed to my feet and I felt woozy. My tongue was thick and my entire mouth tasted of wine.

'Emma, we'd normally have a few more chats in the process, but I have to say you really impressed me. I've been thinking about what was in the room and the password all this time. Now that you've got the job, are you going to reveal it?'

I got the job? I GOT THE JOB?

'Sorry, Donna,' I heard drunk me saying, 'but rules are rules. If you ever do figure out the password though, let me know.'

'I thought you'd say that. Well, I just know you're going to be perfect for the role. For our team. You start in two weeks and I'll have the recruitment team have your contract shipped to your address this afternoon.'

'Great,' I said with a thick tongue.

'Welcome to Maker, Emma.' After she hung up, it took me a minute to realise what had happened.

I had a grin plastered on my face, but then I felt sick. Really sick. As if I'd spent the night shucking and gobbling off oysters-sick, and everything *hurt*. I ran to the bathroom and threw up.

Knowing I needed something to fill my stomach pronto, I went into the kitchen to have a dry piece of toast. As I was eating it, I shoved a fizzy Panadol in water, gulped it down and thought about my list. Number one – get job – had been successful. I should feel happy, but I felt a little guilty too.

I called Tansy.

'I got it!'

'Oh Em! That's brilliant!'

'I'm a little nervous, actually a lot. I think I need to do a crash course in PR or something.'

'What a great idea – there are heaps of online courses you could do.' Tansy was always so supportive.

'Yeah, I'll do that.' I said starting to feel a little better about the role. 'And I need some new clothes on a very tight budget.' There was no way Donna or the rest of Maker would accept me coming into work in my cheaper-style work attire I'd bought exclusively at Primark in the UK: five pounds for a pair of trousers? Amazing! And just a tenner for a faux silk shirt! My UK employers hadn't worried at all that my cheap polyester knit top had made me sweat more than it should, as long as I was filing and sending emails. But I knew Maker was a different story.

Dad walked in the door from mowing and gardening and started washing his hands in the sink as Mum appeared, in the same instant, in the corridor.

'Ted! She's here!' before looking at me and declaring, 'We have somewhere to be.'

'We do?' I asked them both tentatively, hoping Mum wasn't trying to get us to the gym or, even worse, CrossFit.

She held up a pair of keys.

'We're going for a drive?' I guessed.

She shook her head. 'Try again.'

'You've bought me a palace and I'm emigrating to Liechtenstein.'

'No, but close.'

'That's close?' I said incredulously.

'Well, close enough. Keep guessing. Keep guessing,' she said excitedly, using this as her new mantra, rather than 'High knees'.

I laughed. 'Mum. Just tell me.'

'You have a new place. All your things are in the car, and we're going there right now.'

'How can I ...? What new place ...? What?'

Mum held up the keys even higher as though she'd just won the Mum of the Year trophy. 'You're going to be living in your new place tonight!'

Forty minutes later, I was astonished to find myself standing in my new ground-floor apartment in Marrickville, a trendy inner west suburb. My new apartment was a small studio, emphasis on the small. My double bed against one wall, it had room at the other end for a small seating area, and a galley kitchen with two stools made an intimate breakfast-bar area. The storage was next to nothing, but at least there was a wardrobe next to the bed (preventing me from ever getting out of the bed on one side) where I could hang all my new work clothes. The bathroom was long and thin, with a shower, and a large cracked window that made the wind howl as it blew.

Turns out that whilst I'd been sleeping, Mum had been talking down at the local pool about needing to ship me out of the house. A lady had overheard her (which mustn't have been hard, considering Mum was born with a megaphone lodged in her throat), and had offered her son's place whilst he was overseas for the next year. Mum had taken the keys in a second this morning at the pool, without even seeing the place.

Back in the main area, I opened the long brown curtains and looked outside. A cracked stone pathway weaved past a chipped brick fence, a kaleidoscope of spider webs and too many trees to a small barred front door, letting in only a smidge of light, which spilt across the two metres that would be called my living room.

Mum sniffed in the corner of the living room, which was also the corner of the bedroom, and almost part of the kitchen. 'Does it smell a little damp to you?'

'Nothing some spray or candles won't fix,' I said, trying to remain optimistic. It was damp, it did smell like mould, and it couldn't ever fit more than three people, but at least it was all mine.

'I shouldn't have got it without seeing it.' Mum shook her head and got down on her knees, rubbing a stained part of the carpet.

Dad chimed in, 'But it's cheap.'

'I need cheap.' I nodded, thinking of my measly little salary and leaning over to hug my Mum, which I think surprised her. 'Thanks, Mum. I mean it.'

After my parents went home, I unpacked the furniture they'd kindly donated to me. I had two fold-up chairs instead of a couch, I had a plastic dining room table, and an old off-white ottoman, but as I finished unpacking my candles, turned on my oil diffuser with lavender in it, and hung up some paintings, I looked around with a smile – it was beginning to feel more like home, like my home. Sitting on my bed, I took a sip of warm chamomile tea and pulled out my vision board and hung it above my bed. Step 1: Get a job, and Step 2: Get a house. Done. Which left me with one more step.

Step 3: Get a partner. Marry him. How hard could that be?

Chapter 9

Donna Allbright was glossy and glorious, settled on a bar stool in the middle of Maker's open-plan employee kitchen, as she looked at the gathered team of twenty in front of her, who all seemed somewhat besotted by her. The girls especially had all dressed quite like Donna. Which meant I fitted right in, in my caramel heels and red dress.

'Now, before I talk about all the wonderful projects we have coming up, I want to introduce Emma Londstown, our newest recruit.' She flicked her red-nailed hand in my direction. 'Emma wowed us in the interview, so we expect big things.'

I felt a few people eye me up suspiciously. I didn't know what to do, so I held my hand up, and then felt a bit like the Queen, so I started waving it emphatically, as if I were a five year old in the Christmas play who'd just spotted their parents in the audience, and then felt rather idiotic for doing that.

Finally, I said, 'Hey, folks,' unfortunately a bit like Porky Pig might have said it. I hoped everyone would think it ironic – which seemed to be the catchphrase here, because I'd heard two people mutter it in separate conversations in the lift and foyer – but the team just looked at me strangely. Even Donna had a quizzical look on her face.

'So, everyone, let's get a much-needed coffee then we'll break up into smaller teams for the workshops on our newest projects.' She clapped her hands twice and everyone dispersed like ants.

I walked towards the sink and grabbed a cup. A tall man in a purple turtleneck appeared next to me. Ironic? Or was he part of The Wiggles? Were they doing office entertainment now?

'Phil,' he said, nodding his head.

'Emma.' I smiled.

'You mean Porky Pig, don't you?'

'Oh, you got that?'

'Totally. It was ...' he paused, and then we both said together, '... *ironic*.'

'Coffee?' he offered, holding the cup under the automatic machine and saying 'coffee' loudly into the weird robotic AI microphone.

'Double it,' I said, looking at the measly portion tipped into the cup.

'Voila.' He pushed the cup into my hand and made himself a strong tea. 'So, brand spanking new to Maker, huh?'

'Yep.'

'Where from?'

I supposed I was meant to offer my wow career history to this question, but I didn't really have one, so instead I simply said, 'Sydney.'

'Well, that's clear. Look, you're in Nine West pumps and you work at Maker. Of course, you're from Sydney.'

'How do you know these are Nine West?'

'Pfffft.' He waved my words away like a pesty fly.

'OK, so I'm from Marrickville.' I'd never lived south of the bridge before and I was chuffed I was now in a trendy part of town. Even if everything was crammed into one room and it was almost impossible to turn around in my own bathroom and my toiletries hung from a plastic bag on a hook nailed into the ceiling. But at least I wasn't over thirty and living with my parents. As I had been a few weeks ago.

'Oh, honey, no. We don't need to know where you live. Especially if you don't live in Paddington or Bondi like everyone else.' He waved his hand around like Cinderalla's fairy Godmother. 'And on our salaries who could live anywhere but a box in those places?' He leaned in. 'I mean, like a real cardboard box on someone's lawn.'

'Well, my place is kinda small.' I smiled. 'And I do have a few unopened boxes from my move that could possibly provide shelter should I need travelling accommodation.'

'Sounds exactly like my life,' he said warmly. 'Well, I'm the Events Coordinator here, which literally means office bitch. If you need your shoes cleaned or your phone handed to you, that's probably going to be my job.'

He started walking and I followed dutifully like a loving orphaned pup who'd been taken in by the gay handsome hero (in a purple turtleneck). 'Welcome to the kitchen where everything is a bit high tech. Coffee makes itself, just speak into the microphone on the machine. Tea too. The catering we get here is divine. Smoked ginger fish on charcoal platters. Pepper-roasted chicken with potato puree. Sushi rice cream. But about the size of your thumbnail. So expect to go hungry. Going back for seconds is a no-no. We normally don't eat anything here, but we pretend to.'

I forced a laugh because I had no idea what he was talking about, but it sounded a bit more like a wheeze than I intended. He stared at me strangely.

'Lunchtime is legally thirty minutes. But in reality, if you take that long you might be fired. We eat at our desks or on the run. When the bigwigs all gather for their managerial meetings every few weeks, we can skive off for up to an hour – but only then. Otherwise you'll be told you're not a team player.'

We'd walked down a brightly lit white corridor, with streaks of post-modernist pink paint on the wall. Either that, or I was in a leftover haunted Halloween mansion. Or a really bad hospital scene from *Grey's Anatomy*.

'Art.' Phil flicked his hand at the wall then turned and looked at me.

'Ironic?' I guessed. Although I couldn't guess at the type of irony. And I'd used the word so much more today than I think I had my entire life. You know when you've started to repeat a word over and over and it loses all its meaning. Well, irony already sounded really silly.

'Exactly.' Phil nodded, and like a perfect air steward he pointed out the exits, and then the toilets.

'Other things you should know on day one. When Donna claps her hands twice – listen. If it's three times stop everything you are doing. Don't even breathe. It means things are about to explode. Someone's done something. Or hasn't done something.'

I nodded.

'Other thing is, during the peak of our events you'll lose all hours known to man. You'll be here so early and stay so late, you'll forget that you even went home to change or sleep. In fact, sleep becomes optional, and coffee becomes essential. Do you have a boyfriend? A husband? A girlfriend?'

Oh, God. The question.

'Um, no,' I admitted, feeling a bit flat.

'Well, honey, that's a good thing. No one to expect you home or nag at you when you're late. Let me tell you, I'm envious.'

He was envious of my single life?

'Right, here's my desk and here ...' Phil tapped an empty chair next to him '... are you.'

He leaned into my ear and whispered, 'Welcome to Faker.'

That morning we had a meeting about the new artwork that was going up on the walls on a level we never went to. Emails about meetings. Meetings about emails. Meetings to discuss what was the right fabric for a PR night about a million months in the future. And many meeting invites being sent from Creative and Marketing about event nights.

I was introduced to so many new faces, new teams, and everyone disappeared into a really well-dressed, designer blur, except for one guy who kind of stood out. Ryan. He was a Sales Account Executive (I'd had to search what that meant in the bathrooms between meetings) who I caught looking at me several times during the meeting. Each time my eyes would catch his, instead of looking away, he'd smile. Confidence. I liked that. But an office romance? That was the kiss of death in corporate life, so I begrudgingly stopped looking at him.

Besides, I wasn't here to have a romance, I was here to work. And it was taking all of my mental power, trying to concentrate on the PR world around me, because I didn't know what was going on. At all. There were always buzz words I had to try and decipher. That morning Phil and Donna had discussed the 'build buzz' with 'influencers' and all I could think of was the room filling with headstrong bees.

Also, everyone loved to 'disrupt' things. People's actual role titles in our department were Social Media Disrupter or Marketing Disrupter, and whilst disrupting things in most places would not be encouraged (no one needs their sewerage pipes being disrupted), in here it was applauded, often with clapping in team meetings and more buzz words thrown after it like – 'thought leader' and 'demand generation' and 'trail blazer'.

That afternoon Donna called me into her office for our first chit-chat. She actually entitled it that on her subject heading in the calendar invite. Chit-chat.

I wondered if that meant we were close, or would indulge in some girly nattering. Because I really wanted to ask her what products she used on her face – her skin was amazing and didn't seem to have a crease or wrinkle anywhere. How old was she? Twenty-eight? Thirty-five? I couldn't tell.

'How does she do it?' I mused aloud at lunch. One hand on the keyboard single-handedly typing an email to the copy boy – *Could we get more brochures made up, please?* – the other hand on my fork, which was dug deep into my home-made lettuce, tomato and feta salad (I wished it were a cheesy baguette … oh, dreams).

Phil looked up. 'The answer to that question is usually one of the three – Botox, starvation or career prostitution. To any question here, really.'

I nodded, trying out his theory. Why is she so pretty? Starvation and Botox. Why am I working for the same money as a high school student? Career prostitution. He was right. 'Makes sense.'

Donna clapped twice and I realised it was chit-chat time. I hurried into her office so quickly, I forgot what I was doing and almost saluted when I got in there. Thankfully I took a quick breath and realised I was wearing fabulous heels and a knockout dress and I was tres chic. No saluting.

'Take a seat.' Donna smiled from behind her gleaming white desk. Nothing was on her desk besides her extra-large monitor. Just slender metal legs, and the shiny glow of white plastic on top, it clearly cost a fortune. And made her glow a bit angelically. This was extraordinary.

I perched on the end of her white leather couch, which meant I was at a weird angle to face her. I could either face the door and just talk to her without looking at her. Or I had to sit at the furthest diagonal on the couch so I could see her.

'How is everything so far?' Donna crossed her legs and made it look like a gorgeous ballet move.

'Great, really great. Friendly people.'

'And what insight do you have for me?'

'Um, insight?'

'Yes, someone who's so on it like you, Emma, someone with the experience that you have, I'm sure you've got some great insights already.' So I *might* have elaborated a little too much on my PR experience in London on my CV.

Donna was wearing striking black eye make-up today, and pale lips the colour of sand, and she was stunning, of course, but her black eyes were staring at me intently. Waiting for something wonderful to come out of my mouth.

I thought for a second about saying I don't know, or even telling her, *Donna, I'm a little more junior than I may have led you to believe, but I'm willing and able to learn things very quickly.*

But I knew how fast people like Donna turned. I could be her BFF one day, and her mortal enemy the next. Besides, as soon as I'd got the role, I'd signed up for an online PR crash course for the next six months. I was tenacious. I'd learn. This was *Maker*. I'd do anything. I'd be the best PR person they'd ever seen.

Donna was still staring at me, so I cleared my throat and said what I'd heard everyone mentioning at meetings. 'Well, there are clearly some wonderful projects, especially the corporate strategic initiatives. I think people are really disrupting things, and that's something that our competitors aren't really doing, or not doing that well, and it's all about disruption. All about it.'

Donna took a moment. A moment of utter silence. She

blinked a few times. 'Very astute, Emma. On point. Glad you're on the team.' She opened a drawer and pulled out a cream manila folder. 'I knew you were the right person to lead the next big project we have. Because this industry needs a little disruption.'

Oh no. Lead?

She paused and opened the folder. 'Macabre Nights.' She paused for dramatic effect. 'Can you see it?' She leaned over her desk and placed her perfect chin in her hand with her perfect nude nails.

'Oh, yes, I can see it.' I nodded enthusiastically. I could see nothing.

'A tantalising and wonderful event. Our annual charity night. The event of the year, really.'

'Absolutely.'

'It's a Fever Pitch. You don't mind, do you?'

A whatty what? I had no idea what that meant, but I sat with my back straight, as if I was her girl, and said, 'Totally fine.'

'Great.' She handed over the folder. 'It's all yours.'

I nodded and left the room feeling excited and nervous. I had forgotten to ask so many things. Who was the client? What was the budget? What did they want us to deliver? When was the event?

But first things first, I had to google macabre.

At my desk, I opened up Google and typed *macabre*. Wikipedia told me it was the 'Dance of Death' in English. In German the '*Totentanz*'. There were images too of jangling bones. Of wretched souls. And all of them dancing.

Apparently macabre was *disturbing, concerned with or causing a fear of death.* The dictionary also provided a sentence for further context and that was even more alarming – *a macabre series of murders.*

What on earth had I got myself into?

I opened the manila folder and scanned the scant two pages Donna had provided inside. The charity night had been running for years supporting different organisations, with a plethora of annual functions – I scanned the previous themes:

> *Golden Gala*
> *Royal Regatta*
> *Spring Ballet*
> *Oceanic Ball*
> *A Moveable Feast*

So it seemed all the lovely and less sinister ideas had already been used up, and this year they felt the need to go a little out there, a little screwball, and add a heap of murderous darkness to proceedings.

Let me guess. It was the latest trend? It was on point? Add that to the Maker dictionary dialogue alongside ironic. I could probably hold a conversation using just those words.

I read the file. An Australian charity was launching a new logo, which I'd overheard people in the London PR firm say was risky for any brand (I wrote that down – that was a good thing to say) and a new branding concept, to celebrate international charities coming together, for a massive collaboration effort. This event was part of the collaboration, and meant to represent connection and a sense of belonging across the world.

Well, then, why the hell did they want to kill people? This seemed slightly at odds with a charity.

I flicked to the next page with the logo. It was a round pink circle, with a small stick figure head in the middle, and two straight lines on either side, coming out from the head. It was meant to represent a person with outstretched arms – but it looked as if John the Baptist's head had been served up on a silver platter and bled everywhere.

'You have to be kidding me.'

I wasn't aware I'd said this aloud until Phil said, 'Trouble in PR Paradise?'

'More like death.'

'Sounds sinister. Who for?'

I flicked to the second page in the manila folder to see who the international client was. A Kenyan orphanage. Then the word macabre seemed outrageously horrific. Who had chosen this ill-fitting theme?

'Children.' I looked at him with wide eyes. My first PR project and it was lined up to be a complete disaster already. I remembered my conversation with Donna. 'What's a Fever Pitch?'

He looked up at me. 'You got a Fever Pitch?'

'Yes.' I felt totally clueless. 'What is that?'

'A Fever Pitch,' he said simply, 'is when it's down to the wire and you have to pull something out of nothing, in a matter of months or weeks.'

'Because I'm going to get sick?'

He laughed. 'Well, possibly. But also because you'll be

running at such a tempo, it's like you're on fast forward, burning up, like a fever.'

I flicked through the pages, seeing the event date was in three months. *Three months*? Even I knew that most of these large events were planned nine months in advance, either that, or they had an entire team of people on them. I felt a hot flush coming on already. The only thing that had been done was a Save the Date invitation to guests, and the hotel space booked. How the hell was I going to pull this off?

The first few weeks flew by. I got used to being on my feet the whole time, and go, go, go. I drafted press releases, and social media teaser campaigns and Save the Date invitation cards, which were designed on thick white card, luxe and beautiful, with silver inlay – they were so expensive that the bunch of 1000 invitations cost more than my annual rent. Every night I finished at about 8 p.m. and walked home in the last of the summer heat. At home, I microwaved a meal and logged onto my PR course, determined to learn as much as I could.

I was surprised to find it seemed I knew more about PR than I thought I did from all my years sitting in on PR meetings. Turns out I was doing well at my course – actually I was acing it according to my online tutor. Even so, I already felt like I was drowning at work. I thought I'd be managing the guests, the event logistics, the media, writing draft press releases and doing teaser campaigns – all of which I could do, and was doing, for Macabre.

But it turns out, Donna had different ideas. She wanted

me to be across *everything*. She constantly called out to me from her white albatross office, without checking I was sitting at my desk. I became attuned to hearing her, and running back from the kitchen, or the hallway, even the printing room, to scribble down another task on my to-do list.

'Emma – would you work with the chef to create the menu, he is such hard work. You're a gem!'

'Can you choose the fabrics? It would be so much cheaper. Those design consultants cost sooooo much.'

'Em!' It appeared we were on shortened first name basis now. 'Em, you'll need to go to fabric place today, and put in an order, they've got a special on. And where is your concept pitch for the look and feel? I need it on my desk pronto.'

And I responded 'sure' because, well, *career prostitution*, and because I was still feeling a little guilty for fudging my CV a bit, and I wanted to prove myself.

But it seemed I was single-handedly creating the entire event myself. Donna was suddenly expecting me to choose a theme, and the fabrics, and finishing's for the event, and design how they should be set up, and now I was meant to be suggesting dessert items for the chef's menu – and I wasn't sure this was meant to part of my job role at all. To make matters worse, Donna kept sending me emails, lots of emails, even at night, asking for an update. How's the theme? What's the approach? Where are the concept ideas? I was absolutely exhausted. Being in multitasking mode all day, every day was making my brain a frazzled mess. There were things I had to coordinate – guests, media, who was standing where, who was sitting where, what order guests would arrive on the red carpet. Table layouts. Decorations. I had spreadsheets to keep track of my spreadsheets.

If I wasn't in the office, I was at stylists' and designers', picking fabrics for the curtain entrance and choosing the right colour for the table centerpieces and flowers. Crimson or scarlet or carnelian? Ivory or alabaster or opaque milk? The length. The shape.

But I didn't have the theme, so how could I purchase the material? I prayed that the idea would suddenly drop from the skies into my mind. I'd even tried taking up meditation this morning at five, when my alarm went off. I spent the better part of ten minutes willing the force, or the collective consciousness, whatever it was called, to give me the answer telepathically or something, but then I realised the aim of meditation was to clear my mind and be OK with everything, rather than manifest exactly what I wanted. Anyway, it hadn't worked.

Given I had no idea what to pick, I just pointed at a load of different fabrics, telling myself, if we didn't use them now, we could save them for another event. I bought swaddles of every colour combination I could think of – red and white and black, silver and gold, bright green, sunshine yellow and fuchsia pink. And then stared at them clumped together like a big mess. Even the decorating coordinator raised her eyebrows and said, 'So it's a rainbow theme?'

Besides, most of my energy was focused on avoiding Donna. Which was proving very difficult, because she was sending me emails, lots of emails, asking for an update. How's the theme? What's the approach? Where are the concept ideas?

Her emails were getting more and more demanding, and I could feel the suspicion seep out of her words and onto my keyboard. At first, I'd thought I'd finally leapt onto a cracking idea, when I'd remembered an old movie I had loved and suggested the theme The Garden of Good and Evil.

I'd stood in front of Donna's desk, feeling quite theatrical as I'd described an entrance of black curtains. Blood-red stars. White porcelain statues. Two entrances. But which one would you take? Or which one would choose you? Inside, an enchanted garden theme. Fairy lights. Long creeper plants. Ivy. Oak leaves. Black glitter stars. Tables with red tablecloths for evil – quite macabre; white for good and innocence. Donna had held up her hand and said, 'Great idea, Emma, but this was used a few years ago by Maker for a product launch.'

My heart had sunk. I'd scuttled back to my desk feeling defeated, and just wanting to sink my teeth into a very large cheese toastie with a Mars bar chaser, when Donna had emailed saying Glenn wanted an update on the theme by Friday. She even wrote 'tick tock' at the end of her email, like a countdown clock, which made me feel even more nauseous. I sat googling death, hoping no one could see my screen because they might have urged me to phone Lifeline.

At night I wasn't sleeping, because I was starting to feel completely overwhelmed. I tried to work out how I'd got into this mess in the first place. I think I'd done it to please everyone else – to please Tansy who wanted me to stay in Sydney and had gone to such lengths to find me a role and tell them I'd be perfect for them, to please my Mum and Dad who wanted me to finally 'settle down and make something of myself', to show Murray I had what it takes to settle down now I was older, to please Donna who did seem sometimes pleased I was doing everything she asked, but then, at other times, seemed to be aloof and cool about it, as though I was the most insignificant worker in the world. And mostly, I think I'd done it to please all my other friends who kept asking – why do you always *travel*? As if it was a strange habit or addiction I needed to kick in a thirty-day program. The truth was, I was doing it to please everyone, but I didn't really feel that pleased about it myself.

This is just life, I told myself. This is what you do – you go to work at a place you may not love, at a job that requires more than you can give it. You pay bills. You plan holidays for your four weeks of annual leave. You grit your teeth, and you just get through it, and you hope that one day it gets easier.

One night, I left the office at 9 p.m. and realized I hadn't eaten lunch and I started to feel a little lightheaded, and dizzy. I walked shakily into a city convenience store and just said 'sugar' like I was a diabetic. The man behind the counter pointed to some gummy lollies, which I bought, at a whopping seven dollars a packet, and sat on the curb outside tipping the entire contents of two bags down my throat and chewing as fast as I could, until I felt better.

It was a new low. Sitting in that gutter, grits of sugar covering my green faux silk shirt. I almost dialled Donna's phone number and confessed that I needed help, that I felt overwhelmed and I didn't know the first thing about deconstructed desserts and if the chef should make dill and cucumber sorbet or pandan curd, and what the hell was pandan anyway? Or admit that I was not a fabric master and didn't know which would hang better around the pillars, chiffon or organza or georgette.

But then I knew I'd lose my job, and I wouldn't be able to pay my rent, and my Mum had gone out of her way to help me get that unit, I couldn't do what I had done when I was younger – just upped and left. I was an adult now – I had to face my problems, I had to stay and work it out, I had to just keep going and hoping and working as hard as I could.

I was just about to call Donna, my thumb hovering over the call button, when my phone started to vibrate. It was Maggie. I brushed the sugar off my hand and pressed 'accept'. As soon as I answered, she started gabbling down the phone, excitedly talking about Tony.

'Tony?' I said standing up from the gutter, struggling to think of a friend called Tony that we knew.

'Yes, I've fixed you up on a date! Step three, Em!'

'Oh, great.' I should have felt more excited.

'I'm your matchmaker! He likes pizza. Well actually, he makes pizza!'

I swallowed, too exhausted to think about going on a date. 'Aren't you excited?'

'I am.' I said with all the energy I could muster.

'Great! Because I've set it up for Saturday night. Call me afterwards with all the juicy details!'

Not to be outdone by Maggie, Tansy called immediately

after, and said excitedly 'I have a date for you! Step three is in motion!'

'Don't tell me it's Saturday night? Maggie has already booked me.'

'Of course not, we've worked this out perfectly, you'll meet Tony Pepperoni on Saturday night, think of him like a trial run Em. And then you'll meet my guy Peter the following Saturday night. He's the real deal Em, he works in PR too!'

'Oh great, we can talk more about work, because it's not consuming my life enough already.' I half-joked. 'How do you know Peter? And why haven't I heard about him before?'

'He's a friend of an old work colleague.'

'Tansy, have *you* even met Peter?' I said suspiciously.

'Not really, but I hear he's lovely. And Em it was hard to find a thirty-something single guy who wants a relationship but isn't in one.'

'Tell me about it.'

Chapter 10

On Saturday afternoon, I was too exhausted to even get off my couch. I had to down a triple shot of coffee to even consider going on my date. Was this what it was like to work an office job, then crawl back home into bed, and then get up, rinse and repeat every day? How did people go to Friday night drinks? When Phil had asked me, I could barely utter a no before I managed to throw myself on the train, heat up a microwave meal, and get into my sweatpants and sleep until midday.

I knew it was only my first month, but I didn't know how people did this for their entire life. And more, they seemed to *like* this life. *It will get better,* I told myself. Once I knew what I was doing, it would get better. Because it had to.

Now, Saturday evening, I was coffee-amped and striding down Elizabeth Street in very tall heels, with a pencil skirt, and a white silk top with a rose satin bra underneath, which I'd found in my BT (Before Trip) clothes, which meant it was a size, or two, too small and my ample breasts were cut in two, and billowing like a massive cleavage muffin top. I'd told myself it was very French, if only I could figure out a way to sit down for extended periods of time without possibly fainting as the bottom of it cut through my skin and into my actual ribs.

Tony was already there, and he was, in every account of the word, Italian. Short, way shorter than me, and fed on pasta and pizza by his *nonna* or his shop, or both, which had given him a rather rotund barrel sorta look. He had dark brown thinning hair, and a prominent, strong Roman nose. He had a bright smile and was beaming when he saw me. Or rather, when he saw the cleavage pillows nestled in my rose bra. He took one look at them and looked as if he wanted to roost for life – he couldn't stop staring. And I mean ogling. At times, such as when I was telling him that I worked at Maker, or that I'd travelled to Italy, I felt like putting my hands in the air, or bringing up a squeaky toy as I'd do with a child who was getting their photo taken on Santa's lap and I wanted them to 'look here'.

Tony had recently moved to Sydney, a few years ago, from Melbourne, which was – according to him – the real home of coffee and Italians. He was now conquering the world of Sydney melted mozzarella – his words, not mine. Two beers (him) and half a wine (me) later, I was ready to go home. It turned out as magic as pizza is, it isn't worth having a man give you a hug goodnight and putting his paws on your buttock region. *Tony, you may be small, but I'm pretty sure you can reach my back.*

That night, I couldn't sleep. I tried countless times, but my mind kept going over how I was going to get all my work done at Maker. I got my paints out, but I didn't feel like painting a thing. Instead I just drew big, black, round circles until my page looked like a Dalmatian.

Somewhere out on the street, a siren wailed. The couple above were moving furniture around again at 1 a.m. – thud and pull, thud and pull – as something heavy like a couch was dragged across the floor. Since I was up, I thought maybe I should try and get some work done. I turned my artbook over and wrote at the top 'Death Themes'. Just looking at it, I felt overwhelmed. My heart started thudding, and my chest felt tight. My stomach turned and for a second, I thought I was going to throw up. I ran to the bathroom, leant over the toilet and tried to vomit, but nothing came up. Shakily I stood and rinsed my mouth with water, and then ate a bit of toothpaste to get rid of the acidic bile taste in my mouth. *This is what stress does to me.*

Suddenly, I knew what I had to do on Monday morning. First thing when I got in, I was going to tell Donna I didn't have a concept. That she should give the project to someone else who possibly knew about sorbets and organza. Of course, I'd help in every way I could, I'd work around the clock, I'd do whatever it took, but I needed someone leading the way, so that this event didn't become the biggest screw up for Maker. She could fire me. Ice me out with her perfect glacial stare. Yell at me. Or worse, ignore me as if I didn't exist. Whatever happened, I'd take it on the chin.

Exhausted, I climbed back into bed. *It's possible I'm about to have the shortest employment ever – one month.*

After that thought, I was unable to sleep at all. My stomach

115

was in knots. I curled up in bed and left the light on, and scrolled through my phone. Facebook. Instagram. Photos of kids going fishing. And toddlers eating spaghetti and getting it all around their faces. Newborn babies swaddled tightly and sleeping. And dogs being, well, cute and doggy, sleeping on their backs, all paws splayed out. And married couples on date nights – taking photos of their amazing dinners, and expensive, elaborate bright fuchsia and spearmint coloured cocktails with steam pouring out of them, or dry ice, or something like that.

Then I thought of me almost vomiting in my bathroom, and I thought – how do they do it? If this is everyone's life, going to work, feeling overwhelmed and stressed, how do they look so happy?

And then I started wondering why I wasn't sharing date night pictures of my drinks, and my dinner, and my mediocre date with Tony, and then those silly questions tumbled out. Had Murray really been so bad? Should I have stayed with him? At least now I'd have a bigger house.

For some reason, I felt compelled to log onto Facebook. My heart beat wildly, as I typed in his name, as if he could see me do it. As if he *knew* I was searching for him.

Murray Roberts.

There he was – he'd unblocked me. His profile picture was him, awkwardly crouched down at the beach; a young boy, about four, who looked slightly like him with brown hair and pale skin, was wrapped up in his arms. He'd always hated the beach. The sand, the sun. Even though he was pale and awkward, Murray looked happy, and fatter. Middle age hadn't been that kind to him, his hair was receding, but, flicking through his photos, I saw he seemed to have everything he'd wanted. The house was undergoing renovations. They were putting in a pool. He remarked how long it was taking, and how their annual holidays up the coast had had to be cancelled.

I flicked through countless photos of his toddler daughter and son, before I found one of his wife – Stephanie Roberts. And it felt weird, to know she had the surname I could have had. She had shortish brown hair that reached just below her shoulders, and pale skin, she didn't wear make-up in any of the photos, and she was slim, and tall, and quite nondescript. And, I thought, that could have been me. I could have been Emma Roberts. And it filled me with a sense of relief that I wasn't.

Of course, I knew I'd made the right decision. I didn't want annual holidays up the coast, I wanted international flights, and trekking Mont Blanc, and painting Lake Como, and learning Italian, and seeing wolves and polar bears in the wild. I wanted *those* things.

Did I still want them? Tonight I did. Tonight the best thing in the world sounded like a one-way plane ticket out of here. But I couldn't. I couldn't let everyone down. I had to stay, and be resilient, and be like everyone else – and just get through this, and hope that in a week, two weeks, I'd feel a lot better about everything.

Before I shut my laptop, there was one last name that was hovering in my brain. A name that had kept on popping up in my head this past week, even though I'd promised myself not to think about it again. It was a long shot, but I tried anyway.

Nick.

Do you know how many Nicks there are in Sydney? Thousands and thousands. Possibly millions. I tried 'Nick Fiji' and even got so desperate as to type in 'Nick Fiji Timeshare' to both Facebook and Google.

I knew things were bad when I tried searching 'Nick Corporate Long Hours Sydney Fiji' and got a list of flights and business deals in the South Pacific.

By this time it was 3 a.m., and way too late to be thinking about alternative lives and 'what ifs'. I shut my laptop. That was enough reminiscing.

Chapter 11

Monday at work, the first email in my inbox was from Donna. Subject: Melbourne. She wrote:

I'm off to the Melbourne office. Last minute plans. They need someone to head up the new media project down here to ensure it's on point. They'll get someone in as soon as they can. You know what to do.

D

My mouth hung agape.

'Catching flies?' Phil arrived, putting his vintage-find mahogany man bag on the desk between us.

I couldn't say a word. Finally I managed to stutter, 'Sh- she's gone.'

'Who?' Phil yawned and switched on his computer.

'Smug Barbie.'

'Who?' Phil looked at me strangely. He bent down to his computer, read his email and gasped. 'Holy God, she's gone.'

We nodded wide-eyed at each other.

'What about Death Night?' I asked, mewing a bit like a cat.

'What about ...' Phil paused dramatically '... everything?'

'We'll have to spend day and night here just to finish our work. What about her other projects? I don't know anything about them.'

The last of my spare time shrivelled up at the thought.

'I can't handle this so early without coffee. I'm so shocked. Where are the emergency Mars bars?'

I pointed under the desk. Phil dropped to his knees and I heard wrappers being ripped open.

'Phil,' I said tentatively, 'what about the board presentation? Isn't that this week?'

'Our lives are over,' he said, chewing with an open mouth.

As we miserably headed to the kitchen to make a very strong coffee of commiseration, Glenn strode past. 'Oh, Emily!' he said smoothly, not stopping to talk but continuing walking.

I swivelled around and called after him, 'Um, it's Emma.'

'Yes, of course. There's a new man here in the foyer. Taking over Donna's role. His first day. Can you show him around?'

'Today? Already? I thought Donna said ...'

Glenn was already at the end of the corridor.

'Yes, sure I'll do it. What's his name?'

But already I was talking to a closed door that Glenn had managed to slip behind.

Phil couldn't say anything because his mouth was still

full of Mars bar and he was concentrating on directing the machine to put mountainous amounts of coffee into two cups.

'More for me,' I called out, because no matter how much coffee he put in there today, it would never be enough.

As I waited for the lift, I sighed. *This is just what I need,* I thought fiercely. *Donna leaving me an entire new task list and there's not a thing I can do about it.* I hoped the new guy was nice. I hoped he didn't want me discussing sorbets or choosing fabrics for the event. I hoped he would help me choose a theme, because we needed one, like yesterday.

The lift opened and, in the floor-to-ceiling mirrors, I caught sight of my hair. I licked my hand and flattened it down, begging it to behave. My black high-waisted pants and nude silk shirt looked chic, so, hopefully, I'd be able to make a slightly good impression on my new boss, even if my hair had a mind of its own.

The lift rocketed to the ground floor like a shuttle and dinged as it opened onto the shiny black waxed floor of reception, where Bel and Beth (today's morning receptionists) smiled sweetly at every customer and offered them Champagne or coffee.

'Morning, ladies, I hear we have a new starter replacing Donna?'

Beth nodded. 'The man over there.' She pointed under the desk. 'Mr Taylor.'

On the solo black leather couch an older gentleman with white hair was sitting in a smart suit.

With my best smile and a tug at my shirt, I strode over to

meet him. 'Hello, Mr Taylor, I'm Emma. One of your new team.' I leaned over and offered my hand.

The man looked up at me, clearly confused. 'I'm not Mr Taylor.'

'Oh, you're not?' I looked back at Beth. She was shaking her head furiously.

'I'm Mr Taylor,' a voice said. A tallish man with sandy blond hair standing with his back to us, behind the old gentleman, turned around.

My mouth dropped open.

'Hello, Emma. Nice to see you.'

I couldn't speak. I thought I was going to faint. Or throw up. My mouth flung open. My stomach flipped a thousand times. THIS CAN NOT BE REAL. I am *seeing* things.

But I wasn't. Standing right in front of me was a man I'd most recently seen covered in soap suds and standing in a shower.

'You can call me Nick.' He reached out his hand and shook mine.

Chapter 12

I thought I might pass out. The foyer started to spin.

'Well,' Nick said as we waited for the lift.

I took a deep breath, closed my eyes and let the wave of dizziness pass over me. When I opened my eyes, it hadn't been a trick of the light; it wasn't someone who looked liked him. It was him. Naked Nick from Fiji.

His suit was impeccable, starched and sitting perfectly against his broad shoulders. His dark blond hair was wavy, and sat naturally to the side, with a hint of product, but not too much – he looked entirely handsome and I could see the receptionists staring across at him, coyly batting their eyelashes. Those chocolate eyes. Perfectly tanned skin. Square jaw. His hair was slightly longer, and he smelt like leather and coconuts instead of mint – was that a new aftershave?

'W- well,' I stammered, waiting for the lift doors to open.

'This is a—' Nick started.

At the same time I said, 'This doesn't—'

'Ladies first,' he said as the lift arrived.

I walked in and furtively glanced at myself in the mirror.

My hair was half behaving, so I pushed it down, and punched level 29.

I've seen his penis, I thought, *covered in suds.* I immediately shook the thought out of my head.

'You were saying?' Nick asked as the lift doors closed.

Neither of us were looking at each other. In fact, we were facing the large silver doors as if they were a massive TV, playing something interesting.

Still staring at the silver doors, I said, 'So this doesn't look like a country cottage with chickens.'

He gave me a strange look. 'I believe most people call this a lift.'

I gave a little laugh, which sounded like a dog choking on something. 'We talked about country cottages. And veggie gardens.'

'I remember.'

'Fresh herbs. A kitchen so large you could cook a feast.' I couldn't stop talking. 'Dance in it. A kitchen island that doubled as a podium.'

Stop talking.

He looked at me strangely. 'I don't think we mentioned that.'

'Oh, must just have been me.' I was making my head spin, flipping back and forth from the lift to our one night in Fiji, from two professional people to two people sudsing each other up in the shower, before – I couldn't finish the thought. It was horrific. I'd slept with my boss. SLEPT WITH MY BOSS. And in a job where I felt like I am *failing*.

I thought about spilling it all to him. Before I could say

anything else though, the lift door opened, and a woman in a red blouse, black skirt and heels for days walked in, smiled quickly at us both, without seeing us, and pressed level 43.

We rode the rest of the way in complete silence and when the doors opened at level 29, Glenn was waiting impatiently.

'Thanks, um ...' Glenn looked at me with his mouth open.

'Emma,' I said.

'Yes,' he answered, waving his hand to hurry us up out of the lift. 'Nick, we're about to start a divisional meeting, about some, um ...' he looked at me '... pressing things.'

Nick said, 'Lead the way.'

They walked off towards the boardroom at the end of the hall, already deep in hushed conversation.

When Nick turned down the hall, I thought he was turning back to see me and I gave a little wave as if I were seeing someone off at the railway station. He gave a quick nod and walked through the large black doors. And I went into the toilets gasping for air, feeling as though I was about to faint.

I hid in a bathroom stall and sat on the closed toilet lid, thinking I was going to vomit. My head kept spinning. Surely, he was just here temporarily? I'd never thought I'd say this but I'd do anything, *anything* to get Donna back. Thirty seconds passed. A minute. My heart was still beating out of my chest. I had no doubt that I'd have to leave the bathroom some time today, but I just couldn't sit at my desk and act normal.

What would I say? *Hi, Nick, how was the rest of your trip in Fiji? I had a lovely time at that seafood lunch, all by myself.*

Thanks for giving me the wrong number. Oh, Nick, and by the way, I'm drowning here. Completely overwhelmed. Could you help me out? I groaned inwardly.

Shit. This was bad.

I suddenly had the urge to go home, pack all my stuff, and hightail it to the airport. I'd go back to London. I'd work in that Mexican shack again! Happily! I'd serve up half-stale taco wraps with a smile on my face, anything instead of this.

I found my phone in my pocket and put in an SOS call to Maggie and Tansy, managing, somehow, with shaky fingers, to dial both of them into one conversation.

'You'll never believe this. He's here,' I whispered through gritted teeth.

'What?' Maggie almost shouted down the phone. 'Why are you whispering? Who's what, and where?'

'He's here,' I said a bit louder. 'You'll have to say it. I can't talk.' I tried to check under the stalls for other feet, before I said anything I'd regret.

'Santa?' Maggie snorted.

'No, a little further back. C'mon, Tansy, you wanted me to *call* him,' I urged.

'Oh, God, no. Really?' Tansy gasped.

'Yes. *Really*.' I nodded my head with wide eyes, even though they couldn't see it.

'Who!?' Maggie shouted.

'Naked Nick!' Tansy yelled back.

'Oh, my God,' Maggie and I said at the same time. Just hearing his name made me feel faint.

'What are you going to do?' Tansy asked.

'He's at my workplace, what the hell can I do? Pretend nothing ever happened and that we've never met?'

'Uh oh.' Maggie exhaled. 'How does one go from hot shower sex, to professional? You've seen his penis! Was it big?'

'Maggie,' I groaned, then added, 'And yes. Rather.'

Maggie hooted with laughter.

'This is a sign,' Tansy declared victoriously. 'He gave you the wrong number, but maybe there's a valid reason. Maybe he wrote it down wrongly? Maybe you dialed wrongly? Maybe you guys are meant to be together, so the universe literally plonked him in your lap!'

'Not only that, he's my new ...' I gulped '... boss!'

They both gasped. Someone walked into the bathroom.

'Gotta go,' I whispered and hung up the phone, took a deep breath and walked out onto the floor and back to my desk, on high alert for anyone tanned. Nick clearly hadn't been in an office in a while; he'd held onto that summer glow, and wasn't like the rest of us with spray tans, but still looking a little office ghostly pale underneath. Summer glow. I remembered his smooth chest, running my hands down his—

Stop, Emma. Just stop.

Phil cornered me in the kitchen at lunch. 'Spill it.'

'Spill what?'

'What's got you looking like you're a thousand miles away and then suddenly wanting to upchuck every few seconds?'

'Have you been watching me?' I said suspiciously, wondering what I'd looked like as I'd sat at my desk and tried to work, but my mind had been full of Nick. Nick and me pressed against the shower wall. Nick lifting me onto the bed. Nick licking between my breasts.

'Don't flatter yourself. You looked like you were going to pass out or throw up all morning.'

'I'm fine,' I said quickly, but I could tell he didn't believe me. 'And, it's really nothing at all,' I said, my eyes scanning the room in case Nick came in. 'It's, um ...' I stood and walked to the coffee and tea nook, and Phil followed me.

'Tea?' I asked him.

Phil's eyes suddenly flickered with interest. 'Oooh, is it a man?'

'No, as a matter of fact, it isn't.' I reached over him and grabbed two bags of sugar, piling them into a mug before adding hot water.

'Well, it's something because you just made a cup of tea without the tea.' He smirked.

'It's a new thing I'm trying, like sugar water. It's new. I wouldn't expect you to know anything about it.'

'Sure.' He didn't seem convinced in the slightest. 'So, what do you think about the new guy, Mr Nicholas Taylor?'

'I think nothing of him.'

'You must have some thoughts?'

'It's only the first day, so I don't think anything of him yet,' I said, taking a sip of my hot water, which tasted awfully sweet due to all the sugar I'd dumped in it.

Phil sighed. 'I think he's hot.'

'Of course, you do, you think every guy in here is hot.'

'Not true. I don't like Kevin from the copy room. His long greasy black hair doesn't do anything for anyone. But Nick, he's like really, really hot. But he doesn't really know it – which, of course, makes him hotter.'

I threw an empty sugar packet at Phil. 'Just don't go flirting with the boss on his first day. Could be career limiting.'

'Now, are you ready to return to your actual desk?' Phil asked. 'I think Nick's been looking for you.'

'He has?' I said in a small voice, and my heart started beating wildly again. I slowly picked up my sugar water, dawdling as long as I could.

'Chop chop!' Phil said 'Otherwise I'm actually going to physically age in here, under these fluorescent lights, and I've already spent my entire last salary on my Botox maintenance jabs.'

'You get Botox?' I was surprised. Phil looked youthful for his age, which was – actually I didn't even know how old he was, but I'd guessed he was at least thirty.

'You don't?' Phil seemed even more surprised.

Back at our desks Nick was waiting for us with a look on his face that said he was in some kind of mood. 'Emma.'

'Hello, Nick. Hello.' My knees felt wobbly.

He looked at me strangely.

'Hello,' I said again.

Stop saying hello. But my mind was racing, trying to keep calm and appear normal. And hello seemed such a safe word. I was wondering if Nick was feeling as nervous as I was, but he was showing no signs of it. In fact, he kept on talking about work, as though we had actually only just met in the foyer a few hours ago.

'Emma, we haven't really had time to go over your event

in any detail, like the theme, decorations, media, photographers, but you've got it in hand, right?'

Now. Now was my chance to confess everything. Tell him the truth. That I had diddly squat. Less than that. That everyone was going to turn up to an empty hall. Perhaps a good reminder of what death might be like – empty and black. God, how bleak! I hesitated for a second. This was the ultimate chance to tell him, but I just couldn't bring myself to do it.

'Emma?'

I noticed Phil was listening, and so was Daisy from accounts and Karen from business development who had chosen this moment to walk past and was hovering, deliberately trying to overhear. Since everyone knew that the new girl was looking after the charity event, the entire company had become quite intrigued. If I told Nick the truth now, the gossip mill would be in full force, and the entire company would know within the next hour that we were in a bit of trouble. No, I'd tell Nick later, when he was by himself and I had stopped saying hello repeatedly. I mean, he couldn't fire someone on his first day, could he?

I hesitated for a second and then realized with half the floor listening in, I had to pretend the event was in perfectly good hands.

'Everything's just fine,' I assured him.

'Good. Glenn wants the guest list for your event, the seating chart and media campaign as soon as you can. But if you can send it to me first, so I can review it, that would be great.'

While he talked, I found myself discreetly checking out his

body. I'd seen under that crisp white shirt. His smooth skin. His broad chest. Heck, I'd seen under those pants. *No. Stop it. You cannot be thinking about your boss and his under-pants nakedness.*

Nick was looking at me. 'Emma. Can you do it?'

'Sorry, do what?'

'The guest list, seating chart and confirmed RSVPs.'

'Yes, I can.'

I was still holding my cup of sugary water.

'Now?'

I could hear Phil mutter behind me, 'What's going on with you, Emma?'

I sat at my desk, face flaming red. Nick was staring strangely at me too.

'Um, Emma, honey?' Phil said.

'Not now, Phil, I'm busy working.'

'At my desk?'

I looked around. There were photos of Phil's boyfriend, Adam, Phil's shiny black diamanté-encrusted mouse, his stack of PR magazines. 'Yes, so I am. Excuse me.'

I got up, took a step across and sat at my screen, as if nothing had happened at all.

That afternoon, I focused on the seating chart, so Nick and I didn't have to have another awkward exchange, where I said hello a thousand times. I couldn't help but pray to the Gods of Everything – particularly the Gods of Regret, Silly Sex and Office Faux Pas – that he was in meetings all day. I needed some time to process that the man I had hot sex with had turned up at my office. But not only that, as my *boss*.

After three coffees, and two hours of thinking time, I realised I had to be mature about this. And that meant there was only one thing to do. We had to have 'the talk'. We'd got along so well in Fiji, all it needed was a quick conversation. A 'how awkward is this?' five-minute chat, a quick laugh about it, and we'd be fine. We'd be great. After all, we'd had sex. Hot sex. But just sex. It was nothing more than that to him (obviously), and once we had the talk, we'd be fine. Fine. Given his number was disconnected, that meant he had no idea I'd texted him about the seafood lunch. It meant he had no idea I'd got dressed up and waited at Freshwaters. I would never mention those things. I'd forget all about everything. But the other part of the talk was what was making me sweat like a criminal about to take a lie detector. I had to tell him that we didn't have a theme, and more than that, that I was drowning in work and needed help. And I should probably be completely honest and tell him that I'd fudged my CV a little, because I may as well rip the band aid completely off and start with a clean slate.

Right, I can do this.

So I kept watching his office like a hawk, waiting for the perfect moment to descend. But Nick never came back from his meetings, and even though I was at my desk working until 8 p.m. I didn't see any sign of him. On Tuesday, Nick was at an emergency 'offsite' executive meeting for some top-secret celebrity management (read crisis) intervention.

On Wednesday, I was in at 7 a.m., but Nick's door was already open, the light on, and he wasn't inside. He'd beaten me to it. Either that, or he'd camped here overnight (not unheard of in PR). My stomach knotted. I knew we had to speak and soon. But when? How? And how could I do it without anyone else overhearing? This office was a perfect gossip mill; if anyone got a whiff of this it would be across the company in seconds.

All morning, I kept one eye on Nick's empty office, on alert for him to return, and one eye on my screen trying to get the hang of setting up a bunch of social media posts and hashtags for the Macabre PR campaign. I was so intent on talking to Nick, I even skipped lunch. So by 3 p.m., I had the most throbbing headache and I still didn't have any catchy hashtags. Besides, what could I say about a macabre death night?

#comeandgetkilled

#bloodthirsty

#murderisthenewblack

An hour later, all I'd come up with was an inspirational anti-death slogan #livefortoday and that made me want to vomit motivational fairy dust. And I'd tried the serious factor and got #makeitcount #yourlifeyourchoice paired with #atleastwegetachoice. I disliked them all incredibly.

I walked into the kitchen for a coffee and caught sight of Nick at the far end, getting himself a drink.

I knew I'd made a promise to myself to have The Chat, but an open-plan kitchen– anyone could walk in and overhear us. There was a girl I'd never seen before over at the stack of magazines, and a guy coming in to grab an apple. If we talked while other people were around, then it would be gossip mill central. But then he looked up and spotted me, so I couldn't just leave, could I?

'Do you know how this works?' Nick was pointing at the coffee machine.

'Say coffee,' I said quickly, about to make an excuse to leave.

Nick looked at me strangely. 'Okaaay,' he said slowly. 'Do you know how this coffee thing works?'

I let out a loud snort-laugh and then flushed bright red. He thought I was telling him to use the right words. As if he were a child. But he wasn't a child. Not under those clothes. He was a naked man I'd had a shower with – a very, very hot man ... ahem, and now he was my boss. And he was looking at me very strangely.

I licked my lips. 'No, say the word "coffee" into that little speaker thing there.' I pointed from way across the kitchen, keeping more than ten feet distance between us.

'Right,' he said, finally understanding, then he turned and said, 'Coffee,' into the microphone, and the machine rattled to life. Suddenly a whoosh of black coffee came out.

'Did you want one?' He looked over at me and I wasn't sure what to say, so I just nodded.

As he put my mug under the machine, I noticed everyone had cleared out of the kitchen. Perhaps this was the perfect time to smooth over what had happened between us in Fiji, because how could we stand here looking at each other and not mention it? But I had no idea what to say. What could you say? Who wanted to discuss in the lunch room that we'd seen each other's bits? God! Not me! Not at *all*!

He held up the coffee to me and I walked gingerly over towards the coffee machine, determined not to faint. Or say hello a thousand times. *I will not do anything weird. I will take*

this coffee, I will have a mature chat and I will return to my
desk, and all will be well.

When I got to the coffee machine, I made the mistake of
looking at Nick, right into his chocolate eyes. God, he was
really gorgeous this close up. I remembered how it felt to lean
against him. His smooth chest underneath this shirt. How it
felt to kiss him. My mind was trying to tell me exactly what
I *should* say, but my body wanted to tear off his clothes and
touch him. Kiss him. Have a shower with him. Hot sex. HOT
SEX WITH NICK.

'So, Emma—' Nick started to say.

As I said, 'Um, Nick, I think ...'

'Sorry, after you.' He grinned, showing his perfect, straight
teeth, and it felt like he was happy to see me. This was a good
sign.

'Yes, right ... well, I just thought we should be mature, you
know. And have a little chat.' For some reason I'd put on a
strange voice and was talking as if I were about to do a children's book reading at the local library. I cleared my throat
and tried again. 'About, um ... you know what. I just wanted
to clear the air. And say ...' I paused. What did I want to say?
'I had a good time the other night. Other week ... or night.
Whenever it was. In Fiji,' I said quickly.

I wasn't sure what to say after that, but Nick was staring
at me expectantly, and the corners of his mouth were twitching,
as though he was about to smile. So, I just opened my mouth
and let the first thing come out, which I hoped was going to
be, 'Let's be mature about this and professional, and leave it
in the past, and maybe we could get a drink some time.'

I suddenly thought back to that night in Fiji. Us in the shower. Oh his bed. '*I want you*'. Oh, God. A shiver ran through me. Could he ever see me as professional after *that*?

What happens when I get nervous, is I become unable to communicate, and say things without a filter, so it ended up as, 'I'm sorry about saying I wanted you. You know. On your bed. That was uh ... uh ... not *me*.'

A shadow appeared on Nick's face, and I nervously kept talking. 'I mean it *was* me. But not normally what I'd do. You know? I wouldn't normally ... I want you to see me as a professional, and ... I mean I don't *want* you. Just in case you think I'm standing here thinking that I want you. I'm not. Not at all. Far from it. Not even in the slightest.' *God, stop talking.*

I was interrupted by the loud ringing of Nick's phone. He pulled it out of his pocket, and I glimpsed the name as he looked at the screen. Chloe calling.

'Sorry, Emma, I need to take this.' He walked away murmuring into the phone, as my face flushed a deep red of absolute shame. What timing!

So much for having my mature chat, instead I'd just had the most explosive case of verbal diarrhoea in my life. But it wasn't over yet, I still needed to tell him about Macabre, so instead of leaving him to his phone call, I busied myself with getting a water. And when he still hadn't finished his chat, I sipped that water s-l-o-w-l-y, then refilled my glass.

When Nick walked back over, he seemed different. Brisk. His eyes had darkened but the rest of his face remained completely unreadable. Who was Chloe and what had she said to him?

'So, Emma,' Nick started.

'Yes?' I said, wondering what he wanted to say to me about Fiji, or what I'd just garbled at him.

'Can you have the seating chart to me soon?'

The seating chart? Clearly, Nick wasn't thinking about Fiji *at all.* Now I felt really silly.

'Uh, sure,' I said quickly, standing up straight.

'Great. So, I think we're good,' he said completely professionally, handling this situation as I wished I had, rather than being all strange about it. Nick was cool, calm and collected and focused on work. As I should be. God, how *embarrassing.*

I opened my mouth to say 'one more thing ...' when suddenly the room filled with the strongest scent of opium and musk. It took all I had not to cough and choke. And that could only mean one person had entered – Sadie. Sadie had clearly smelt Nick out, as sharks could smell a drop of blood in a thousand miles of ocean. She was wearing a tight-fitting designer dress, and her hair was in a perfect blonde bob, as it always was, sprayed into place with a thousand cans of hairspray. I knew this because she left cans in the bathrooms to spray in-between meetings.

Phil had told me to avoid her if I could, and I could see why: she had small eyes that darted everywhere and took everything in (sharky) and a very pointy long nose (sharky), and a way of looking as if she wanted to devour any good-looking man (picky sharky). Once she'd caught me staring at her neck in a divisional meeting, because I was sure if I looked hard enough I'd find gills.

Her tight white dress ended just above her knees, hugging every inch of her slim self. She was tall, and athletic, with well-defined legs and arms that no doubt she worked out every morning in the gym, before spraying an entire bottle of hairspray to keep her hair in that bob. Holding that hairspray can alone was enough to give her those biceps.

She slid right past me, as if I didn't exist, and put her hand out to Nick to introduce herself, literally saving me from the most awkward conversation, and it took every ounce of energy not to scream at her, THANK YOU SHARKY SADIE!

Instead, I said quickly, 'Oh, hello, Sadie,' and then, 'Have you met Nick?' I felt like adding, *he likes naked walks, and hot shower sex and then turning up in my office place.*

'This is Sadie, our Senior Manager of Sales and New Business.' *She likes hairspray, and tight clothes, and men, and more hairspray.*

'That's executive, Emma,' she said, staring straight at Nick.

'I'm sorry?'

'I'm an executive, not a manager.' She gave a little laugh. 'Anyway, Nick.' She directed all her attention towards him. 'I've heard of you before, from the old Burleigh days? Five Star PR! Hilarious. Do you know Paul Clark? Matt Palmer. Josh Ng. Katerina Fowler?'

They were both considerably taller than me, and I felt a bit like their child, craning my neck and looking up to see what the grown-ups were talking about.

Sadie was tossing her hair around and had a gummy smile

on her face that she only ever did in front of clients or men she liked.

I felt strange about standing between them, so I excused myself in a tiny voice that neither of them heard, and slid away from the coffee corner, vowing to finish The Chat later.

Even if it meant getting fired, I was going to tell Nick the truth.

Chapter 13

'OK, Emma.' Nick was standing at the door to his office, with a smile on his face. 'You wanted to chat?'

I looked at Nick and wondered how many more days I'd be working here, once he knew the truth. With a deep breath, I picked up the folder that Donna had given me on my first day and stepped inside his office.

Nick closed the door behind me. 'Take a seat.' He motioned to the leather couch, where sitting for even a minute could make your thighs stick to it. I couldn't imagine how grand and graceful I'd look if I got stuck to his couch and he had to pull me off.

'I'd rather stand, thanks.'

'OK, suit yourself,' Nick said, looking at me as I teetered over his desk uncomfortably.

But then, I realised it might be a long meeting and my feet were going to get achy in my heels, so I sat on the sticky couch anyway.

'OK, so ...' he said with a smile as he sat behind the desk. His eyes looked kind, and for a second I had a feeling he was going to take this moment to try and clear the awkwardness between us after Coffeegate, or give me a pity 'are you still thinking about me after Fiji?' and that wasn't something I wanted to revisit, so I thought it best to get the first word in.

'I don't have an event theme,' I said quickly, leaning across the desk, handing the manila folder to him.

'What do you mean?' He flicked through the folder, and then came to a page that made him stop. 'This says death.' He raised his eyebrows and pointed to a pencil marking on the front of the file, as though I'd given him the wrong file.

'Oh, yes.' I nodded. *Here it comes. Here it comes.*

'*This* is your event?' he asked, his face suddenly serious and white.

'This is my event.' I was nodding blankly, and just repeating everything he was saying, because I knew what was coming.

'What is this?' Nick said, bewildered. He looked at me as though I had suddenly grown two heads and, even with two brains, I still couldn't understand what was going on. 'This is going to be a PR nightmare. You put one word out there, in this current newscape, one word that says you're mixing death with orphanages, and we'll be ruined.'

Finally, someone else who agreed with me. I smiled out of sheer relief, but he thought I was smiling at the theme, because his entire face went white. 'Emma, what were you *thinking*?'

What was *I* thinking? He thought I came up with this horrible event? His words stung a little. Was that what he thought of me? For a second, I didn't know what to say. But I couldn't let him see that I wasn't professional, especially after Coffeegate. I had to be ultra professional.

Instead I took a deep breath, gathered myself, and refound

my words. 'Hang on a minute. I didn't come up with this idea. I'm not *simple*.' I shook my head. 'This was Donna's idea. And I just walked in and was handed this ... this mess!'

'Donna's idea?'

'Yes, your predecessor, the person who hired me,' I confirmed.

'You didn't come up with this?' He looked genuinely surprised.

'Give me some credit. I may not be a PR bigwig, but I can tell when an idea is a bad one. And yes, this is a car wreck. But when I brought up the idea that mixing death with an orphanage was insane, I was told, by Donna, to make it work. Apparently, Maker is so edgy that this is us pushing the boundaries.'

'Of insanity,' Nick said, shaking his head and looking strained.

'Agree,' I said. 'But we have to make it work.'

Nick had tensed up and was massaging his temples as if he had a throbbing headache. 'Hmmm,' was all he was saying. 'Why would Donna ... and Glenn ...? Death ... How do we ...?'

'You see the turmoil I've been in? Trying to think of a creative way to approach this that might actually work.' I shrugged. 'And nothing. *Nada. Niente.*'

'But didn't you say you had this in hand, Emma?'

The way he said my name made me feel extra guilty. He was right, I had said that. 'Ahhh, I, ummm. I'm really sorry about that. I really am. I thought I had something. But if it counts for anything, everything else is on track. The invites.

The guests. The press releases. The social media. It's just the theme that's missing.'

Nick put his hands firmly on the desk as if preparing himself for what he was about to say. 'Well, we are going to have to come up with something. Brainstorm. Get creative. Anything. We need to figure this out.'

'We?' I asked tentatively.

'Yes, Emma, I'm not going to leave you to do this on your own.'

'Oh, thank God,' I said, a wave of relief washing over me that I wasn't in this by myself. But the relief quickly turned to worry. Wait, spending time with Nick? The two of us, alone? I felt a deep unease settle in my stomach. What could be worse than us being in confined spaces, and me trying to come up with ideas that were probably going to sound terrible, given I didn't actually have any experience in events or PR? God, why had I got myself into this mess?

Would it get awkward? Or tense? Would I be able to look at him without thinking about our shower? I must have looked worried, because Nick pointed out, 'It's probably easier to do it together, rather than coming at it alone.'

'Just like life,' I said without thinking.

Nick gave me a strange look. 'Sure, OK.'

'Not that I'm alone.' I gave a little laugh, and then felt as if I needed to explain a little more, otherwise Nick might think I was sad and alone and thinking about Fiji every night. 'It's just some people are. I'm not ... alone, that is. Actually, I'm dating.'

What was I saying? Oh, my Lord.

'Well, that's, um ...' Nick looked at a loss for words '... nice.'
I kept nodding. 'Yes, it's very nice.'

I squinted at Nick, trying to figure out what he was thinking. He seemed to be fine, and taking everything in his stride. As if nothing bothered him. He didn't seem to mind that just a few weeks ago we'd been swimming naked together. He'd built us a fire. We'd kissed each other's slippery skin in the shower. How did you go from having great sex with someone, and then just turn up and be cool, calm and collected and work with them?

What an unnecessary distraction, I thought. And how annoying that he was even here in the first place. If only the sex had been bad. Or his eyes didn't do that thing to me – make me act all strange and nervous and just babble like a bit of an idiot. It wasn't like I *liked* him or anything; I hardly knew him

'We need to start right now. Clear your diary and meet me in the breakout area.'

I nodded. Great. Just great, I thought glumly. Me and Nick alone in a room. What could go wrong?

Chapter 14

For the next two hours Nick and I brainstormed ideas and came up with absolutely nothing. At 1.30 p.m., he said he needed a break and then came back with a packet of chocolate biscuits in his hand.

'Here you go. Snacks.' He leaned across offering me one. 'Found them in the kitchen and thought they were better than apples.'

'Chocolate at Maker? They're probably a hundred years old.' I started to check the use-by label, but I could see it was a peace offering for our tense chat before, so I grabbed a Tim Tam and popped it in my mouth.

'What about an evil versus good battle?' he said, talking aloud. 'We could have macabre evil side, black and death, and then a saving the world, with light. Light. Light,' he mused. 'Maybe even lightsabers. Maybe *Star Wars*.'

'You want a *Star Wars* theme?' I said incredulously. 'That's a bit geeky, isn't it?'

'Totally geeky.' He grinned like Fiji Nick, and for the first time the tension around us seemed to relax. 'I thought I was out of the nerd closet, but appears I hide it well.'

'Don't tell me you like *Star Trek* too? And playing computer games?' I said, slightly teasing, forgetting I was being Professional Emma.

'Not a Trekkie.' He shook his head. 'Definitely not. But I played a lot of Nintendo when I was younger, and Game Boy.'

'Oh, Game Boy! I was obsessed with Tetris.' I laughed. 'I used to play under my blanket at night, trying to hide it from my mum. I think I existed on three hours' sleep for the entirety of year two.'

'OK, so I'm in geek-friendly territory?'

'A little. But I never watched sci-fi movies.' I held up my hands to plead my case, as he looked at me, completely astonished. 'Guilty as charged.'

'So, what movie did you watch over and over when you were young?'

I cringed a little 'This is going to tell you a lot. *Anne of Green Gables. Little Women.* And *My Best Friend's Wedding.*'

'Well, you've lost me on the first two, but the last one, I agree. It's a pretty good movie.'

I absolutely loved movies, and I couldn't help myself. Professional Emma had flown the coop. Left the building. And it was just me, Everyday Emma, getting excited about rom-coms.

'Except for the ending! I watch it until twenty minutes before the end and then, boom.' I clicked my fingers. 'I have to turn it off.' I thought about my favourite scene, and my heart beat faster. 'Remember the scene where they're on the boat—'

'And he's singing Frank Sinatra like a boss?' Nick nodded.

I laughed. 'And Julia Roberts is so into it, then she's about to tell him she loves him, but then the moment passes them by. Urgh! It gets me right here.' I clutch at my heart, laughing. 'I feel like crying every time.'

'I never took you for a romantic.' He said it lightly, but I wasn't sure if he meant it was a good thing or not.

His phone started ringing on the table. Being a little nosy (OK, a lot), I glanced at it. Chloe calling. He said sorry, and excused himself to step outside the room and take the call. I wondered if Chloe was someone from work. Once I'd checked that he'd left the room, I quickly clicked onto Maker's people directory and searched for a Chloe. There was a Chloe Maxwell in Printing and a Chloe Gerrard in Human Resources. It could be either. Or it could be someone else entirely.

I was hoping Chloe was no one, because Nick and I seemed to be getting on really well; our conversation flowed and I was enjoying being with him. On a professional basis, *of course*.

'Sorry about that,' Nick apologised, his tone back to professional. 'OK, where were we, before I think we got slightly off track?' And just like that Fiji Nick and Fiji Emma left the room and the work versions of both of us reappeared.

'Unfortunately, your idea is good, but it's been done before.' I told him what Donna had said about the garden of good and evil.

We both lapsed into silence as we thought about other

possibilities. I stared at my watch, and looked out of the window at the blue sky. In the distance, I could just make out the shape of the moon.

'Wait, I think I have something!' I said excitedly.

'Cityscape?' he asked, walking over to where I was sitting, and staring out of the window. 'Traffic?'

'Shhhh,' I told him as my brain chugged around.

'Isn't it career limiting to shush your boss?' He smiled so I knew he was joking.

But I didn't respond, because something was formulating. I stared out of the window as the idea started connecting in my mind. But then I realised that he was standing near me. And I made the mistake of looking up at him and into his eyes. And just like that – the chemistry between us was palpable. I was jolted back to that night, my hand on his neck, his muscly neck, kissing him. *Warm suds*.

'Earth to Emma.' He broke the spell. 'What did you have in mind?'

'Yes, um, so I was thinking … stars. Heaven,' I said, looking back out at the sky. *Focus, Emma, focus*. 'Then we can segue into glitter, planets, cosmos, ethereal – anything really.'

'Good one.' He wrote it on the board. But then he stood back and shook his head. 'Heaven, it's a little religious, isn't it? And we're trying to have an event of collaboration, not religious divisions.'

'Oh.' I felt deflated. 'You're right.'

'Death, death, death.' He pondered. 'You know, this is the most I've thought about death – especially in a work context.'

'Me too.' I opened up my laptop and busied myself with searching. 'OK, I'm going to try searching it. Again. For the millionth time.'

I typed in *death* and *word association*. 'Oh, God, there's an app that reminds you five times a week that you're going to die.'

'What?' Nick said incredulously.

I read out from my screen. 'It's called WeCroak and it's meant to remind you to keep living. You get text messages every day and it's meant to encourage "contemplation, conscious breathing or meditation".'

He raised his eyebrows in shock. 'Why would anyone want that? Hold on. Maybe that's an idea – doing a take on carpe diem, seizing the day and living!'

But when he got to the board, he didn't write anything. 'Living isn't really the same as death, though, is it?'

'Nope,' I said glumly, drumming my fingers on the table. 'Do you see the nightmare I've been in?'

'Why would Donna—?'

'Do that? I know, right?' I said, then I thought, maybe she wanted the event to fail. She did say it was a Fever Pitch. I tried to keep to myself what I thought about Donna, but I was eager to know what Nick thought. 'Did Donna mention anything to you?'

'About this? No,' Nick muttered. Before I could ask what they had talked about, he checked his calendar and said, 'At least we have the guests confirmed. They just don't know what the theme is.'

'Right, which, by the way, I'm getting a load of calls. People want to know what to wear.' I mused for a second. 'Is it too late ... or do you think we could lose the macabre plan?'

Nick shook his head. 'I texted Glenn earlier. Donna, in some way, managed to convince IAH's CEO and board that this was the way to get attention, and be edgy. God knows how.'

I knew how – through her pure, tantalising Goddess self. She was stunning. Even when she was coming at me like a predator, she was strikingly beautiful. Part of me wanted to just pop her on my mantelpiece and stare adoringly at her all day. She didn't even have pores. I knew, because I'd got up close to her one day in a meeting, when we'd almost bumped into each other, and even then, there was just glacial smoothness across her cheeks and nose. I knew the power of beauty (the kind of power I'd never had myself, but had seen countless times). She only had to breathily purr, 'Let's do macabre as an event,' or even, 'We should kill someone,' and the IAH people would have been jumping up and down, with their hands up, hoping they'd be chosen.

For the next hour Nick and I brainstormed further, did more word associations and came up with pretty much nothing. Finally, my stomach started growling. 'Chocolate biscuits just don't cut it for lunch.'

'How about we get a pizza delivered?' Nick replied, clearly hungry too.

'Pizza!' I said, shocked. I didn't know if Maker had ever entertained the idea of *takeaway pizza* inside its walls.

'Yes, it's this round dough thing with cheese on it.' He grinned.

I looked around sneakily. 'Perfect. Just don't let anyone see you carry it, or eat it, for that matter. Eating that kind of food around here is one of the cardinal sins.'

He laughed. 'I'll take my chance. What's your order?'

'This is where it's going to get weird.'

'Oh, mine too. Go on, then, do your best.'

'Double cheese, double pineapple, pepperoni and triple barbecue sauce.'

He laughed. 'You win. Mine's a supreme with crème fraîche instead of sauce.'

I wrinkled my nose at the thought.

Nick laughed. 'I thought the same about yours. It will be swimming in barbecue sauce – the toppings will probably float away. Shall we do half and half?'

By 2 p.m., we had an empty pizza box, and nothing else written on the board.

Nick yawned from the other side of the table and said, 'Death. Sleep.' He paused. 'I could do with some sleep. Or coffee. I worship coffee. It's a Godsend on days like today.'

Death. God. Rivers of barbecue sauce. I held up my hand as an idea started to take hold in my mind. 'I've got something!'

Nick looked at me expectantly.

'Hades and the Underworld,' I said excitedly. 'Picture this. They arrive to a hooded figure on the steps, and perhaps a glowing, gleaming red and black River Styx, maybe to get to their seat and tables they had to travel! Even by boat.' Now I was just getting carried away. 'There could be creatures of the Underworld and of course Persephone, Goddess, glowing white and bright. And the meals could be crimson and black and white – or a take on those foods. It will be opulent, and majestic and magical!'

Nick grinned at me. 'Emma, I think you've got it.'

And him just saying that made me feel amazing.

Chapter 15

'You're still here?' Nick stuck his head out of the office. 'It's 8 p.m.'

'OK, OK, maybe one more little thing?' I promised. 'By the way, how do the new logos from Tim look?'

He pulled them off his desk and brought them over. Tim had done just about next to nothing, except change the angle of the outstretched arms to be more on a diagonal so now the logo looked like a martini glass, and the head was a bouncing olive at the bottom of the glass. He'd also tinted the soft-bleeding pink to a deeper maroon, still in line with their brand colours. 'Thoughts?' he asked.

'No longer John the Baptist.' I nodded, feeling relieved. 'So that's a plus.'

He pointed to a large A3 sheet on my desk. 'Is that the seating chart?'

I nodded. 'Trying to get it to you by the end of today, but I'm just making some final adjustments.'

I'd been juggling with it all afternoon, trying to seat people who liked each other together, and who hated each other very far apart. We were also expecting some VIP celebrities, including Honey Clark. Honey was a well-known Australian actress that had been in the US for some time where she'd had a little run-in with the law for a DUI and a dodgy boyfriend. But thanks to Maker, she was planning to come to Australia and was perfectly positioned to be the new face of IAH, which was all part of her new do-good image. Even though she'd never done an ounce of charity before. That was what we did at Maker. Celebrity management. Spinning crises in new directions. Basically, we took the seedy underneath and made it look clean and sparkly again.

'Yep. Want to see?'

'Sure.' He walked behind my desk and leaned over. I could feel his warmth above me, and the hairs on my arms and neck started to stand. He still smelt as fresh as he did in the mornings. How did he do that?

'You've put Jessica Cohen next to Brian Jones?' he queried, running his finger across the chart. Jessica was a newsreader, with a side hobby of spinning the charity circuit, and Brian Jones was a footballer, and spokesperson for IAH.

'I shouldn't have?'

'They used to date. Ages ago. Maybe years.'

'Oh, right.' I picked up an eraser and rubbed out Jessica's name, replacing it with Gwen Herceg, a beautiful silver-haired patron and benefactor, who'd previously been the curator of the NSW Art Gallery. She was always lovely on the phone, and when I called I got to speak to her directly, rather than her assistant, which was the case for most of the other VIPs. 'Better?'

'Much.' He looked over it again. 'Did you want to go through the whole chart? I know we haven't had much time to discuss it yet.'

'That would be wonderful,' I said gratefully.

'Now?' he asked, checking his watch. 'At this point we may as well sleep here.' I must have given him a look of shock, because he said quickly, 'Not together.'

For a second neither of us moved. I refused to look at him, but, even so, I was sure I could feel something between us. A connection. Even if just for a second. I was sure of it.

'Great.' I followed him into his office, and he sat on one side of the couch, and I perched on the other side, more than a metre away. Nick took the pencil and made a few more changes, explaining who he was swapping with whom.

'How did you know about Jessica and Brian?' I watched him work. Trying desperately not to stare at the muscular curve of his neck.

'Experience.'

'Have you always worked in PR?'

He looked up. 'I have. It's been years now.' He calculated it. 'About fifteen. No, wait, eighteen. And you?'

I squirmed a little, then said, 'It feels like eons. Like a hundred years!' I said lightly, hoping it sounded believable.

'I know what you mean,' he said, scribbling on the seating chart. I watched as he swapped Charles and Bryce. 'Old feud.'

'Really?' I said, intrigued.

As he sketched he told me about the business wars and the lines of battle drawn. 'Yeah, local squabbles. Since you've been overseas, you wouldn't really know much about it.'

I nodded and tried to take in everything he was teaching

me – if the seating chart had gone unnoticed it could have caused some issues on the night. Thank goodness he'd been here to check it.

'Oh! Katrina.' He'd reached the VIP table that had Gwen and Honey on it. Katrina, I'd learnt, was a top charity strategist who had single-handedly spun many charities into the mainstream attention, with the help of Maker. She'd worked with Maker as far back as a decade, possibly even two.

I leaned over and watched what he was doing, as he finalised the names across the VIP table.

He passed the chart back to me. 'So, I think we're done here. A perfect seating chart.'

'Thank you,' I said gratefully, meaning it.

'Katrina needs to be next to Honey on VIP. We need as much media attention on Honey as possible. Positive attention. Honey is gorgeous and gets a lot of press. This will be good for her. And good for Maker.'

Everything Nick said was completely right, but all I could hear in my mind was: *Honey is gorgeous.* I suddenly felt really frumpy in my dress, because mine was a snug size fourteen, and Honey was a stick size six, and was that what constituted gorgeous?

I decided not to say anything else, so instead I just nodded and said breezily, 'Great. Exactly what I was thinking. So, thank you again for your help.' Professional Emma all the way.

Nick smiled warmly. 'You're welcome. Now, go home. That's an order.'

While I was waiting at the lift, Nick appeared. I felt myself freezing up a little – now work was officially over, what could we talk about? I gave him a quick, awkward smile. He smiled back – but with way more ease – and seemed fine.

We caught the lift down in polite silence, and I was wondering if he was feeling as strange as I was. When we stepped outside it was warmer than I expected. I took off my jacket. The air conditioning in the office always made it feel freezing, as though icicles were about to start forming on our computers.

'I'll walk you home?' Nick offered. 'Or to the station?'

I looked at him, surprised. 'You don't have to.'

'I do.' He smiled. 'It's almost ten. Can't have you be taken down by a bus, or Godzilla.'

I laughed. 'Or turning into a pumpkin? OK, the train is fine, because I live far, that way.' I pointed towards the inner west – at least I hoped it was west; being in the centre of the city I lost my bearings a bit being surrounded by so many tall buildings. 'But wait, first this girl must Clark Kent herself.' I bent down and took off my heels, and replaced them with ballet flats. 'Ahhhh, that is good.'

'Why do you bother wearing heels at all?' He stared at my feet. 'They look like weapons of mass destruction to me.'

'To all males, I think. Apparently, it's a Maker thing. Well, a corporate thing. It gets easier after a while just walking on tiles or carpet, but not outside on cobbly pavements.'

We crossed busy Elizabeth Street and started walking down the wide stretch of path in Hyde Park, right in the middle of the city. The traffic noises were hushed by the large rows of trees that bloomed in front of us. Far off in the distance, the Archibald fountain, baroque and beautiful, was being held up by a chorus of bronzed Gods and Goddesses. Twinkling fairy lights lit up the sky like tiny stars as a summer thunderstorm cloud was being blown in by the wind. With any luck, I'd make it home without being drenched.

We walked side by side, and I was conscious of how close we were to each other, the only people strolling through the gardens at this late hour. *Careful,* I told myself, *I'm a professional, I can't have an office … Fling. Crush. Distraction.* And Nick, I could tell, could become a giant distraction. And he already had been these past few days.

God, he was walking closer to me. I was sure of it. I stepped away to the right, and walked further away from him – so far that at one point I almost mounted the kerb and went into a garden bed. Thankfully he didn't seem to notice.

Nick looked over at me. 'If we are going to dress up for this ball, as Gods and Goddesses, who would you be?'

'Sounds like you have an answer already.' I looked at him as I almost stepped up on the pavement kerb, now a good two metres from him.

'Apollo, like the statue up there.' He pointed to the fountain.

'Isn't he the God of War?' I said, astonished. 'That sounds, awful.'

He ignored my surprise. 'You mean Ares. No, Apollo is the God of Light, but many people don't know that. Actually,' he started, 'if you want a history lesson—'

'I don't,' I interrupted him, then laughed when I saw the pretend look of sadness on his face. 'Fine, then, show off your geeky knowledge.'

'Well, he's actually the God of sun, and healing. He's also

160

known to stop us from repeating our mistakes over and over again. Of course, he's also immortal, and gets to carry a bow, so what's not to like?'

'I could do with an Apollo at times,' I admitted.

'I think we all could,' he said, and we continued walking down the pathway. 'So, who would you be?'

I thought for a while then said, 'I think most girls would say they'd be Gaia or Diana, you know, mother earth, or all wise. Some women may want to be Persephone, she of the underworld, with a darker edge, but I'm going to be honest and dig back into my grade six mind, when we studied mythology, and say I'd be that old guy, Cronos. Didn't he start the world? Or start something. Anyway, I know he ate his sons and all that, and, since I get hungry quite a bit, I think a God-sized snack would really satisfy me.'

He laughed. 'Even after a large pizza?'

I looked shocked. 'That? That was hours ago. I'll have you know I'm excited to get tucked into some serious mac and cheese when I get home.' And I wasn't joking. *That's it Emma,* I thought, *talk about eating large amounts of food.* It's very unromantic and a *great* strategy for office distractions.

'What's your favourite thing to eat?'

'Maybe a really good burger. Chicken. Beef. It must have pickles. Lots of pickles.'

Good, good, food was a very safe topic.

'But I haven't eaten a burger in ages.' He admitted.

'Really? Why not, if it's your favourite food?'

'Well ... uh, it used to be a thing me and my ex did. Have a weekly burger night. And uh, we broke up two years ago, and it was a bad break up. I haven't really had a burger since then.'

I felt bad for him then, I felt like I wanted to tell him about Murray, and being left at the altar, so he knew I understood, what it was like to have a bad break up. It had taken me years to get over it properly. Instead I said 'I'm really sorry to hear that. That sounds tough.'

'Yeah, it was. We tried again but it's hard to get trust back once it's broken.'

Ahhh Chloe I thought. That must be the Chloe who keeps ringing him. Or maybe that's his new girlfriend. Or one of many who he likes. Of course Nick would be surrounded by girls. Hot girls. Model girls. Influencer girls.

For some reason I felt a bit deflated when I thought about it. Of course, he'd never be interested in plus-size, average looking, somewhat ambitious, not very successful yet me. But why was I even thinking about that? Being with your boss, or even liking your boss, was *career suicide*.

I mean, how many office relationships do you know that succeed? In my experience, a total of zero. At first, they're hot and lusty and sexy – meet me in the broom closet, the stairwell. But soon the novelty wears off, and they're full of tiny arguments and tension – why didn't you sit with me for lunch? – Who's that marketing girl you're spending time with? And then, after a series of larger fights, silent treatment, accusatory glances and needy texts, the romance is over. Kaput. Done. And you must try and avoid the kitchen, the meetings, their desk, your desk. It's a *headache*. Every single office relationship I have seen always ends the same way – with one person resigning and leaving the company, and the two never talking again.

I purposefully switched our conversation back to a safe topic. Work. 'You know I'm sorry I didn't tell you straight away about Macabre and not having a theme. I suppose I should also tell you that Donna has asked me to do quite a bit for the event, and I do feel a little overwhelmed.'

Nick stopped and raised in eyebrows and a glimmer of concern crossed his face. 'Like what?'

I told him about the sorbet, the crazy chef, the fabric, everything I could think of that Donna had asked, I rattled off the list.

'You should not be doing all those things Emma. How are you even standing up right now?'

'Today Emma is brought to you by copious amounts of coffee, and the words "Get It Done".'

He grinned but then the smile fell off his face. 'Are you ok though?' That was the nice thing about Nick, he was always caring. 'And what were you thinking saying yes?'

'I guess I wasn't. I just wanted this to be the best event ever.' I shrugged.

'But you know these aren't PR tasks at all.' He paused. 'Right? I mean how long have you worked as a PR Advisor?'

I opened my mouth to tell him the truth, but I couldn't. I felt like I would let him down so much. And his words echoed in my mind – *it's hard to get trust back once it's broken.* 'Four years. In London.'

'Well you should understand then, you need to focus on managing the event and the public image of it, that's your main job, not working on desserts with a chef. First thing tomorrow, let's find someone else to do this. Like the designers and the actual chef – since it's their role.'

I suddenly felt like a weight had been lifted off my shoulders. 'Oh that is such a relief. Thank you, Nick, you don't know how good I feel hearing that.'

'Well good, just let me know if there's anything else on your mind. I'm here to help.' He smiled reassuringly.

We kept walking in silence for a little while. The last of the summer crickets were buzzing in the bushes. The night was beautifully warm, but the breeze was starting to whip through and grey clouds were gathering overhead. I peered up, and the stars were all covered.

'Isn't it funny,' Nick remarked, 'how this is the first time all week we've been able to properly talk to each other?'

'You do realise we talked pretty much most of today.' I looked over at him strangely. 'And some of yesterday too. Or did you forget that already? I hear early onset Alzheimer's is a thing.'

He laughed. 'I didn't know you were keeping a log of our conversations. And apparently the trick to knowing if you have Alzheimer's is to smell peanut butter. I had some on my toast this morning, and the verdict is – I can taste and smell it.'

'Peanut butter?' I said incredulously.

'Yep, it's one of the first signs of getting Alzheimer's – you lose that particular scent,' he said, nodding.

I stared at him dubiously.

He held up his hands, as if to say, *I'm just the messenger*.

'I bet I know exactly what you're thinking. You're going to tell me this isn't true at all. Then you're going to get home and open up the jar in your pantry, and take a deep whiff. You'll be relieved you can smell it. After that, you're going to investigate to see if that's an actual fact, because you don't believe me.'

'Pretty much, except I may investigate first, save me from having my nose in a jar.'

'Suit yourself. I bet you're too curious though, you'll have your nose in a jar anyway.' He grinned at me. 'Anyway, what I meant was this is the first time, without people around at work, that we can chat.'

I braced myself for a serious talk, but instead he was looking at me with a slight smile on his face.

'Tell me, what do you think about us working together?' he asked as we walked past the rose garden.

The blooms smelt sweet as sugar, and – WHAT THE HELL WAS THIS? A romantic movie? I looked around me. Since when was Hyde Park suddenly so wonderfully set up for a lovers' tryst? This was extremely distracting, more so because Nick looked very hot under this light, under any light for that matter. His lips were full. His eyes were crinkled as he smiled. His broad swimmer shoulders looked wonderful underneath his slightly see-through white shirt. I could have put him in one of those blue-lit-can't-find-your-vein public toilets, and he would have made it look like a high fashion model shoot.

I focused very hard on looking around at the grass for things that were not so romantic and felt relieved when I saw a really large dog poo, and further down a discarded old wine bottle, and some cigarette butts. Poo. Bottle. Butts. I repeated it like a mantra. Poo. Bottle. Butts.

'Um, it's fine.' And even though it felt far from fine, in fact it felt rather ... rather ... I couldn't put my finger on how it felt actually. Strange? Ridiculous? As if fate was having a good old laugh at me. *Let's send you a really hot guy that you totally connect with, but we'll make him your boss. Totally off limits. See how you go with that* 'How do you feel about it?'

'Well, I never thought my new job would deliver this kind of surprise.' He laughed. 'And it *was* a surprise. It's not often you find a free spirit trapped inside an office.'

Oh, yes. That. My face suddenly flushed red, and thank goodness it was dark, so he couldn't see it.

'How's Alaska going?' he asked wryly. 'Seems quite warm for winter this time of year. Snow hasn't kicked in yet.'

I laughed. 'OK, OK, I'm not in Alaska, yet. I didn't say I was going right away, just I was going. Am going. Just need to save up a little more. One day. Soon.'

He looked at me with his eyebrows raised as if to say, 'Oh, really?'

'Soon-ish?' I wheedled. Then remembered. 'But apparently you're meant to be in London? So that doesn't look like Big Ben, does it?' I said pointing to Centrepoint Tower. 'Or London Bridge?' I pointed off in the direction of the harbour bridge.

'You're pointing to Darwin, so, yes, further north west, that is vaguely in the direction of both those iconic structures.'

I felt like playfully swatting him, but I couldn't do that. Thankfully, I stopped myself – you couldn't go touching your boss. Not when you'd seen his penis. He'd think I was trying to, you know, insinuate *something*.

'So, we're both here, even though we said we wouldn't be,' he said. And I couldn't tell if there was something he was trying to hint at. He stopped for a second. 'It's a little weird, isn't it?'

I stopped too and he turned to look at me, so we were staring at each other. Did he mean weird good, or weird bad? I couldn't tell. The trees overhead started rustling, the breeze sent cool air over my bare skin, and even though it was still summer I shivered with anticipation. I couldn't help but imagine if someone saw us from afar, they'd think we were together. I knew it was Nick, my boss, but also it felt a bit as if he were my boyfriend. And I found myself shocked to realise – I *liked* it.

Suddenly, the sky let out a swift sound, like someone cracking a whip. And then, before I could look up, heavy rain started pouring down, soaking us in seconds.

'Over here!' Nick yelled, pointing to a small awning, but I could hardly hear him from the downpour. We ran towards the small stall, a pop-up pancake place, already closed for the night, but thankfully, offering a small alcove, about two metres or so, of protection from the rain.

We huddled beneath the very small awning as the water gushed around us.

'That was unexpected!' I said, laughing, crossing my arms across my chest to keep warm, and trying not to look at him. Was my make-up running? I tried desperately to remember if I'd worn waterproof mascara or not. Had I? Or did I have panda eyes? And was my foundation still in place, or was it running off my face, and revealing my tired, sleep-deprived eyes?

'You're shivering,' he said, quickly taking his jacket off. I could see what was about to happen: he was going to put his warm, woodsy-smelling jacket around my shoulders – and that was the *ultimate* distraction. It would feel as if we were on a *date*. Worse still, I noticed with his jacket off, it exposed *everything*. His white shirt was completely soaked and sodden and clinging to every part of his perfect body. Nothing was left to the imagination. *Smooth skin. Warm suds.*

He was walking straight into my personal space, and part of my mind was going all gooey and melty, and the other half was yelling, GET OUT. RUN. NOW. God, was he going to kiss me? I wasn't drunk. I hadn't had a drop of alcohol. Would it be like before? Was this about to *happen*?

Suddenly, I knew what would happen next. Because he was so lovely, and smart, and gorgeous, and such a gentleman. Once he'd put his jacket on my shoulders, I'd completely melt and would have to use every inch of my willpower not to say, *Let's get coffee. Let's get married. Let's make a baby with a vanilla-scented head.* Then it occurred to me that if we didn't keep moving, if we stayed here standing, staring at each other, under the canopy of oak trees, we might have started, I don't know, *kissing* or something.

He was my *boss*. I was his *employee. C'mon, Emma,* I thought. *Get a grip.*

To kill any mood – if there even was one – I opened my

mouth and said the first thing that came out, which happened to be, 'So giant lizards didn't kill me!'

He stopped in his tracks, his jacket hanging on his hands, with a look of genuine incomprehension on his face. 'Giant lizards?'

'Godzilla!' I said hastily. 'You know? Before?' I tried to laugh, but didn't quite pull it off. I looked at my watch. 'Gosh! Is that the time? Wowser. It's late. I better be going! Tootaloo!' *Tootaloo!?* Who the hell said that? But I needed to get out of this Nick vicinity and immediately.

Even though it was absolutely pouring with rain, I started almost jogging, well, sprinting really, as fast as I thought I'd ever run, towards the entry to the station, which was about fifty metres away.

Nick called out above the rain. 'Hey, Emma?'

I spun around, in the rain, breathlessly yelling, 'Yes?' Don't let anyone ever tell you jogging in flats is easy – it is very hard, and can lead to exhaustion after just ten steps.

'Thanks for your help today,' he yelled kindly, raising his hand to wave. 'Get home safely.'

God, he was so nice. Which meant I had to chant this on the entire train ride home. *No distractions. No distractions, No distractions.*

Chapter 16

It began the way all mature dates should. With fancy expensive wine from Portugal and Bordeaux, and slabs of blue and smoked cheese arranged on a very small platter in a tres-chic Sydney wine bar. I was dressed in a silk green chiffon, three-quarter-length dress, with mid-thigh slits for a bit of mystery. I loved the way the dress fluttered in the breeze when I walked – I was sure I looked Italian, walking on a cobbled little Florence laneway, rather than waiting at the lights at George Street, and avoiding mud puddles from the recent rain, in miserable Sydney.

Peter was tall and broad, with a nice face and brown hair that had a cowlick at the back. He wore a heavy brown coat and tweed-like pants with a crisp white shirt. He looked positively English even though he was from somewhere outside Brisbane. He arrived before me and was waiting at a small table in the corner of the bar.

'Peter.' I smiled.

'Emma,' he said.

I went to shake his hand, but he leaned in to kiss my cheek and so I awkwardly stuck my hand into his slightly soft stomach. 'Oh, sorry,' I laughed and blushed a deep shade of red. He leaned in and tried again, landing a slightly wet-lipped kiss on my right cheek, which I immediately wanted to wipe away. Instead I tried to feign I was brushing my hair out of my face, whilst using my pinkie finger to gather the drying saliva. Gross, I thought, wiping my hands multiple times on my napkin.

'That's a nice shirt,' I said, sitting down as he pulled out the chair for me, then sat opposite me.

Peter looked down. He seemed pleased. 'You know Tarocash?'

'Yes.' I nodded, thinking that was where my nineteen-year-old cousin Brad shopped for his first business outfit, because he got a full suit for forty-nine dollars.

He smiled at me. 'This is it.'

I took a large gulp of wine and Peter filled up my glass. He smiled. 'How long have you been single?'

'A long time.'

'Me too. Five years. It's hard dating in Sydney.'

'Yes.' I took another sip of wine.

For a few minutes neither of us spoke. I didn't know what to say, so finally I said, 'So, do you watch much TV?'

'I love that series about a drug dealer, in Columbia. You know it?'

I shook my head.

He grinned. 'And, guilty confession, I like *Star Trek*. You?'

'Um, *Kamikaze*.'

'Oh, I don't know that one.'

'It's Japanese, people compete on water obstacles, but mostly land in the water, awkwardly.' I gave a strange laugh. 'That made me sound like a sadist.'

He nodded and there was another long silence.

'I'm not a sadist,' I quickly said. 'Just to clear that up.'

More silence.

Peter smiled awkwardly. 'Are you on any dating apps?'

I shook my head. 'You?'

'Yeah, I've done most of them – Tinder, Plenty of Fish, RSVP.'

'And?'

'Well, a lot of first dates, some second ones, but nothing has really stuck.'

'Oh?'

'Yeah, still looking.'

There was more silence.

'What hobbies do you like doing?' he asked.

'Oh, um, I like swimming in summer. Movies. Dancing badly.' I laughed. 'You?'

'Football and car racing.'

More silence.

'And you work in PR?' I asked.

'Yeah, in fleet and overseas luxury cars. And you?'

'Yes, PR, and Events.' I waited for the rush I usually got when I said I worked in PR, but strangely it didn't come this time.

He nodded. 'More wine?'

I nodded. We sat there in strained silence for ten minutes before I excused myself to go to the bathroom. When I came back my wine glass was refilled – he really was attentive – and we tried to talk about pets. I used to have a dog. And he wasn't allowed any, and now had allergies to most animals. Even, he said, prawns.

'Even when you're swimming around in the sea?' I said teasingly.

'No, on my plate,' he said seriously, totally missing my joke. 'I have EpiPens.' He opened his jacket pocket, showing me where he kept them.

I nodded politely and swallowed a lot of wine, and made hmmm noises, as if it were very good wine. Then I had to use the bathroom. Again. To his credit, he stood every time I left the table. Which was a lot (at last count – three). I have a teeny bladder.

In the bathroom for the third time, I texted Tansy.

On date with Peter. Bad conversation. Have almost run out of topics.

She wrote back immediately.

Is he cute? Is he nice? Has he ever been in jail?

I wrote: *Kinda. Yes. I doubt it!*
She took some time replying and with it came a list of questions to ask on a first date.

When I returned from the bathroom there was Peter standing up again, then offering the cheese knife so I could sample the brie. That was very sweet of him, and I decided maybe it was just first date nerves, and I needed to give this another chance.

'What's your favourite holiday destination?' I asked him with a smile, armed with my new conversation topics.

'Oh, fishing in a little spot off the coast. Do you like fishing?'

'No.' I really hated the idea of catching some poor little fish with a metal hook in its mouth and neck. 'It's just never hooked me.'

He seemed to miss the pun; instead he smiled at me pleasantly. When he didn't ask me what my favourite destination was, I decided to tell him. 'I loved Peru. The mountains and landscape there are breathtaking. Have you been?'

'No, I haven't been to South America. Or America. I went to Hong Kong once to watch car races and rallies.'

'Oh.'

He smiled at me. 'I much prefer camping locally.'

I took a sip of wine. 'I don't particularly like camping at all really. It makes me itchy.'

He nodded and we sat there in silence. Again.

I didn't know what else to say, but there was still half a bottle of wine on the table, and some nibbles of cheese, so I had to stick around, didn't I? I didn't remember dates being as painful as a visit to the dentist, and this one felt like having a tooth pulled, except without the happy gas high.

While I sat there pretending to listen to Peter talk about the best camping spots, I started thinking about Nick, and what he would say if he were here. We'd be talking about living in a country cottage. Or penguin training as a career. Or he'd be trying to teach me about Sirius or some other star cluster, and I'd be telling him he was just a big old nerd.

Peter excused himself to the bathroom, and, because I was

slightly tipsy, it was making me reminisce about how Nick and I connected in Fiji. I kept thinking of calling him, or texting him, but what would I say? Then I had another thought – were we even friends? I wasn't sure. I thought we were colleagues, and that was about it. And sending a slightly tipsy text to your boss about a date was not professional at all. I put my phone away quickly.

Peter was suddenly back on the stool in front of me. 'So, this was fun, should we do it again?'

I opened my mouth, and realised I was about to say – *sure*. Because isn't that what you say on dates, and then you never call them again, and you avoid their calls and you hope that they get the picture. But ghosting wasn't that kind was it? Wasn't it better to tell the truth?

'You know Peter, you're lovely, but I'm just not feeling it, really.' I swallowed hard, feeling bad, really bad.

'Oh yeah, yeah, me too actually. Yeah I've got another date later anyway, later this week.' We both knew he was lying.

'Oh that's great Peter.' I tried to nod enthusiastically.

He stood then and said 'I don't think we had that much but this should cover the wine.' He opened his wallet and left a fifty-dollar note on the table. 'Bye Emma, thanks for a good evening.'

And then I watched him walk slowly out of the bar. God, I felt awful. You tell a lie – you feel bad. You tell the truth – you feel bad. How could anyone win?

Chapter 17

'**I** hate it.'

'Y- you hate it?' I stammered.

'Hate it,' Glenn repeated after Nick and I had just revealed our Hades and the Underworld theme. I'd spent the entire weekend feeling great about the fact we had an event theme all planned, even to the point that I wasn't that perturbed by the fact that I'd not really done anything beyond my date but catch up on sleep and vacuumed my apartment. All two metres of it.

I'd gone out once to get the paper, just to the mailbox, but the fresh air I'd had for those twenty seconds had been nice. Other than that, I'd spent a few idle hours watching YouTube videos on Gods and Goddesses. I'd felt so positive coming into this presentation, Nick had given me a thumbs up in the meeting room when he'd come in, and I'd been sure Glenn would love it.

Apparently, he didn't.

'It's almost exactly the same theme that Hive did for the Warners account. Some Mount Olympus shit with Gods and Goddesses, and a whole room dedicated to the underworld.'

177

Hive were our prime competitors, and there was a massive rivalry going on, always had been. A bit like deciding if you were Team Jacob or Team Edward, or Team Aidan or Team Big, Hive and Maker had a rivalry so long, no one could point out when it actually began. The way it had been discussed in the office, playing hard and playing dirty was expected between the companies. Even stealing accounts from each other. Trying to hack into emails to get juicy gossip. Nothing was off limits. Thankfully, Maker had taken the high road lately and seemed to be winning accounts without getting all guerrilla warfare, but apparently we'd failed to nab the Warners account.

Nick nodded and his lip quivered the way it seemed to when he was concentrating. 'Yes, they did, you're right. I remember now hearing about it last year, and about Maker's top-level pitch.'

'That we didn't win,' Glenn said, sounding bitter. He checked his mobile and, while scrolling through emails, he said, 'So, second options?'

I shot a panicked look at Nick, who faltered, before he quickly said, 'We've got something else, but how about we present that to you later this week? We just need to clarify a few things.'

'Get Kerry to book you in,' he said, standing up and leaving without looking at us.

For the rest of the day, everyone wanted to know what was happening with Macabre. Who was the entertainment? What colour theme had we chosen?

In meetings, Nick took charge, saying, 'Guys, it's top secret,

178

and hush-hush, so we have a small party of need-to-know people only.'

And when Nick wasn't there, I smiled secretively and put a finger to my lips, as if to say, I'm sworn to silence.

Which just made people want to know more about it. By lunchtime, there was a rumour going around that Macabre was *the* event of the year. By mid-afternoon it had spread like wildfire to our clients, and I got a steady stream of calls, people throwing around their titles, as if that would make me give up the secret.

'Well, the hush-hush thing has worked,' I said to Nick when I saw him in the corridor. 'I suppose that's the best lesson to learn in PR. Mystery sells.'

He stepped in closer to say something, and I found it extremely hard not to look at his eyes, his warm melted-chocolate-pool eyes. *Distraction!* God, this was not a good idea.

In fact, it was a very bad idea, because standing this close to a hot guy, a very hot guy, for whom I might have been harbouring feelings, very small feelings, but feelings nonetheless, meant my willpower was at a level zero and falling.

This could only end in disaster. Like me trying to inhale his aftershave. Or losing all word control and just gummily smiling and drooling at him. Or, even worse, asking if we might find an office closet and get down to some frisky Fiji business. I stepped back and tried not to flinch at my uncontrollable thoughts, but I saw him register the look on my face. And he must have misread it for me not hearing him properly, because he leaned closer. *Closer!*

And then ... Too late. I'd smelt the lingering of his aftershave. His mint toothpaste. Saw the strong muscles at the back of his neck. His lips. And my imagination immediately propelled us into the future, and I was seeing us in his Fiji timeshare, a small beach wedding, hibiscus flowers. Bright pink. Damn it. I shook my head and focused, very hard, on listening to what he was saying.

'We can't keep this up with Glenn or the other execs for long. They're going to want to be let in on the secret.'

'Yes, I can't keep this up,' I agreed, wondering if we had enough money to get a Balinese timeshare too.

'When you think about death, what do you think of?' he asked, clicking his fingers.

Thankfully, this jarred me out of my made-up couple bubble. 'Cemeteries,' I said quickly, thinking of zombies and horror movies – which scared the bejesus out of me. All horror movies. Even the slightly silly ones where the guy had an axe – or was it a chainsaw – and wore an ice hockey mask.

'OK, why don't we take a walk in a local cemetery then? Maybe that will help jog our memories. Get outside,' Nick suggested.

'OK, that's a bit creepy,' I said slowly, waiting for him to come up with an idea that didn't include me and him walking together again. But he was looking at me expectantly. I swallowed hard. 'Oh, you're not joking?'

'Right now, I'd happily perform a sacrifice to get an idea for a theme.'

'Slow down, Satan worshipper, no need to go that far,' I admonished him, and stepped back again, to give us at least a metre distance in between. We stared at each other, helpless, no ideas coming in.

'OK, the cemetery.' I was regretting it immediately. 'But not at night time. I'll have nightmares forever.'

'How about sunset?'

'When?'

'Tonight? We need to get this sorted soon.'

'As long as you don't want me to visit a crypt or anything scary. And I put my foot down to visiting the crematorium.' I imagined terrible flames and burning bodies.

Nick looked horrified at the thought. 'Never. I don't want to breathe in ashy people air.'

'Ew!' I said, laughing. 'I never thought of that until now.' This topic seemed very safe, talking about dead bodies; it wasn't romantic in the slightest, so I was silently grateful for that.

Phil came around the corner, so Nick whispered, 'Cemetery tonight?'

I nodded and he walked down the hallway, saying hello to Phil on the way.

Phil caught up with me and we walked back to our desks.

'Did I just hear the word cemetery?' He squealed a little. 'I knew it, you're doing a take on Michael Jackson's *Thriller*.'

'Ironic,' we both said in unison.

'But wrong.' I winked at him.

Over the next few hours Phil popped his head above my computer, with a series of guesses.

'*Fright Night? Return of the Dead? Halloween?*'

'No. No. No.' I shook my head at each of them.

At one stage, Nick was coming back to his office and overheard Phil say, 'A take on *Pet Sematary*?' and shot me a look of apology, then shrugged. We both knew there was nothing either of us could say to stop people from guessing about the event theme we didn't have.

'Why the secrecy?' Phil asked me as I was packing up my desk for the day.

'Because of big mouths like you,' I teased him. 'We can't risk it getting out.'

Phil eyed me up and down. 'You don't have a theme, do you?'

I hesitated. 'Of course, we do,' I said hotly, trying to pack up as quickly as I could and shut down my laptop. He had a keen sense of figuring people out, and now the Phil spotlight was directed towards me, I needed to get out of the office, like *now*.

I considered, for a second, telling Phil *everything*. It would be nice to confide in someone, especially Phil, who knew me so well already. And who knew Nick too. But once you told one person, you could never guarantee that it wouldn't just get out. These things might just pop out in conversation. No, I couldn't risk it.

'Then what's got into you? You're more ansty than normal.' Phil narrowed his eyes and leaned forward, placing his chin in his hands. 'What's going on that I don't know about? I can sniff something different about you.'

'Firstly, that's disgusting. Stop, er ... smelling me,' I said, horrified. 'Secondly, we do have a theme, it's just top secret.' I prayed he would buy it.

'I know what it is!' He snapped his fingers.

'You do?' I looked at him nervously.

'You're dating someone,' Phil declared.

I thought about Nick, his broad shoulders, his chocolate eyes and how they unravelled me. Had I been acting strange around the office? 'I'm dating someone.' I meant it to sound like a question, but it sounded more like I was making a grand admission.

'I knew it!' Phil looked happy with himself. 'You're seeing someone! What's he like?'

Nick was inside his office, but had left the door open. I made a motion to Phil to shut up, otherwise we'd be told off for gossiping instead of working.

'I don't do sign language.' Phil looked at me weirdly.

I tried again to silence him by putting a finger on my lips, but he ignored me.

I just needed to get out of there before I had to pretend I was dating someone. 'Chat about this later,' I called out over my shoulder, moving quickly to the lift and hitting the button five times.

Chapter 18

Waverley Cemetery at sunrise was always beautiful. It overlooked the eastern beaches of Sydney, and was perfectly positioned on a rounded grassy hill, with a view straight out to sea. A few years back developers were going to take it over and start building high-rise buildings atop, well, dead bodies. Which was strange and creepy and absolutely guaranteed whatever would be built there would be thoroughly haunted. Luckily, the court ruled against development, and now the dead could enjoy their view in peace.

But at sunset, Waverley Cemetery was extremely spooky. The tombstones held a ghoulish red glow in the evening sun. I felt as if I were walking onto a horror film set. Whose silly idea was this? The sun would be setting shortly, and then Nick and I would be here in the dark, like a pair of idiots.

I was waiting by the statue of Mary, as planned, at 6.30 p.m., wearing a long blue maxi dress, a white cardigan and red converse. The wind was cool, but the earth still felt warm, after being baked from the hot summer months. I realised it had been a long time since I'd just gone for a walk or been outside other than shuttling back and forth between work and my flat. I looked at the ocean, and tried to take a deep breath and forget I was in a cemetery, but my eye caught the glint of sunlight reflecting off a large cross, and I suddenly felt as if Dracula were going to fly down, transition from bat form, and fang me.

Nick called out, 'Emma,' from the bottom of the cemetery, waving hello. He was wearing cargo shorts and a navy-blue jumper and his legs looked still summer-tanned and slim. By the time he made it up the hill, the ocean horizon glowed as if on fire.

'Who in their right mind does this?' I hissed. 'A cemetery. At night.'

'Mrgherhewh brains,' Nick said in a zombie voice.

Being out of the office, he felt like less like my boss, and more like my friend, and before I could think better of it I playfully hit his arm with the palm of my hand. 'Seriously, don't start with me. I'm going to lose it.'

'Hitting your boss now?' He clutched at his arm, overreacting and stepping backwards. 'I believe that's a case of harassment.'

'Let's get this over with quick.' I pulled a large flashlight out of my bag.

'Oh, folks, she's armed and dangerous, watch out. Or she'll get you with ... dum dum dahhhh the light!'

'I'm about to clock you with this if you don't shut up.'

'Challenge accepted.' Nick looked around the cemetery. 'So, what's the plan?'

'I was about to ask you the same question.'

'Well, let's walk and see what happens. Death-wise.'

I shuddered. 'That sounds like one of us is going to die.'

Nick started walking ahead, and I stepped in behind, single file, between the burial plots. It felt extremely eerie and strange. Due to seeing too many horror films when I was younger, I half expected a hand to stick out of the dirt and try and grab at my leg. So, I kept watching the grounds, and because I wasn't looking where I was going, I kept bumping into things – my hip went into a tombstone, I nearly tripped over a small concrete plaque and finally I made a quick save when I nearly fell over nothing at all.

Nick led the way into a darker patch of the cemetery, with large trees that shrouded us in shadow.

'What was that?' I said, jumpy, sure something had just touched my neck.

'What was what?' Nick said.

'It feels like a cold patch of, um, air, which they say reveals ...' I couldn't finish the sentence.

'Reveals what?' Nick turned and looked back at me, lifting his arm to block out the flashlight's strong glow. 'God, Emma, if you're about to say ghosts.'

I was shivering a little from the adrenaline pumping through my body, because, yes, that was exactly what I was thinking. We were, after all, disturbing their final resting places.

'Because do you know what else it means?' Nick asked.

'No.' I shook my head and put down the light, spilling it out across my feet. 'What?' I asked, intrigued.

'Cold air in a cemetery often means,' Nick whispered,

leaning towards me so close I could smell his woodsy scent, 'that it's night.'

'Ugh.' I flashed the light straight into his chocolate eyes.

'Ouch! You're blinding me.' Nick threw his hand up towards the light.

'Continue on, blind one!' I told him, laughing. 'And don't say you didn't deserve that.'

He turned around and blindly stumbled for a few seconds, before his eyes adjusted. We walked for another few minutes between smaller tombstones, and a few more plaques and crosses.

'So, is this working?' Nick called out over his shoulder.

'I feel we have to be quiet and respectful,' I whispered.

'I don't think they can hear us,' he whispered, then said in a normal voice, 'Do you think it's working?'

'I don't think so. All I keep thinking about are zombies and ghosts and wondering who is trying to clutch my ankle.'

'Your ankle?'

'Never mind.' I paused to readjust my flashlight, which seemed dimmer than when we'd started. 'It looks like it's dying a bit – does it to you?'

Nick grabbed the light, switching it on and off. 'Maybe.' Then he switched it off, and we were standing in total darkness.

'Nick?' I could barely make out any shapes, or Nick. 'Nick, this isn't funny, turn it back on.'

To my right I saw a shadow move out of the corner of my eye. 'Nick!' I said in a high-pitched voice. 'Where are you?'

In an act of desperation, I reached out to grab the light, and as I did Nick turned it on, up against his chin, so it made his face look grotesque, and he let out a horrible low moan, like a disturbed ghost.

Petrified, I opened my mouth and shrieked like a banshee, a bit like Britney Spears did when she shaved off all her hair (well, as I imagined her to be doing in all those photos of her), and I couldn't stop.

'Shush. Emma, it's me,' Nick said, dropping the flashlight, which fell to the ground and switched off, so we were standing there in pitch black again. I thought I felt something on the back of my neck again, and I was thinking of all the horror movies I'd seen, especially the horrible devil thing at the end of *Paranormal Activity*, and I couldn't stop screaming.

Suddenly, Nick reached out, his hands found my arms, and he pulled me into his broad chest. 'Emma,' he said, and his mouth was warm and so near my head. Being against his chest as I had been in Fiji jolted me out of my banshee state. He felt so warm, and strangely familiar. And I could feel my heart pumping hard, and tiny little bolts of electricity run through my chest. 'I'm sorry. I had no idea that was going ... Are you OK?' And he felt so wonderful. I literally thought I was going to lean up and kiss him. But I couldn't. That was entirely inappropriate and unprofessional.

Suddenly, I had a brilliant idea to get me away from Nick's wonder-hug *and* to exact my revenge for him scaring the bejesus out of me.

I pretended to run out of breath and faint, collapsing in

his arms. It sounds romantic, but it wasn't. Nick staggered around for a bit, trying to keep me upright, with some over-exerted 'ooofs' as I made sure my legs were like jelly. Eventually, he managed to lay me down on my back on the ground.

'Emma? Emma?' I could feel him peering over me. 'God, Emma, are you OK?'

I stayed silent, eyes closed, trying not to laugh.

'Emma,' I could hear him fumbling around for his mobile phone, 'Emma talk to me. God are you still breathing?'

He leaned his ear over my nose and mouth and I held my breath.

'God, hold on, Emma, I'm calling someone.' He sounded panicked. I could hear him press the keys on his phone to dial someone; just before he finished, I grabbed his knee with my hand.

He let out a yell and dropped the phone.

I sat up cackling evilly and said, 'Ha ha, sucker.'

He fell back, panting. 'Oh, my God. I nearly had a heart attack.'

'That makes two of us,' I said happily, switching the flash-light app on my phone on. In the light, Nick's face looked sweaty and red, and I almost felt bad. Almost. 'You deserved that, and you know it.'

His eyes narrowed but I could see he was trying not to laugh. 'Did I?'

'Yes!' I stood and dusted myself off, and picked up my flashlight, which was well and truly broken.

He got up and still looked a bit shaky. 'I thought you'd totally passed out, or ...'

'Or you'd killed me?' I couldn't help but smile. 'Sorry, because then maybe my funeral could have been the macabre event.'

'At this rate, it will be yours and mine together. If we don't have something for Glenn tomorrow.'

'Possibly. But, unfortunately, I think the only thing that's dead around here is this light. Now, before we meet a ghost, let's get the heck out of here.'

On the walk out of the cemetery, I suddenly realised all the excitement had made me really hungry. 'Do you want to get something to eat?'

'I'm not sure,' Nick admitted with a glint in his eye. 'You almost killed me.'

'And you almost scared me to death.'

'So, we're even?' he asked.

'I believe I still owe you one shark scaring at sea ...' I teased, before I could think about what I was saying. Then I realised I'd inadvertently brought it back to Fiji and the idea of us together, and the seafood platter. And put my foot in it again. God, I had no filter.

I couldn't read his face, but he ignored that comment completely, and I wasn't sure what that meant. 'Well, there's a pretty good Mexican up the road.'

Over burritos and bottles of cheap beer, we chatted about other ideas for the macabre night, until I said, 'I can't talk about death any more. It's so depressing.'

'Shall we talk about Santa instead?'

'The tooth fairy?' I grinned.

'Easter Bunny and a round of chocolate?' Nick took a swig of beer. 'So, what was that back there?'

'I think, mostly, that was you trying to scare me, and me getting you back,' I said, licking a clump of yummy black beans and cheese from my fork. 'Even better, if I do say so myself.'

'And then you falling into me, like you were some sort of damsel in distress.'

'Correction – you grabbing me because you scared me to the point of banshee screaming. Did someone mention harassment?' I smiled at him, to show I was completely joking.

'Yeah, I'm pretty sure I'm not supposed to hug my employees.' Nick ate a bite of his beef burrito then said in an offhanded way, 'Especially since I heard Phil talking about you dating someone. Wouldn't want to make someone jealous.'

Jealous? I couldn't work out what he meant by that. It could have been totally innocent, but also it could mean ... *no*. I wouldn't obsess over one word, and overanalyse it as I'd done with every other guy previously. Nick was my boss. And was clearly making conversation. Nothing more, nothing less.

I snuck another look at him as he took a swig of his beer. His hands were so perfect. If only he weren't so good-looking, so kind, so nice, so funny. Damn it. No, I wouldn't think about how it felt to hug him back there. Or the way I wished he would hug me again. Even thinking about it made my heart start pumping so loudly I thought it was going to bounce out of my chest, and come to rest on Nick's plate, yelling, I THINK I LIKE YOU.

'Oh, you heard that?' I said, trying to downplay the conversation. 'You better watch out, he'll be offering his set-up dating services to you, if you're not careful.'

'Actually, Phil has already poked his head into my office and asked me if I wanted any help on the dating front. Twice,' he said.

'He did?' I laughed at Phil's gumption. That took guts, offering to help your boss out in the dating stakes. 'And you said ...?' I was intrigued to find out if Nick was single.

'I said I didn't need his help. He seemed a little gutted.'

Oh, so he *was* potentially seeing someone.

'I think he wants a new career as a matchmaker,' I said, looking at Nick. Even slightly hot and sweating in the burrito shack, he looked gorgeous, with his dark blond hair tousled to the side, and his T-shirt revealing his wonderfully smooth tanned skin. 'Besides, there's no time for anyone to date at Maker. I mean, my crazy boss is making me work very long hours.'

'Oh, is he?' Nick shook his head and made tsk-tsking noises.

'You'll never guess what his latest idea was – that we go walking in the dark in a cemetery.'

'He seems interesting.'

'You got interesting from that?'

'Yes, at least he's not vanilla,' Nick pointed out.

My hand froze in mid-air with the chilli bottle in my hand. 'What did you say?'

'Vanilla. You know boring, plain—'

'I know what it means. I've just not heard anyone else say that. It's what I normally say.'

'Great minds think alike.' He leaned his glass forward as if to cheers me, and I felt unable to drag my gaze from his hand. He had great hands. Big hands. Great. Finally, I lifted my beer to meet his.

Nick was still speaking. 'So, then, if you're not vanilla, what flavour of ice cream would you be?'

'Tutti frutti,' I said quickly. 'Full of surprises. You never know what you're going to get.'

'Also,' Nick pointed out, 'a flavour that no one chooses.'

I stared at him. 'Are you seriously saying that, when I have the chilli bottle and could douse your entire dinner in ...' I read the label carefully '... level nine, hot crazy sauce?' For extra effect I popped a dash over the end of his burrito. 'Did that even come out?' I asked and tipped it up for a few more splashes but the bottle appeared to be blocked.

Nick took the bottle out of my hand, and slightly grazed my fingers, which gave me a warm tingle up my arm. 'I think we should put that down,' he joked. 'And I meant that particular flavour isn't something people choose, so maybe you're not that. Maybe you're something else.'

'Like?' I prompted him.

'Like ... gimme a minute.' He looked up at the ceiling, carefully considering it.

'Well, what would you be?' I asked, taking a bite of my burrito.

'Easy. I'd be peppermint chocolate chip. Peppermint is refreshing, it always feels new. And, well, chocolate is strong and resilient. There isn't a situation that can't be made better with chocolate.'

I held up my hand. 'Wait a second! I'm sure there are situations that chocolate doesn't come in handy.'

'White chocolate and butterscotch,' he said quickly.

'What?'

'You'd be white chocolate and butterscotch caramel. Mostly white chocolate, but some globs of butterscotch caramel, that catch you unaware, by surprise.'

How on earth did he come up with that? Nobody liked white chocolate; I mean, technically it wasn't even chocolate. And a glob? A *glob*? To be globby felt big, or fat. I suddenly became aware that I was eating an entire burrito plate. For a moment, I almost stopped eating. But then I thought *screw that*. I loved tortilla wraps with refried beans with cheese.

'So, basically, I'm the white version of you? Besides, white chocolate isn't even chocolate,' I pointed out. 'It's just a whole load of milk and sugar. Like vanilla.' And the word, as it always did, spun my mind back to seven years ago. Murray. Busline. Suburbia. Long service leave. My wedding dress had been the colour of French vanilla. The colour of my thighs when we were together had been vanilla, because he hated the beach and being out in the sun. And honestly, Murray was vanilla. Come to think of it, most things that were white were really bad. Or at least I thought they were.

I bet some people out there loved vanilla. Loved security and stability and having salmon Mondays and chicken Tuesdays and tuna casserole Wednesdays, and going to Bunnings hardware stores every weekend for a sausage sizzle, before taking the two kids to the park for a bike ride. But that life seemed like my worst nightmare. I was never made to be vanilla, and Murray was, and that was just how we were.

We'd never belonged together. Suddenly I realised all this time I'd felt guilty that I was too much of a free spirit, and maybe I should have settled down. Maybe I should have taken that house on the busline. Maybe I wasn't grown up enough.

But suddenly I saw it so clearly: Murray was vanilla and that suited other vanilla people. And I was tutti frutti, or globby white chocolate, and both those flavours needed something else completely. I felt a fierce jolt through my veins, because I realised it wasn't my *fault*. It felt electrifying. I shook my head and said with confidence, 'Plain, simple vanilla is not my style. At *all*.'

'Why do I get the feeling we're not talking about ice cream any more?' Nick put down his beer and looked at me, waiting for me to speak.

'You're right,' I admitted. I wasn't going to say anything, but when I looked up at him, his unshakeable chocolate eyes looked so kind, it all just came tumbling out. 'I dated someone vanilla once.' I paused. 'And it went well for a while, until it didn't go well at all.' And suddenly I was spilling parts of my past I'd promised never to tell anyone again. And once I started, it all fell out, including The White Horror.

When I finished, I picked up my beer and downed it in one gulp, then asked the waitress to bring me another. Then I gave him a small smile. 'Sorry, I don't know why I'm talking about that. It was a long time ago. But I think what you said the other day rung a bell with me. Once someone breaks the trust it's hard to get back. Not even with the same person, but with different people too.'

Nick looked at me intently, and said softly, 'I get exactly what you're saying.' He took a swig of beer, as if he was building to say something. 'Something about me that I don't tell many people: a few years ago my partner of eight years cheated on me.'

I grimaced.

'Yeah, it gets worse,' he said with a tight smile. 'With her work colleague. Isn't that like so clichéd? And not just once, they were seeing each other for a while – a year, I think.'

I shook my head. 'Gosh, I'm so sorry.' I gasped, feeling so bad for him. I wanted to hug him, and it was all I could do not to lean over the table and touch him. I literally had to put my hands on the table in front of me, almost wedge them under my plate.

'And Emma, I'm sorry. Being left at the altar, even if they're not your person, is not OK. Ever. I'm so sorry that happened to you.' And I was sure he went to put his hand on top of mine, but then he stopped. Because he was my boss? Because he thought it would give me the wrong idea?

I took a sip of my beer. 'Thanks. I think when it's the right person, you just know. Even if it's after a day, a week.'

Nick and I stared at each other and it felt *dangerous*. There was something there, I was sure of it. I was starting to have thoughts like – maybe some office relationships can work. Maybe we're the one per cent.

I was about to suggest we have one more round of beers,

when Nick took a bite of his burrito, then quickly spat it out, fanning his throat. 'Hot, hot,' he spluttered.

Oh, God, the sauce.

'Water,' he said in a strangled voice.

I shoved his glass of water in front of him. He downed it in a second, so I shoved my glass, which he downed too.

'Milk, please!' I called to the waitress, who brought over a glass of milk and some rice.

'Rice!' she said. 'It helps.' We were both looking at Nick, who was going a deep shade of redish-purple, and drooling out of the corner of his mouth.

He started spooning in rice and then throwing down the milk. I couldn't help but laugh as his face went back to just a red colour. 'Do you think chocolate would have made that situation better?' I teased, thanking God it felt as though the awkward moment was over and we were back to normal. So, it turned out that was all you needed to clear up a bit of awkward tension – choking.

Finally, he managed to talk. 'I think I'm dying,' he said, falling back against the wall, sweaty and hot.

'Oh, my God, that's it!' I looked at him with glee. 'The theme to our event!'

Chapter 19

Thankfully, Glenn loved the idea. When we pitched it, he actually had a smile on his face, something I'd never seen before.

'Inspired by Día de los Muertos. Mexico's Day of the Dead,' I said, flicking to our presentation, 'a day when the veil thins between the two worlds, the living and the dead. And the spirits come back to their family for one day to join the living.'

I paused. 'It's macabre, because we'll decorate the place with traditional Mexican skulls, but there will be the typical festival celebration feel to it, and the area will be decorated with marigolds, candles and rosaries. But our event will honour unity – it will celebrate all countries, all cultures, and all people. From Africa to Asia, we'll have cultural dancing and music, from each country IAH is established in, to celebrate the spirit of family and coming together. And also act as a remembrance for those on the other side of the veil.

'Instead of the staid sit-down meals, the three-course dining, the elegant tables, we at Maker live on the edge,' I continued. 'We're pushing the boundaries by asking people to enjoy international Michelin-starred food carts set up around the room. They will be able to choose for themselves what they want to have, and then take it back to their tables.'

I clicked to the next slide, and continued. 'This is not your average sit-down ball. Yes, people will wear ball gowns, but they will be treated to a feast for all the senses. They will really feel like they are in Mexico. Or Japan. Or India. A completely submersive experience.' I smiled. 'People will talk about this for ages.'

When we finished, I almost felt like bowing, especially when Glenn said, 'Call in the clients, Nick. It's ready to show them for final sign off. And don't tell anyone about it. Keep the mystery, it's getting everyone talking. I even had the CEO of the *SydneySider* magazine ring me the other day, dropping her title and wanting an exclusive.'

Nick smiled. 'That's great. We'll wait until the day before to do a press release about the theme, until then, you got it – no one but the three of us, the executive clients and the designers will know.'

Glenn's phone started ringing. He held up his hand, to signal it was important, and left the room to take the call. When he came back, his face looked dark. 'Honey is on her way home, on the plane. We have to meet it.'

'Problems?' Nick asked.

'Another run in.' He shook his head. 'It will be splashed all over the media tomorrow. This time, she's been charged with ...' he paused and shook his head '... assaulting a police officer.'

Nick and I shared a look that said 'holy crap'.

'She needs babysitting, twenty-four seven. I don't even know how we'll spin this, to line up with her as the new spokesperson for a charity.' He shook his head again. 'Christ. We need to go into crisis mode. Immediately.'

'Fine, Glenn, Emma and I will look after it, twenty-four seven.' Nick nodded.

We would? This was news to me.

'Who can pick her up from the airport?'

Nick looked at me. 'I would, but I have plans that can't be moved tonight, so, Emma?' It didn't sound like a question.

'Me?' I asked.

'At 8 p.m. tonight.' Glenn nodded.

I fidgeted in my seat. Tonight was meant to be my first night off since I started. I was meant to be leaving here at 5 p.m. No work. But here was my opportunity to show how dedicated and professional I was, that I was really part of the Maker team.

'Of course, I can. No problem. Leave it with me,' I said smoothly.

At 8 p.m., I was standing in the arrivals section of Sydney international airport, waiting for Honey. And yes, that was her real name. Honey was one of the country's TV screen darlings, and one of very few Australians to make it big in the US. She'd literally transitioned straight out of wearing a school uniform in *Home and Away*, onto the Hollywood big screen in a period historical piece, where she'd got rave reviews. She'd followed this up with several other blockbusters, where she'd worked opposite Chris Hemsworth, and even one with

Ewan MacGregor, who Tansy and Maggie agreed was the most gorgeous man, like, in the *world*.

Of course, the media was always looking for a good story, and soon articles were popping up everywhere, saying the fame had gone to her head, because she was out partying every night. There were photos of her stumbling out of nightclubs and falling asleep in taxis, but being in PR had taught me you couldn't believe anything you read in the papers. If the photographers took a photo of you blinking your eyes, it could make you look half-asleep or half-drunk too.

But when Honey breezed out of the airport VIP area, she looked just like you'd expect a celebrity to look: long grey pants, a woollen white jumper on her slim frame, the shoulder peeking out of the side, just to remind everyone she had the best collarbones in the business. Her long, dark blonde hair was silky and full, and she wore it in a messy bun, but it looked perfectly messy, as if she'd had a band of hairdressers doting on her. She had not one skerrick of make-up on, but looked as if she could pose for a L'Oreal beauty campaign. She didn't look as if she'd just been cramped on a plane for the last thirty hours, but then I guessed first class wasn't all that cramped.

'Honey!' I exclaimed, waving and walking over to her. Glenn had told me to give her the five-star treatment the whole way. I grabbed her bags and gave her a big smile. 'Welcome home.' She looked less than thrilled.

'I'm so tired,' she said in the softest voice, which sounded as if she were at the bottom of a well; it instantly made me want to reach out and help her out. 'That man snored the entire trip. Even my first-class pod wasn't able to block it out. I had to put my earphones on and turn them up. High.'

'That man?' I looked around for the evil snorer, but no one else was in the hall.

'Thank you.' She looked at me as I struggled to wheel her extra-large Louis Vuitton luggage out of the door and towards the waiting Uber Black, a large glossy SUV with super-dark tinted windows.

'Celebrities,' Glenn had said, 'don't want to be seen, until they do. So dark tint always. Have umbrellas even if it's not raining. Always bring extra-large sunglasses. Or hats. Keep the mystery, keep the celebrity's happy.'

Glenn had rattled off an entire list of things for me to remember, as he was pacing in front of Nick and me. Half the time he'd been mumbling to himself: 'Can you imagine any shots of Honey coming home looking tired? They'll be spread across the entire front page, about her being hungover, and up will come the same old DUI story again.' I'd nodded, dutifully taking notes. Tint. Umbrellas. Hide.

When the two of us were safely in the tinted Uber, and on the road, Honey finally put down her phone, looked outside at the night sky and said, 'Where are we going?'

'The Sheraton Grand.' I smiled. A beautiful five-star hotel opposite Hyde Park, near the office. Glenn had told me, amongst the other thousand things he'd said, that the hotel had to be the best for our clients. The Langham, which came in at a whopping thousand dollars a night, was booked out, so it was off to the Grand for eight hundred dollars a night, which was still more money than I could afford in a month, for, well, *anything*.

'What about stopping off for some drinks?' she asked with a gleaming actress-perfect smile. Her teeth were pure white amazing, but not too white. If they were fake or veneers, the dentist had done an outstanding job.

'No, straight to the hotel,' I said firmly, not looking at her large round 'help me' actress eyes, for fear I'd cave in.

'A little one. With dinner. Some Champagne.' She pouted slightly.

'Sorry, PR orders. Straight to the hotel.' I smiled apologetically.

Honey went back to scrolling and messaging on her phone, smiling every now and then, when her phone kept beeping.

I tried to stifle a yawn, but Honey didn't even notice. I was hoping to just drop her off, but when we got to the hotel, she said, 'Aren't you going to stay?' and pouted a little again, before adding, 'I'll get bored.'

And I knew what bored meant: it meant she'd go out drinking, and getting into mischief, and the paparazzi would be on her like sharks smelling a drop of blood in the ocean. Tomorrow, the photos would be splashed over the front pages of the papers. I could see it now. *Horrific Honey Can't Stop Her Vicious Cycle. Drunk And Disorderly*. I shuddered at the thought.

I nodded, trying not to think of my comfy bed. 'Sure, I'll stay a little while.'

Her penthouse suite was so large it almost took up the entire top floor. Expensive rugs with real gold thread adorned the floors. There was a lounge, a large bedroom, and a bathroom with a tub bath and a separate dining area that seated six, with a full kitchen complete with marble countertops. A note on the bench read in neat handwriting, 'Your chef is ready to cook for you any time, anything, anywhere, in your room or delivered. Just call 111.'

The bedroom was darkly opulent with crimson velvet cushions, and deluxe grey blankets. Two plush chaise longues overlooked the bed, in case one wanted to swan around and drink tea, or Champagne. There were a total of three balconies. Three. Each one gave a different uninterrupted view, with a choice of Hyde Park, St Mary's Cathedral and Sydney Harbour.

I'd never known a hotel room like this was possible. The room even had electric blinds and curtains. You could operate everything from a remote control, whilst lying in bed. On the coffee table there was an extra-large fruit bowl and expensive crafted chocolates with a handwritten note from the General Manager welcoming Honey. She sniffed at it, and walked past.

So this is how the other half live, I thought. What I would have done for just one night in here, tied up in a bathrobe, like a fat happy sausage, eating those caramel chocolates and having a movie marathon.

Honey fell onto a chaise longue and sighed. 'Tea?' she asked me, and I guessed she wanted me to make a cup. 'Earl Grey. A splash of milk.'

I put the kettle on, and busied about getting a tea ready, with the most delicate fine-boned china tea set I'd ever seen. I took extra care not to break it, because it looked expensive.

When she had her tea, I smiled and said, 'Ready for bed?' As if I were her mother.

I desperately hoped she'd say yes, because I was absolutely exhausted, and also questioning why I was babysitting a twenty-four-year-old celebrity at ten at night. 'Maybe we could watch a movie?' Honey said happily. 'And once I'm asleep, then you're safe to go.' She winked at me, as if she knew the drill.

I got out the remote control and started flicking through the channels.

'It's always so boring being babysat.' She sighed, and stared out of the window.

'Um, Honey, can I ask you a question?' She nodded and sipped her tea. 'Has this happened before?'

'Where I've got in trouble and been on media watch? And babysat so I don't go out drinking? Maybe once or twice.' She grinned. 'But the PR team in California thought this time it was better to go back to Australia, and Maker agreed. Apparently, I need some time out of the camera, so people forget.' She almost laughed. 'Thankfully it only takes a week or two over there for that to happen, then I can slip back into my life, like nothing ever happened.'

'I don't know if this is speaking out of turn, but it just seems, like you're so sweet ...' I trailed off, because I was speaking out of turn. But she really did seem just like a very young, sweet girl. I couldn't imagine her trying to hit a police officer.

'That I wouldn't do the things you've heard?' Her eyes sparkled. 'Sometimes I don't mean it, but sometimes I just get bored. And we just have a few drinks, then a few more, and the next thing you know ...'

'You're swimming naked with a man you've only just met,' I said, then realised I'd said it out loud.

She let out a hearty laugh. 'I've never done that! Or, actually, have I?'

'I was just using it as an example,' I said quickly.

'Everyone's done *something* in their lives. It's just I'm in the spotlight.' She took another sip of tea. 'What about you, Emma? I'm sure you've done something you wouldn't want splashed on the front pages of a newspaper.'

Well, that was entirely true. Starting with Nick. 'Maybe a few things,' I admitted.

'Like?' She leaned forward excitedly as if we were besties and I was about to confide in her. And for a second, I thought, why not? I could tell her everything about my night with Nick, but give him another name, so she'd never know.

But eventually I said, 'Oh, this and that, nothing much really.'

Bored of the conversation, she went into the bathroom and changed into a silk white nightgown, then curled up in her super-king-sized bed and asked if I wouldn't mind handing her her pink sleep mask. I flicked through the movies until she eventually picked *The Proposal*. I sat on the chaise longue to watch it with her, praying she'd fall asleep fast. Checking my phone, and stifling another yawn, I saw it was almost midnight. I couldn't believe I was still 'on the clock' and at work whilst Nick and Glenn were probably tucked up in their beds. Here I was, glorified tea-maker and babysitter, not even being paid for overtime. *So much for my wonderful Maker career,* I thought glumly.

I was debating in my head if this was better or worse than working at that Mexican dive making stale burritos look appetising, when Honey sat up in bed. 'Could you make me another tea?' she asked, batting her eyelids, and I wondered if she'd ever heard the word no.

One green tea later, thankfully Honey was fast asleep. I switched off the TV just before one in the morning, and slipped quietly out of her room, feeling every bit like a nanny. And not at all happy about it.

Chapter 20

'Call the paparazzi,' Nick repeated.

'What?' I said for the second time, doubting I'd heard the right words.

'Call the paparazzi and line them up for where Honey will be this morning.' He checked the schedule on his laptop, 'Bluebell Café at 10 a.m., drinking herbal tea, meeting with the head of IAH, followed by a brief workout in the park opposite.'

Nick smiled and sat back in his chair, wearing a white linen shirt that was unbuttoned, and made him look extra tanned. He'd paired it with a perfect pair of light tan pants, and square-toed shoes. He looked immaculate, of course, and his hair, a little longer, had more of a tousled look. He'd walked in that morning with a large grin, as if he were on top of the world, and asking how my day was.

'Long already, and I need coffee.' I'd smiled bleakly, given I'd only managed to get four hours of broken sleep each night since Honey arrived two weeks ago, I'd been looking after her while Nick was in long budget and strategy meetings and Phil mocked me endlessly. It was a thankless task and I kept dreaming about making the wrong cup of tea. Honey was nice enough, but she took demanding to a new level. Phil had recently taken to calling me Cinderemma and asked if I lived in the ashes and had two wicked stepsisters.

Looking after Honey was like having a newborn baby. I was interrupted at weird hours because she wanted to talk. Or eat donuts. Still keeping strictly to LA time so she didn't miss out on any updates from her friends, she had no concept of time and boundaries. It was a thankless task. She was nice enough, but she took demanding to a new level. She'd called me once at 2 a.m. asking me why Instagram wasn't uploading her selfie and when would it be working properly. I barely slept through the night anymore.

'But I thought paparazzi hid in bushes, and stalked celebrity clients, and we hated them, and now you're saying we're going to call and tip them off?' I asked, astonished at what I was hearing. Was this really how it all worked? I thought back to all the 'Stars in the Street' and 'Stars without Make-up' articles I'd read and believed. Was it *all* fake?

'That's exactly what I'm—' Nick looked at me quizzically. 'Who did you work with in the UK? They didn't have the same set-up?'

'Oh, mostly government officials.' I swallowed. 'Not really paparazzi lovers.' I tried to gloss it over, because it had been true over there, the tabloids didn't want to photograph the backbencher for the Conservative party doing their Sunday groceries at Tesco's – 99p tin of spaghetti and a loaf of brown bread.

'Here's the number.' He handed me a Post-it note that said

'Tom', and underneath it 'TakeOutMedia'. Oh. I nodded approvingly; I liked what he'd done there. TakeOutMedia as an acronym became Tom. Clever.

When I picked up the phone and dialled the number from my desk, I felt strange, and breathless, as if I was doing something wrong.

'Hello?' a strong Australian accent and smooth voice answered.

'Um, hi, Tom?'

'Yup.'

'This is, um, Emma, from, um, Maker. We're ringing to, um, tell you about Honey,' I said, then added quickly, 'And where she's going to be today.'

'Great, let me get a pen,' he said smoothly, as if this happened all the time.

He took down the notes, and then with a polite but curt tone said bye, hung up, and I was left listening to silence down the line.

My strange day didn't stop there. I was also on Honey patrol again. Or Honey babysitting. At 9 a.m., she needed help dressing so that the colours in her fake paparazzi shots made her look glowing. There were a thousand photos on my phone now of Honey, courtesy of Glenn, Honey's Californian agency and Honey herself, in all colours under the sun. If anyone saw them, they'd think I was a Class-A stalker.

According to her, yellow made her look washed out. Red was too strong. And beige was too mumsy. I mean, I thought she looked wonderful in everything, but, sitting in her hotel room, Honey was staring at her thousand selfies critiquing every one.

'We need to have her look healthy,' Glenn had noted, 'not hungover, never hungover.' She ended up in a soft powder-blue top, white tight pants, and some slip-on white Prada espadrilles. She looked as though she were Elle Macpherson's daughter, arrived refreshed from a top beauty spa.

Unfortunately, Honey was still on LA time and having trouble remembering the key messages I'd created for her, at her staged morning tea, with the head of the IAH charity. So now, it was me, not the paparazzi, that was hiding in the bushes. Well, near the bushes. Near enough that I had to lean into a bunch of leaves to hear what was being said on the other side. I was thirty minutes in and prickling. I had to overhear what she was saying and my job was to cough if she said anything inappropriate, and then she'd excuse herself to go to the bathroom, where I'd meet her and remind her what to say.

I couldn't be seen in any of the paparazzi photos because then the magazine editors would know it was set up.

So instead I was in a bush. Hadn't they heard of MI6 and earpieces? Wasn't this the technological age? Couldn't I sit in the air conditioning of the car and listen via a tiny chip of some sort? Nope, not at Maker. Apparently bush listening and coughing were the approach. Let me guess, it was *ironic*.

Thankfully Honey was staying on script for now, and saying things like, 'It's for the children, which I think is the most important thing.' And she was a good actress. No, *great*. Even I was buying what she was saying. And, thankfully, it appeared the IAH head was too, because he'd needed a little convincing when Nick and Glenn had suggested Honey was the new spokesperson. He'd only agreed to it when he'd realised her next movie coming up was a blockbuster with a budget of a billion dollars, and she was going to be the lead role, in a dystopian future, where children were hunted by machines. Now *that* was macabre.

I leaned back in, to hear Honey agreeing and saying a lot of 'mmmm's and the IAH head was talking about statistical rates of something that I couldn't quite hear, and I knew, despite her acting skills, that she was bored silly. Even I could tell that.

Whilst I was mid-bush listening, Tansy called. Since Honey was doing so well, and they had almost finished the faux morning tea, that neither of them had touched, I thought I'd be able to take a quick call.

As soon as I picked up, Tansy almost shouted, 'Oh, my God, Emma, you *are* alive! Where have you been?'

'With Honey Clark,' I whispered.

Tansy said breathlessly, 'Wow. How's it going? Gosh, I feel your life is so glamorous.'

'Glamorous?' I spluttered. 'I'm in a bush.'

'Whose bush?' She sounded horrified.

'Um, a restaurant's.'

'Oh, thank goodness. Listen, have you had *the* chat with Nick yet?'

'Which talk?'

'Where you tell him you have feelings for him!' Oh Tansy, ever the romantic.

'I have never ever said that.'

'No, but you talk about him all the time, and you drop him into conversation whenever we chat, and so, I mean hello, *you* like *him*.'

'I do not.' I said hotly, because it was kind of true. A few weeks ago, when we were at the cemetery, I had thought I did really like him. And I'd even thought it was possible he liked me back. But more recently, he'd seemed distracted, and I couldn't really put my finger on why or what had happened.

As if on cue, I looked down at my phone vibrating with another call. It was Nick. 'Gotta go, Tans.'

I hung up and pressed receive to Nick's incoming call.

'Um, hi, can't really talk right now. I'm hiding in a bush.'

He laughed. 'We need to get paparazzi shots of that!'

'Please don't. I have a reputation to uphold, as a celebrity babysitter. They can't be led to believe that I plant-sit too, otherwise my schedule would become overly demanding,' I said wryly.

'What type of plant are you sitting now?' he joked.

'A prickly one. Seriously, I'm getting prickled as we speak.'

'Well, we've lined up a press conference for tomorrow, and you'll be pleased to know there's no bushes in sight at the building. And we had confirmation from the Californian office, we just need to keep Honey clean and happy for another few weeks, and then she'll be back on a plane to LA.'

'Are we going to babysit her the entire time?' I felt concerned thinking about all the work that was sitting back on my desk that I had to do.

'Well, Phil's picked up your event schedule and is looking

after all the caterers and menu options,' Nick said. I thanked Phil silently. 'And I'll come and do a Honey shift now, plus if you take this week, I'll take the following one, if that helps.'

'Thank you,' I said gratefully. 'It does.'

When Nick arrived after the morning tea and successful faux gym session, Honey immediately perked up, and I could see why. With his open-collared white shirt, and designer black sunglasses, admittedly, he looked quite lovely. OK, I'll admit it, he looked *hot*. So, I could see why Honey was suddenly retouching her shiny pink lip gloss.

'How's the prisoner?' He walked across the park to me, taking off his sunglasses and hooking them on his open shirt.

'Oh, she's fine, just done her workout,' I said, picking up the call sheet, and filling up Honey's water bottle by the fountain.

'No, I meant you.' He smiled warmly.

'Oh, well.' I shoved my arm out. 'I look like I'm the lead character in some kind of *Outbreak* movie.'

'The one that gets a mysterious rash, and dies first?'

I laughed and said, 'Patient X. Yep. That about sums it up.'

Honey trotted over, with a smile and glossy, perfect lips. 'I'm Honey,' she positively purred, smiling at Nick.

'Nick.' He grinned and took her hand. 'Nice to finally meet you.'

'So you're, um ...?' She looked at me, then Nick.

'My boss,' I said. 'Nick Taylor.'

'Oh.' A large smile took over her face. 'And my new minder?' She was actually batting her eyelashes. *You can't be serious, I* thought. No one would buy this. But when I looked at Nick, it seemed he was buying every bit of it.

'Right, well, I better get packed up,' I said, leaving them to it, because the pretend gym equipment we'd had on the lawn for her workout session wouldn't pack up itself.

While I was picking up her tiny pink dumbells, I caught a glimpse of Nick and Honey still talking over by the fence. Honey was tossing her hair back and forth, and giggling at something Nick had said. At one point she even put her hand on his arm, delicately. I stopped for a second to see how he'd react, half hoping he'd step away, or pull back, but he just let her keep her hand there until she finally removed it, and put another layer of lip gloss on her perfect lips.

I should be taking notes on how to flirt like a gorgeous actress, but I was too busy folding up her yoga mat, kneeling on the wet grass getting green stains, sweating in my heavy maroon dress, and wondering how I'd got here. Just a few months ago I'd been travelling in the French countryside for a weekend, and now I was babysitting a girl so she didn't have a drink and get behind the wheel, or throw a punch at a policeman.

When I finished packing up the gear, I went back to where Honey was fixing her hair, looking at her iPhone and taking a range of Snapchat selfies with the butterfly filter, so it looked as if actual butterflies were flying above her head.

'Emma, get in on this!' she said, laughing and trying to point the phone in my direction.

'Um! No, thanks!' I ducked down into a squat, behind the stone fence she was sitting on, which I knew looked ridiculous. But I didn't want to go out live or viral, or what-ever, on Honey's social media with fake yellow wings batting above my head. That wasn't the idea of what a classy PR person did. Plus, I was also sporting some very large undereye bags that my cheap five-dollar night cream wasn't getting rid of, as it promised, and standing next to Honey I would have looked sagging and flabby, as if I were a hundred years old.

When she put her phone down, and it seemed safe, I stood and gave a quick glance over to see where everyone else was – thankfully it seemed all the photographers had packed up and gone home, and no one had seen me squatting by the stone wall. 'OK, Honey, anything else you need before I head back to the office?'

'Well.' Honey smiled, picking up her phone again, and scrolling through Instagram, then glancing over at Nick, who was at the other end of the park, speaking to some guy sitting on a black scooter. 'I thought we could go to Feast.'

'Feast?' I asked, trying to think if that was a new style of eating, or a place.

'Jimmy Loudin's new restaurant,' she said, and whilst I was wondering who was Jimmy Loudin – was he a celebrity? Or a chef? Or both? – she smiled. 'I love that you don't know the latest places. It must be so nice to not have to keep up appear-ances.'

Was that what I was doing? Not keeping up appearances?

Honey looked at me through her large bug-eyed sunglasses. 'You know, that boss of yours is pretty cute.'

'Is he?' I said, trying not to look at him.

'And maybe, I was wondering,' she started, 'if Nick could take me. To Feast, I mean.'

'Nick?' I repeated.

She nodded and smiled. 'Do you know if he's single?'

Suddenly it felt as if she'd punched me in the stomach. 'Uh, I'm not sure.'

'Can you find out?' she asked, as easily as if she were asking me to pass her a pen.

'Sure ... I'll ask,' I said, wondering how the hell I could ask Nick that question.

'Now?' Honey smiled sweetly.

Now, in a park? While Honey was watching? I wanted to tell Honey to ask him herself, why did I have to be the middle man? But Glenn had said, 'Anything Honey wants, Honey gets.' My stomach sank. How I could be subtle and professional about this? The answer was, I couldn't. I wished I'd packed a hip flask of whisky along with this damn yoga mat. I could really do with a shot or five right now.

'Sure, uh, now is fine,' I agreed, feeling slightly ill at the thought of what I was about to do.

OK, here goes. I took a deep breath and started walking over to where Nick was still chatting to the scooter guy. I decided it was best to just ask Nick, straight away. Not wait for a second, because then I'd chicken out. Just walk straight up, rip the Band-Aid off and ask.

Trying not to concentrate on the butterflies in my stomach, I marched right up to Nick and said straight out, 'Hi, Nick. Um, I need to ask you something. Are you single?'

As soon as I said it I cringed inside, because this was *not* the kind of question you should ask your boss. Ever. Nick looked shocked.

'I, uh ...' He looked uncomfortable. He fumbled a bit and it was almost endearing that he was having so much trouble answering what should be a very simple question.

The guy on the moped removed his helmet, revealing green eyes and dark hair, and olive skin with a few wrinkles. He looked about forty. He leaned in, interested in Nick's answer. Who was this guy? A friend?

'Maybe we could chat over here.' Nick gave a quick goodbye nod to the guy on the bike, and then walked away, turning around a few metres later to say, with another one of his unreadable poker faces, 'Emma, do you know who that was?'

I shook my head.

'Tom, from TakeOutMedia,' Nick said.

'*That* was the Tom?' I'd expected paparazzi to look dirty, maybe even sleazy, but that guy looked as if he'd actually just be an everyday guy who spent Saturdays playing basketball with his friends.

'You can't ask those questions,' he said, 'in front of people like that.' He nodded towards where Tom was still sitting on his moped, unsuccessfully trying to listen in over the steady stream of traffic in the background.

'In front of the people that we've staged photos for, we can't talk about whether or not you're seeing someone?' I asked, dumbfounded.

'Well, yes, people can make anything look real if they hear rumours. Put two and two together, make five. Especially around people like Honey.' Nick looked over at Tom, who was finally leaving, and seemed to relax a little more knowing there were no eyes on him.

Nick turned back to me. 'And, more to the point, why do *you* want to know if I'm single?' Nick said, staring into my eyes. His wonderful chocolate eyes. TURN AWAY, EMMA, NOW. I looked at the ground.

If he was single, wouldn't he have just said yes? The way he was talking suggested he was well and truly not single. For some reason, I felt a little clench in my stomach.

'It's not for me. Honey's asking,' I said, still looking at the ground and then my fingernails, as though they were suddenly very interesting.

'Oh. Right.'

As if on cue, my phone beeped. It was Honey. She wrote: *FEAST? NICK?* I looked across the park at her, but she was too busy scrolling and pretending not to look at me.

I tried to keep a steady tone, and keep one shred of dignity, but I thought I'd lost all of that by now. 'Honey wants me to ask you another question.' I felt as if I were back at high school.

Nick raised his eyebrows and when I looked up from my phone, I could tell he definitely looked as uncomfortable as I felt.

'She wants to go to, uh, dinner with you,' I offered Nick.

'Does she?' he said, and I tried reading his face, but I couldn't tell how he felt about it. He would have made a great poker player.

'Should I, um, arrange something?' I probed, now burning with curiosity to know if he would accept.

He looked at me for a while, again with the unreadable face, and it was impossible to tell what was going on behind those chocolate eyes of his, before he said, 'Sure. Yes. Do that. I think Oil and Salt is good, for Friday night. Would you mind making us a reservation for 8 p.m.?'

And just like that it hit home. Maybe Nick liked Honey. What man wouldn't love her? Heck, she had driven me almost crazy these past few weeks, and still I found her endearing. Her large eyes. Gorgeous hair. Glowing, young skin with zero wrinkles and a mischievous smile.

Of course, Nick liked her. And now they were going to dinner together. And clearly, my job was not only to be Honey's babysitter, but also restaurant coordinator for the gorgeous Honey and the man I'd once had sex with. How low could I go?

I suppose I *could* go lower; I could be expected to hand-wash their underwear whilst they had loud and amazing sex upstairs. I wondered if Honey was the kind of person who screamed loudly and whispered dirty things, and I decided she very much was. People who hit police were always a freak in the sheets. And Nick liked that. *Shower. Suds.* I gulped.

'Actually, she wants to go to Feast. Tonight.'

'Well, what Honey asks for—' Nick started to say.

'Honey gets,' I finished for him.

He nodded. 'But I can't do tonight, I'm afraid. Would you mind stepping in? I promise I'll do Friday.'

'Sure,' I said, mentally wiping away my social calendar. I mean, it wasn't as if I had an exciting week of events planned.

'But I can't say Honey will be pleased to have me opposite her at the table.'

Nick grinned. 'I can't see why not. Tell Honey I will gladly see her at Oil and Salt on Friday.' He pulled out his calendar on his phone. 'And if you wouldn't mind confirming the media rules for Honey's press conference. Remember they can't ask about the DUIs or her romantic life.'

'Got it,' I said, taking a deep breath. Romantic life. Did that include him? Honey and him on her chaise longue. Doing it on the terrace with a choice of uninterrupted views.

Honey arrived with an extra coat of shimmering nude lip gloss on her lips, and asked Nick if he was ready to go. He opened the car door for her, and she got in, saying something about desperately needing a coffee after such a boring morning. Nick laughed at something else she said, and the two of them looked like the most perfect couple, taking off and giving me a wave.

Right, back to work, I reminded myself, determined to never again think about Honey and Nick having hot sex.

Chapter 21

Wednesday's press conference was full of eager young journalists trying to trip up Honey, but she handled it like a pro. Her acting ability came out in full force. Even I started to believe that she really did care about the children and the orphanages.

Nick and I were standing at the back of the room, listening as Honey was describing how she was going to Africa next.

'News to me,' I said to Nick with my eyebrows raised.

'And me.' He grinned at me.

'Don't tell me – I get to book those flights, maybe even go with her?' I whispered with a smile. 'She loves the way I make a cup of tea.'

'Good try,' Nick said, smiling back at me, with his gorgeous straight white teeth.

See, there you go – we were smiling at each other, as if working with each other was all too easy. Colleagues. That was what we were. Sharing a work joke. And I was absolutely fine …

Nick asked, 'How was the dinner at Feast?'

'Fancy. I had the best wagyu beef I've ever tasted.'

'And Honey?' Nick asked, probing a little more.

'She had the salmon. And then tried to flirt with some hotshot real-estate guy at the table next to us, who turned out to be waiting for his wife.'

'Oh.' He looked at me and I could tell he was twitching not to laugh.

'It's not funny!'

'Maybe a little?'

'Maybe,' I said wryly, because the look on his face was almost contagious.

As the press conference went on I could tell the journalists were really warming to Honey, and why wouldn't they? She was graceful, and beautiful and poised and sat like a ballerina. Plus, she was saying all the right things, just as we'd prepped her to say.

'You know, these are perfect media bites leading up to Macabre,' Nick said, looking so pleased that I wondered if he was thinking about his date with Honey this Friday too.

'The event that I feel so behind on,' I said, worried.

'Do you need help?' He was looking at me so sympathetically I almost said yes.

'Should be fine.' I wanted him to know I could do this myself. All alone. 'But I'll be working late tonight – what should we do with Honey? I'm not sure she wants to hang out at the office. Could you help out?'

'Oh, Emma, I'm really sorry,' Nick said. 'I have something that I can't move. Normally, I'd take this one, because I know you've been doing a lot, especially with Honey. Would you mind?'

'Me? Tonight?' Well, it wasn't as if I had anything else to do. Oh wait, except plan a massive event.

'Yeah, she wanted to go to Pool, that new club,' Nick mentioned.

'A club? That can't be good.' I wondered how I'd be able to keep her away from the bar.

'Better a few drinks than telling her she can't have any, then I think we'd have anarchy on our hands. Thanks for doing this, Emma. You're a champ.'

A champ? That was the equivalent of patting me on the back and saying, 'Great job, mate.' It was what guys said to each other. *Friends. Great,* I thought glumly, *I've had sex with a guy who turned out to be my boss, and now I'm babysitting his new crush, and a 'champ'.*

My life truly felt as if it was heading down the gurgler.

On Thursday morning, I sank into my office chair, and had to resist letting my head rest on my desk, because I'd surely fall into a deep, snoring kind of sleep. I'd been at Pool all night, then up at 5 a.m., because Honey had a hankering for donuts. Donuts.

But not any old donuts, *the ones with extra sugar and glaze,* she texted, *you know the ones I mean xx,* which meant I had to take a taxi out to the airport to pick up a batch. Problem was they didn't open until 7 a.m. and the taxi left, so I waited in the cold out there, without so much as a coffee to keep me going.

I desperately wanted to go home and curl up in bed, or call in sick, because I had the shakes from lack of sleep, but

I couldn't because there was *so* much to do. There was media to confirm, and more Honey interviews, and paparazzi pics to stage (sigh) and a final press release to announce the theme of the night – which we'd managed to keep a secret this entire time – and quotes, and the daily media alerts and ... My brain was jumbling at the thought of my to-do list. I even considered snorting donut sugar just to get through the day.

By the time I got into the office, I was so exhausted.

'How was Pool?' Phil asked as soon as I got in. 'Looks like you were there all night.'

'Except for the three hours I've slept, plus the dawn donut run,' I said, resisting putting my head on the desk. It just looked so ... *comfy*.

Phil raised his eyebrows.

'Oh, yeah, Pool is amazing, if you like your head being beaten by duff-duff music around a small little pool, where people were literally in itty bitty bikinis, and Honey complaining that I couldn't get her into the VIP VIP section. There are not enough vodkas in this world. Or coffee,' I said, taking a large gulp of my extra-strong, double shot cappuccino. 'Speaking of coffee, where is our quick catch-up meeting this morning? And do you know where Nick is?'

'He's been in meetings. By the way, there's a rumour going around that there's a girl he's seeing, or into.'

'Oh.' I felt a bit sick all of a sudden. I tried to ask casually, 'Any idea who?' Hoping he wouldn't say Honey.

But before Phil could answer, Paige Drews, the entertainment writer for *More!*, was calling my mobile. Usually I'd think that was very cool, having a journalist call *me*. But I was so tired that it took everything I had just to muster up the energy to answer the phone and say hello.

'Can we confirm that Honey was at Pool last night?' Paige cooed down the phone in a fake friendly tone.

'Yes, confirmed,' I said, stifling a yawn.

'That's not great for her new scrubbed-up image, is it?' Paige baited me.

I had to think quickly, on my feet. 'Actually, Paige, she was there to consider using Pool for a new launch. I can't say any more yet, but you can pull all the footage and photos, and you'll notice she had two vodkas. The entire night.'

Thank goodness, I thought, that I'd almost murdered Honey when she'd attempted to drink more, and she'd only relaxed because I'd shunted her into the VIP section with some actor called Harry and Tom the paparazzi guy. How a paparazzi guy got into the VIP section, I had no idea.

I was beginning to think this media vs celebrity thing was just a giant ruse, and the poor public really had no idea in the slightest. Of course, Tom and Harry had literally fawned over Honey, and, receiving all this attention, she hadn't noticed I'd swapped out her vodka limes for just lime and tonic.

'Ooohh ... Sounds intriguing. Can we set up an interview with her, to find out more about this launch?' Paige said in a saccharine voice as if I were her new BFF.

'As soon as we can say more, Paige, you'll be the first to know.'

Another lie. I hung up the phone feeling another shroud of guilt descend upon me. I'd lied so much, I realised I was actually now comfortable doing it. No, more than that, it came to me now like second nature. I was shocked to realise that was what we did at Maker; we called it bending the truth, or 'spinning' something, but really my job consisted of Honey babysitting and lying.

Lies that Honey was actually interested in charity work. Lies that said she no longer wanted to drink. Lies that she really wanted to settle down. Lies about why she was at a club. Lies on my CV. Lies to everyone when we didn't have a theme. I felt sick realising I'd become one of them. A Faker.

I tried to shake it off and focus on work so I didn't have to think about it. The rest of the day was spent doing design and event checks and confirming the entertainment – some very authentic Mexican dancers and musicians – and trying to keep Honey excited about trailing along with me. Donuts and coffee only bought me an hour, and mostly I spent the day doing my work on the run, mobile in one hand, and directing taxi drivers with the other, running errands for Honey. Dry-cleaning. Nail appointment. Picking up some weird pickled Japanese salad that was supposed to help with losing weight and was in all the latest Insta stories she kept scrolling through and then shoving in my face – except she had no discernible weight to lose.

On Friday, she decided she wanted to get her hair dyed beach blonde. Then she changed her mind so we went back to the salon to go a darker blonde with highlights. Why she couldn't have just taken an Uber on her own I didn't know; she was an adult, she had a functioning phone and able thumbs. But Glenn had told me Honey was now very fond of me. Of course, she was. I'd be fond of someone who did late-night runs to get me burgers and donuts too.

Speaking of which, I'd not yet figured out how she could eat all that fast food I was getting her and not put on an inch of weight. It was beyond me. And, honestly, made me feel a little sad about the extra weight I was still carrying on my thighs.

Thankfully, I was off the clock at 6 p.m. on Friday. Honey was now in Nick's hands (possibly literally) for their dinner at Oil and Salt, which I was trying not to think about. I'd also managed to get the entire weekend off, by convincing Honey to go to a lovely retreat spa for the weekend, with a strict no-alcohol policy. Which meant I could sleep in for the first time in forever, and then hopefully do something fun. Something that didn't remind me of work.

But all my friends were booked up or were too tired to call or chat or go for coffee. I offered to bring takeaway coffee to them, even with hot, piping banana bread and loads of butter, but they said, 'Sorry, we haven't slept in days,' with big sighs that sounded as if they were eternally exhausted.

Sydney wasn't like London. I couldn't be in Paris in a few hours. I could be on the central coast, but that required a car, and I didn't have one. I could have gone to the markets, the cinema, a cute little French restaurant that had opened up, but it just wasn't as much fun by myself. I pictured myself sitting at the restaurant.

Emma, what would you like?

Oh, Emma, I think the snails, sorry, escargot, it's very French, isn't it?

Brilliant idea, Emma! Exactly what I was thinking …

Twice I'd thought about logging onto the dating app again, but then I'd remembered how disastrous my last attempt at online dating had been.

Instead, I slept in until 1 p.m. on Saturday. Then I cleaned, went grocery shopping, did a quick park walk, meal prepped for the rest of the week (because wasn't that what single, fabulous women did?), and attempted to paint a beach scene I remembered from a weekend in Samos, one of the Greek islands, but ended up stinking my unit up with oily paint smell, and then having to air it by opening every window. And even then it was only 5 p.m. I looked at my phone, half hoping Honey would text me. She didn't. I sat on my couch and watched *My Best Friend's Wedding* – which was exactly what I shouldn't have done, because that made me feel more alone and single than ever. And, it made me think of Nick and Honey. I was dying to find out how their dinner 'date' had gone, but it wasn't professional to text and ask. Was it?

By Sunday morning I had cabin fever. I knew I needed to get out and I found myself scrolling on an online app, ConnectM8e, a site where groups of strangers met for walks or coffee or kayaking. On a whim, I saw a coastal walk over at Bondi, and clicked, 'Yes! I'll RSVP!' And then felt a pang of regret. It just seemed a little … forced.

I pulled on comfy black leggings and the only black singlet I'd brought back from London, which had a large rip under the right armpit so you could see my white sports bra that was so old, it had turned grey after too many washes and wears. I made a mental note – buy more singlet tops and sports bras. Thankfully, you could only see the rip if I lifted my arm up, and I wasn't considering that a required motion for walking. I wore a black cap and no make-up. And I noticed, staring into the mirror, that my skin was starting to break out around my chin and cheeks from wearing so much foundation during the week. And possibly lack of sleep. She had no concept of time and boundaries. But now, I was doing something weird, and missing her, so I knew I *had* to go on this walk.

My phone beeped. It was Honey: *Met a very cute boy xx.* I replied: *Who is this boy? Make sure not journalist!* Because you could never be too careful. She replied: *Thanks mum, he's kinda in marketing!* I wrote: *Almost as bad.*

It sounded as if she'd met someone new at the spa, which was typically what happened to gorgeous girls whose lives were like actual rom-com movies. Because when I went to the spa it was full of middle-aged women who complained of being too sweaty and had toes full of gout. But what did 'kinda in marketing' mean? Maybe the dinner with Nick hadn't gone so well after all. The thought of them not getting on, and not having hot sex, I couldn't help it – it made me smile and feel a little happier.

With my new surge of excited energy, I took the cliff walk pathway from the bus stop to the start of the walk, heading south towards Bronte, trudging through a park where people were throwing balls to their excited dogs. Off in the distance a slim girl with long blonde hair wearing a pink sweater was laughing and linking arms with a man in a red plaid shirt, as their French bulldog was bounding about, a little out of hand. They looked really happy. *I want that,* I thought.

I wanted a someone to do things with on the weekend. I wanted a someone that would be at home in bed, waiting to hug me, when I returned exhausted from a night of celebrity babysitting or from a really bad day at work – because I was having more and more of those. When my friends were all busy on the weekend, I wanted the feeling of knowing there was someone I could do things with, rather than doing it how I was now. Solo.

Being single for a small period of time could feel liberating and empowering. Being single for seven years felt like an entirely different world altogether – a very empty world. And now, I had signed up to go on a bloody walk with strangers.

The meeting point was at the rear entrance to the park, and a group of people was already milling around. There were two large middle-aged women, a pair of tiny girls who looked very young and I assumed were students, and a very tall, thirty-something guy, who was very pale, and had thick dark hair. He was awkwardly hunched over as if he'd been embarrassed about his height all of his life, which reminded me of Lurch. We were a giant pack of misfits.

'Er, hello,' I said to the very muscular and stocky guy standing with a giant red flag that was stuck into the top of his cap. 'Are you ...' I scrolled my phone to see the leader's name '... Patrick?'

'Yes, how did you know?' he greeted me in a loud, booming voice.

'Um, the flag?'

'Oh, right! Yes! The flag.' He hooted, reaching up and touching the flag. 'There it is!' Everything he said sounded as if it had exclamation points ready.

'So, team!' Patrick called out. 'Are we almost ready to get going? Get walking? Get our heart's rate up? Get dating?'

Wait. What!? Dating? My heart sank. Had I clicked on a romantic walk? I scrolled through my phone, and there it was, a Lonely Singles Walk. How had I missed that? Even worse, had my brain seen the word lonely and single, and thought, *Oh, yep, that's me?*

I looked around this group of misfit people and it hit me then in a heartbeat – these were the people I spent my time with on the weekends. I mean, I'm sure they were lovely, but they were strangers, single strangers, and that spoke volumes.

I stood in line at the nearby coffee cart, and ordered an extra-large cappuccino, whilst I debated if I was actually going to go on the hike. As I stood in line, I heard a small voice in my head. *I think I'm lonely.*

The thought sank in.

God, I'm really lonely.

It was so palpable, I almost said it aloud.

If I was being truthful, my entire life felt a bit off. My friends were always busy. I couldn't get past a first date with anyone. I hadn't started the diet I'd been promising myself I would, because every night I just wanted to comfort eat. And then there was my job at Maker. It had felt like the offer of a lifetime. But now that I was doing it, working so many hours, for such little money, I didn't really know what I was thinking. To buy a place? Let's be real, I couldn't buy a place in a hundred years on the salary I was making. And whilst my studio unit was nice enough if you liked living in one damp room, it wasn't a cottage. It didn't have a garden, so I could never grow veggies. Or have chickens. Or a dog.

I ordered a banana muffin. Then changed my mind and made it two.

'Are you here for the singles in love and fitness walk?' Patrick called out with so much enthusiasm I thought he might pop a vein, to a person approaching the coffee cart. I winced and turned away, pretending not to be on the walk either, when I heard a soft, whispery voice order a non-fat latte, hold the sugar. I *knew* that voice. I looked up.

'Honey?' I said in astonishment, because she was meant to be at a spa right now, getting a facial.

She looked over, giving me a slow up and down. I wished I were wearing tight jeans, a pink wool sweater and little ankle boots like her – not my holey active wear. 'Emma?' she queried hesitantly, looking over the top of her sunglasses. 'You look so different on the weekends. Is that a new hipster thing you're trying? Because I'm not sure it suits ... anyone.'

Just then the French bulldog bounded over and started nosing itself into my shin. 'He is gorgeous,' I said, bending down, ignoring her last comment. 'What's his name?'

'Sherlock,' Honey said without looking at me.

I scratched Sherlock's ears and he jumped up excitedly, finding my lips and giving them a big doggy lick. 'Whoa.' I laughed. 'Gotta be careful of boys that want to kiss me without buying me a drink.' Honey's partner jogged up; I could only see his two large feet in white sneakers. Standing up, I put out my hand to introduce myself, but looking up I saw familiar eyes staring at me. 'Hi, I'm—' I stopped cold. The blood drained out of my face. *You've got to be kidding,* I thought.

'Nick?' I asked, feeling sick, grabbing back my hand. Then realised that was awkward, perhaps rude, so I put my hand back out, where it hung for a few seconds, unsure and outstretched.

'Emma.' He looked just as astonished to see me. He looked at my hand as if I were offering him a snake.

Eventually, I put my hand down, then started doing arm stretches as though that was what I was doing the whole time. Honey peered at me as if I'd gone strange. No one said anything. I looked from him to her, and back to him. *Do not lift your arm,* I told myself. Grey old sports bra. Grey old sports bra.

'Guys? You coming on the singles' walk?' Patrick pointed at Honey and Nick. I wanted the entire earth to open up and swallow me whole.

Honey didn't even turn her head, as though Patrick didn't exist. I blushed. Nick stared at me and then at Patrick, before he managed to finally say. 'No, thanks, mate.'

'Are you with those people?' Honey asked, looking confused.

'Oh, no, I'm not with them.' *Those* people looked at me strangely, because I was dissing my type. Dissing the misfits. 'I'm just here for the coffee.' I tried to smile.

'Isn't that a long way for you to come?' Honey cocked her head to the side. 'Don't you live, somewhere, west?' She said west like that was where drugs, and crime and general gang warfare occurred.

I nodded. 'Somewhere like that.'

The misfits were getting ready to leave. I could see one of the ladies swinging her arms around. She'd realised there was no other men, and noted Patrick had a shiny wedding ring on; she'd zeroed in on poor Lurch. I didn't know who I felt more sorry for. Thankfully, I hadn't told Patrick my name, otherwise he'd likely be yelling, 'Come on, Emma! Get a move on!' loud enough for the entire park to hear.

The silence between the three of us was deafening, until finally I managed to splutter, 'Honey, I thought you were at the spa?'

'Oh, I was.' She waved a perfectly manicured hand at me. 'But I got bored, and then I bumped into someone.' Honey smiled sweetly at Nick. 'Also, we had a lovely dinner, thanks for setting that up.'

We had a lovely dinner. She was speaking in 'we's' already. I looked at Nick and suddenly I realised what 'kinda in marketing' meant. She meant PR, but she didn't want me finding out about her and Nick. So it was hush-hush, this little love affair, was it? And now, it appeared, I was in on it too. Wonderful.

She smiled. 'Nick's a real gentleman. Not like my ex in the States. So immature. Can you believe he lives in a shared house? Like with *other people?* And he doesn't even have Instagram!'

A real gentleman. I imagined Nick pulling out her chair. Offering his jacket. Putting a strand of hair behind her ear. Just as he'd done with me. I felt sick to my stomach at the thought of them eating together, and even sicker when I thought about them kissing.

Nick cleared his throat uncomfortably. 'Honey was nice enough to lend a hand this weekend,' he said quickly, 'when something came up at work.'

Lend a hand? Honey? I almost snorted. Unless it was to eat an entire plate of donuts, I couldn't see Honey helping out with anything, at all really, especially to do with public relations.

You guys have been working in ... the ... park?' I asked, looking between them. 'Are we featuring your dog in some new campaign?'

Honey laughed breathily, as if I'd said the funniest thing, and shared a look with Nick. 'That's not his dog.'

'It's not?' I asked, bewildered.

'No.' Honey tossed her hair back over her shoulder. 'It's Gabe's.'

'Gabe?' I felt as if I were on a different planet and didn't know the language. Who was Gabe?

'Nick's friend,' Honey said.

At the same time Nick said, 'No one.'

'Nick's so lovely.' Honey seemed to be the only one not realising the tension in the group. 'Looking after his sick elderly friend.' She gave a melodious laugh. 'I'm not sure I could.'

Looking after his sick elderly friend? I raised my eyebrows at Nick, who looked away uncomfortably, as if someone had taken away his power of speech. If they weren't together, how did Honey know so much about his life?

Finally, Nick said, 'It's nothing.'

'It's not nothing.' Honey smiled sweetly at him, and the

way she slightly leaned into him made me think it was something way more than just work. I hated to admit it, but they looked cute together. Looking at them was like watching the end of a Hallmark movie.

Honey was still gazing at Nick and rattling off all the kind things he did. 'You walk his dog, and do his shopping, and take him out.'

Suddenly I felt I was in the middle of a very loved-up-couple moment. It was extremely uncomfortable and I wondered if I could pretend my phone was ringing, or just turn around and leave. Thankfully the barista shouted out, 'Soy Cappucino', literally saving me.

I grabbed it and my two muffins and said, 'Well, gotta run.'

'You're going running?' Honey asked, her eyebrows raised as if the thought of running was rather hideous.

'Sure, a little.' I shrugged. Pointing to the cup. 'After my coffee.'

She eyed up the two muffins in my hand, and I felt as if I needed to make an excuse. 'I'm meeting someone.' And I held up the second banana muffin as if it were proof that I had someone waiting for me, not that I was just hankering for a carb-fest. 'So see you next week, Honey, enjoy your, um, weekend. Bye, Nick,' I said quickly and turned around before anyone could say another word. Suddenly, I was jogging across the park and back to my cliff walk so fast my coffee spilt half of its frothy foam out of the lid before I could even take a sip.

My mind was racing. What was going on? Were they a

couple? From the looks of it, of course they were. I sat on a park bench and took a sip of what was left of my coffee. I tried to shake off the idea of Honey and Nick cuddling on the couch. No, they wouldn't cuddle, it would be more like she'd be a Spooning Seductress, lying perfectly on the couch, her petite frame, her perfect long blonde hair; she'd be holding a glass of three-hundred-year-old Chablis as if it were a glass of water and didn't cost an arm and a leg – what man wouldn't swoon? Oh, God, he was with Honey. They were, like, a *thing*. And I'd helped them get together. *I* was their matchmaker.

My appetite for exercise and being outside suddenly disappeared. Besides, I didn't want to accidentally run into them again. The ocean breeze picked up. I shivered and walked quickly, head down, back to Bondi. Now, I was even more confused. Was Nick a nice guy who looked after his sick elderly friend? Or was he the kind of guy that dated girls that were fifteen years younger than him, who were obsessed with taking the perfect Instagram photo? I remembered back to our night in Fiji, and I was sure that was something we'd joked about, how people lined up for hours to perfect their poses, with filters and airbrushing, and what the hell was the point? But now, here he was, with someone exactly like that. I couldn't work him out, no matter how hard I tried.

On the bus ride home, I stared at my reflection in the window and thought, *Gosh, I look tired.* But I didn't just look tired, I looked older. *Must be all those late nights,* I thought. When I got off the bus, I walked passed a shopping mall and maybe it was how tired I looked, or felt, or that I wanted to feel better about my grey bra life, because I made a split decision.

Five minutes later, I was sitting in the hairdresser's, staring in the mirror, at my long wavy hair. I wanted something sleeker. More mature. Something that said PR Woman. Something that said 'Maybe with a New Haircut I'll Like My Life in Sydney'. Even though I knew that sounded ridiculous.

When Jo, the hairdresser, asked if I wanted a trim, I pointed to the girl on the cover of a *Vogue* magazine and said, I want *that*.

Chapter 22

'**W**hat is that on your head? WHAT IS IT?'
      I grabbed at my head. 'Oh, God, I don't know!
What's there? Is it a spider?'

Phil leaned back in horror. 'I think it's a fringe,' he managed
to splutter.

I sighed. 'Oh, yes, funny one, Phil.'

And that was how my day went. Everywhere I went. Every
phone call I took, every meeting I attended. There was Phil
whispering comments, and when he couldn't speak he'd write
them down in meetings and hold them up so only I could
see them.

Emma, 1980s called. They want their fringe back.

Hey, Lily. LILY. LILY ALLEN. Oh, sorry, Emma.

Ems, why are you wearing a helmet on your head?

*Why are you sporting a skull-shrinkage device? I thought
torture was out ruled in 1600s?*

Oh, piss off, Phil.

Thankfully, Nick wasn't back in the office until Wednesday, and by then I'd almost managed to make my fringe look presentable. Or so I thought.

Except Nick looked at me strangely as he and Sadie passed our desks heading towards his office. Sadie peered at me. 'There's something different about you today, Emma.'

Phil piped up, 'You can't see her eyes any more?'

Sadie laughed. 'Oh, Phil.' Phil looked pleased with himself.

Suddenly, next to Sadie, I felt more like a schoolgirl than ever, with my silly fringe. Her hair was perfectly straight and sleek, falling in a chic bob around her angular chin, lacquered with spray so not a hair moved. She looked amazing, her long legs, nude high heels, and a tailored navy dress falling above her knees, showing off her athletic body, and a scarf tied casually around her neck. I glanced at the label. Hermes. Her scarf cost more than my entire outfit. More than my monthly food shop. More than my life. Sadie was channelling PR Success Woman completely, and I was channelling Year Ten Schoolgirl.

'Looks, uh, nice, Emma,' Nick said kindly, even though we all knew he was lying.

Sadie and Nick went into his office and closed the door, and every time she trilled with laughter I felt as if someone were running their nails down a blackboard. This horrific sound continued for an hour.

Mid-morning, I was in the kitchen dunking a tea bag

repeatedly into a mug of boiling water. I kept trying to turn my head around so I looked like Lily Allen in the microwave window reflection, at least from some angle.

I didn't.

What had I been thinking?

Anyway, I couldn't stop to think about my hair disaster; Macabre was fast approaching and all my focus had to be on that.

When I got back to my desk, Nick was standing chatting to Phil, then smiled at me. 'How are the media alerts, anything about Honey?' Again, he was cool as a cucumber, the consummate professional, as if I'd never seen him at the park with her.

I was almost tempted to ask him what 'work' Honey had been helping him with, but Professional Emma was in full force. Even with a fringe. 'No negative coverage, a few small mentions, but all good. I emailed them to you this morning.'

'And the runsheets for Macabre?' He looked as if he was checking off a list in his head.

'All done.'

'And the budget sign off?'

Oh, no.

That was the one thing I'd forgotten, when I'd thought I'd been on top of everything else. With everything being so hectic, I'd completely forgotten about the budget sign off from the CFO, Charles Newton.

I nodded again. Another lie.

'So you got it all? Without a problem?'

Thankfully, my phone started ringing. It was Honey. 'Sorry, I have to take this.'

Honey declared down the phone that she wanted Chinese food, particularly lemon chicken, but without onions, and with free-range organic chicken. I had to call six places before I found one that said they were organic. I wasn't sure I could trust them because they kept saying yes to everything I asked, but I figured Honey would never know if it was actually organic or not.

When I arrived at her hotel suite, she was curled up in her white silk gown, at 2 p.m., as if she'd slept all day. She took the chicken from me, and said, 'Care to join?' and I had to say no, I had work. But she wanted to talk about what she was wearing to the next press conference, and to the event, and she had an arsenal of questions, which I tried my best to answer, and not let myself fall asleep on her actual bed. Gosh, it looked comfy.

Thankfully she didn't say much about Nick, just prattled on a bit about how he was a gentleman, and did I know how lovely he was? How smart he was? How witty? To which I replied 'hmmmm' and then prayed she would change the subject, because thinking of the two of them together, from underneath this fringe, made me feel a little claustrophobic.

I stayed for as long as I could, hiding out in Honey's room, listening to her natter on about her new nail colour and handbag purchases, and I put up with all of it, with a smile on my face, because all of this was better than seeing Nick and having to admit I didn't have the budget approved or signed off. When I finally got back to the office it was past 5 p.m., and I knew Nick would have already left for the offsite IAH client meeting. I strode straight to my desk, picked up the phone, dialled Charles' EA and requested an urgent meeting.

Chapter 23

'There's a solid increase.' Charles scrutinised the pages from behind his large black desk that had been sheened to perfection. It was a place that would keep fingerprints forever if any ever got on there. 'Why are the expenses up ten per cent?'

'I'm not sure.' I stood awkwardly to the side of Charles' desk and looked out onto the city at dusk. It was 6 p.m. and I was crossing my fingers this could be done and dusted and back on Nick's desk for the morning.

'Well, I can't sign the budget off, unless I know more of a reason than ...' he put his glasses on and peered over and read '... than "unexpected increase to forecast".' He paused. 'And if you want this signed by the expiry time on this paper, which is ...' Charles checked his calendar '... tonight, then I suggest you get going, because I'll be leaving at 8 p.m., for the airport.'

'Yes, sure, on it!' I said a little too anxiously. Because how was I meant to get Nick's explanation since he'd already gone home? I took the budget papers back to my desk and picked up the phone, calling Nick's mobile. It went to voicemail. I left a quick message – 'Can you please call me?'

I sat there drumming my fingers on my desk, waiting for the return call. After ten minutes I sent him a text – *please call asap, quick question*.

I watched in anticipation for the three dots to appear on my screen, suggesting he was writing me back, but there was nothing. I could see it hadn't been delivered at the bottom of the text screen.

I looked around the office. Phil had gone home. Sadie had gone home. Glenn was in a meeting. Who else could I ask? Finally, I picked up the phone and dialled HR, in case they had any other ideas. A girl I'd met at a department meeting, Gaby, picked up.

'Oh, that does sound like you're in a pickle!' she said when I'd told her the situation. 'Look, I normally wouldn't do this, but I know how hard it is to juggle so many priorities. Plus, I know what Glenn's going to be like if you don't get this. He'll probably fire you and Nick!' She laughed. 'Sorry, I'm not meant to say that! I do have an idea of how to get ahold of Nick, but you can't tell anyone.'

'Absolutely,' I said, eager to hear her idea. 'I won't tell a soul.'

Gaby whispered into the phone. 'OK, so I'm going to give you his address. Do you have a pen?'

His address? I was going to his house? After hours? 'Yes, I have a pen,' I said, my palms sweating.

'It's Unit 800, 45 Bayside Road, Hyde Park,' Gaby said. 'OK, I've gotta go, so don't tell anyone you got it from me, OK?'

'OK,' I said thickly down the phone. When I stood I felt a

bit woozy. I was actually going to go to Nick's place. Nick's place. I opened the fridge door and took out a beer from the corporate stash and skulled it over the sink. Nick's place.

On the way over in the taxi, I felt dizzy and clammy. Would Honey be there? Would I be interrupting something? The cab arrived at Nick's place, a swanky apartment block that was ultra-modern with a large glass door, and inside industrial cement and marble lined the hall and walls. It looked exactly like where someone who worked at Maker should live.

A doorman held open the door for me. 'Madam?' He had a doorman!

Taking a deep breath, I signed in and walked over to the large lift, my high heels echoing against the cool tiles. At the lift I pressed number 8, which said 'Penthouse Suites'. God, he was in a penthouse.

When the lift door opened, I checked in the mirror that my navy pants and cream top were in place. Staring at my reflection, I saw that my cheeks looked red and my eyes a little panicky but there was nothing I could do about that.

At the top the hallway was entirely black. After the glare of the mirrored elevator, I could hardly see a thing. It took a minute for my eyes to register, and then the small ground lights came into focus, and I followed the sign to Unit 800.

I raised my hand and knocked. I took a deep breath. A few seconds passed. Maybe he wasn't home. I knocked again.

'OK, OK,' a muffled voice shouted. Nick opened the door wearing a long white bathrobe. His hair was wet and tousled. 'Emma?' He looked completely shocked.

God, I'd interrupted his shower.

Shower. Fiji. Warm suds.

'Charles needs you to write more in this section,' I said, shoving the paperwork towards him, my finger pointing to where he needed to fill in.

He still looked surprised to find me on his doorstep, as if he wasn't registering.

'I tried your phone several times,' I explained. 'Emails, texts, calls ...' My voice trailed off.

He reached down into his pocket and pulled out his phone. 'Oh, my battery must be flat. I didn't realise, I was in the shower.'

'So it seems.' *Berry foam. Lathering. Slippery thighs.*

He looked up at me. 'How did you know where I lived?'

'Um, I ...' I stammered. 'Someone at the office knew.'

'They did?' He looked confused.

'Well, can you sign this?' I tried changing the subject so I didn't get Gaby in trouble. 'It's on a deadline.'

'Oh, sure.' He looked down. 'Did you want to come in? This could take a few minutes.' He said it so casually, as one would say, 'Oh, did you want to see my new orchid?' Rather than, 'Hello, person I've had sex with before, did you want to come into my *house* whilst I'm wearing a *bathrobe* and possibly *nothing underneath?*'

'No, I'm fine,' I said, shifting in my high heels, feeling it was more professional to stand at the door.

'Suit yourself.' He walked down the hallway and disappeared off to the left. I could hear some banging of drawers, and then silence. Five minutes later he came back, papers in hand.

'I'll get these back to the office now,' I said, because I was almost used to this life now, working late each night, living off coffee and microwave meals, and having zero social life. I dashed back down the lift to my waiting Uber, and then back to the office. Thankfully it was only 7.30 p.m. so Charles was still in his office, and signed the papers happily, telling me the funds would be released the next day.

'Oh, Emma?' Kyle called out to me in the hallway, from his office next to Charles'. I stiffened. Kyle was Glenn's boss. One of the bigwig executives who looked after all Sales and Marketing, and I hadn't even thought Kyle knew my name. I whirled around and walked quickly into his office. He was sitting at a desk, which was larger, if that was possible, than Nick's entire office.

'Did you just say that you saw Nick?' he said without even looking at me.

'I did. Just now.'

'The swimwear art campaign needs Nick's signature ASAP to go to printing.'

'Sure. When?'

'Tonight.' He pointed to a load of files, still all without looking at me. 'And take the latest marketing figures he wanted.'

'Right,' I said, picking them up, expecting him to at least thank me. He didn't. Which felt slightly unfair, because it wasn't my job to give him the figures; I knew it had to be someone's, but it sure wasn't mine. Until now. *Looks like I'm not going to be home before 8 p.m. after all,* I thought bitterly.

I knew Glenn and Kyle were still working at night, but I could guarantee they were getting paid six-figure salaries at least to do the extra-long hours. What was I getting? About a quarter of that, maybe an eighth. Literally. No one seemed to care that I was working fourteen-hour days, every day, and was literally doing two full-time jobs between Macabre and Honey. I felt super unappreciated and as I sat in the Uber on the way back across the city, I felt a pang of jealousy for those out enjoying their lives or those in bed.

By 8.30 p.m. I was back in the lift at Nick's place. This time when he answered the door, he was wearing dark brown pants, tapered at the ankle, and a white open-collared shirt and no shoes. He smelt fresh, like mint and deep forest woods again. His smell.

'Emma. Again.' He looked surprised.

'Yep. Me. Again,' I said, feeling exhausted. 'Kyle said you need to sign off on the final art campaign for Tiger tonight. Finance have already okayed it. And here are the latest marketing figures.'

'OK.' He nodded, flipping through the files. 'Thanks for coming back so late.'

I sighed, feeling flushed and drained; it had been a big night and the longest of days. The only thing I wanted to do was fall into bed and sleep for a hundred years.

'Did you ... ah ... want to come in, for a drink?'

'Am I taking the cover art back to Kyle?'

'No. I can email it.'

'Well, I don't need a drink, but I could do with some battery – I'm down to two per cent and I have to get an Uber home.' I held up my phone.

I followed Nick through his dark hallway, where at the end it opened up to an open-plan living room, set three stairs down from the hallway, with scallop-shaped couches, in black and brown leather, and an entire one-hundred-and-eighty-degree view of the city.

'Wow,' I said.

'Breathtaking, isn't it?' Nick said, hooking up my phone to a charger. 'How about a tea while you wait?'

'Sure.' *It can't hurt, sitting on the couch,* I thought.

Nick switched on the kettle.

'How long have you lived here?' I looked around the impressive lounge.

'Five years. My idea was to renovate a place in the inner west, have those DIY projects on the go, keeping me visiting hardware stores every weekend. But then I found this place, and the idea of easy living sounded a lot better. So now I get to enjoy a piece of urban paradise.'

He poured me a tea. 'Milk?'

'No, just plain is fine.'

'There you go.' He passed it to me carefully, his hand briefly grazing mine as he held it out. He slid in next to me on the couch, holding his own cup of tea.

I tried to ignore his touch. He was my *boss*. And he was with Honey. But I couldn't help but imagine him leaning over and kissing me.

'Do you live here by yourself?' Then I caught myself. 'Sorry, that was prying. You don't need to answer that.' I hesitated, because I was burning with curiosity.

'Not alone, unfortunately,' he said. 'Brett, my good friend, lives in that room over there.' He pointed across the hallway. 'He's in Melbourne for a sales trip at the moment.'

Nick's phone buzzed and he excused himself to take it. I could hear mumblings from the hallway. 'No, I'll email it to you. The figures? Yes, the ones we talked about earlier. Yeah, first thing tomorrow.'

When he came back, he seemed more distant, his mind on other things, as if he was slightly closed off. 'Sorry, what were we saying?'

'Living arrangements.' I felt awkward so I kept on talking. 'I live in the tiniest little studio in Marrickville. Talking of do-it-uppers, that's definitely a trash not treasure place.' I looked around his house. 'Judging by your style, you'd hate it.'

'Oh, this? Sarah, my ex, did all this. Years ago. She's very minimalist. Chic-urban, she called it. She put in the new range, the kitchen, the wall colour painted that muted oatmeal, that's what she called it. But I think it's nude. Or taupe. Actually, I don't know what it is. She had the couches ordered from some German-Melbourne designer. They cost, like, half my annual salary.'

'Well, they're very comfortable, but now I'm feeling like I shouldn't drink tea on it.' I went to stand.

'No, that's fine, sit down, really.' He smiled.

Suddenly I remembered Honey. 'What are you doing tomorrow night?'

'Um.' His forehead creased in thought. 'Nothing at the moment. Why?'

'Oh, it's Honey. I think she wanted you to have a babysitting shift.' I couldn't bring myself to call it a date.

'Oh, OK.' He didn't seem as excited as I had thought he would. 'Do you ever get the feeling it's like we have a child?'

I laughed. 'Sure do. At least she doesn't want to crawl into my bed at night and co-sleep.'

But then I thought, a child? Why would he speak about his girlfriend like that? I couldn't work him out.

Nick sounded amused. 'Co-sleep? That's a thing?'

'I have lots of friends with kids and, yes, apparently that's a thing, sleeping with your child for years, I think. I'm not sure. I have lots of other child knowledge too – it doesn't stop there. I could also talk a lot about sleeping patterns, mastitis and potty training.' It fell out of my mouth before my brain could filter it. I had just referenced *poo* and also *sore red nipples*! I was so used to discussing these things with Mags and Tansy that I forgot non-child humans probably didn't chat about this. The look on his face seemed to be one of disgust, or was he trying not to laugh? I couldn't tell. God, someone get me something stronger than a tea.

Something started vibrating. Nick leaned over and lifted up another phone that was plugged into the wall. 'Sorry, I've got a work phone and a personal one. Too many phones. Hold on.'

He took the call, out in the hallway, but I couldn't hear what he was saying.

'Did you want a whisky?' he said, coming back in looking a little strained. I wondered who he'd been talking to. I nodded. Actually, a whisky sounded perfect.

He settled back onto the couch when my phone started ringing. He laughed. 'This time it's you.'

It was Tansy. 'I'm going to take this,' I excused myself and slipped down the hall. I needed to hear a friendly voice.

I whispered hello into the phone, and she whispered hello back. 'I just put Brie and Toby and Addy down all before nine, so I thought perfect timing for a long-overdue catch-up call! But I have to be quiet. So don't tell me any exciting news.'

'OK, I promise.' And made sure I wouldn't tell her I was in Nick's apartment, otherwise I was sure she'd let out a big girly scream and then want to plan our wedding. 'How are you?' I asked her as I stared at Nick's black walls.

'Same as always here. Sick from Toby. This time it's a really nasty fever virus thing, which makes me unable to hold more than one thought in my head.'

'Oh, God, I'm sorry. Should I bring you something? Panadol?'

'A new life. Or a hazmat suit,' she joked. 'Anyway, how are you? I haven't heard from you in ages, and I wanted to check in.'

'I'm good,' I said stoically.

'That's great, Em, so why don't you sound like yourself?'

Suddenly exhausted, I felt myself get a bit teary. 'I don't?'

I walked further down the hallway and slipped out of the front door, so Nick couldn't hear me.

'You sound exhausted. Like you did before, when you worked in marketing, remember? You ended up hating that job.'

I thought about it for a second. 'Yeah, you're right. I am really tired. Most days I'm literally rolling up yoga mats, and getting Princess Honey donuts at dawn. I feel a lot more like I work as her PA rather than in PR.'

'Is she awful?'

'No, she's actually quite nice. I mean, she's a typical millennial, always scrolling. And very demanding, because she's used to getting everything she wants. But she's nice.'

'And what about your event?'

'Well, I can't really concentrate on that, because I'm basically babysitting Honey, and staging paparazzi shoots so we can spin her PR. I think I liked it better when I was struggling to find a theme for the event, at least that felt genuine.' I sat in the hallway. 'It just feels like I'm lying all the time. And I hate that. It's not me. And no one appreciates that I'm working fourteen hours a day for literally no money.' I sighed, sobering up at the thought of my situation. 'Sorry, I know I'm going on a bit of a rant.'

Tansy put on her brightest voice. 'You're doing well, though, aren't you? Don't they love you?'

'I'm doing OK. And if you mean, have they realised yet if I elaborated on my CV? No, I don't think so,' I whispered into the phone.

Although there had been a close call the other day when I was about to send the final confirmation email with the event details, and Phil had stopped me with horror, almost shouting. 'You have to blind copy them! They can't get each other's email addresses,' he'd said in complete shock, staring at me, saying, 'Emma, these are celebrities and top VIPs, if you gave away their personal details, there'd be murder.' Then he'd shaken his head as if I were absolutely bonkers. I'd had to tell him it was a silly mistake because I was so tired, but I'm not sure he bought it completely.

'And to top it off, I don't really have a life any more. During the week it's work non-stop, and on the weekend, well, I sleep and clean, and make bad hair choices. Oh, I got a fringe, Tansy, and it's a bit hideous.'

She tried to hide a laugh. 'Surely, it can't be that bad? I remember you looked rather sweet in grade two with one.'

I tried to give a small laugh. 'Tansy, my life is just not going according to The Plan. I'm not sure Step 1 is going to plan, and Step 2 is a damp flat. And, you know, Step 3 is failing big time. Trying to find someone I really like in Sydney is really hard. Besides, I don't even have time to go to the toilet at the moment, let alone go for a drink,' I said, feeling miserable.

'Em, is that what you actually want? To date someone in Sydney?' She knew me well, almost too well.

I gulped and said nothing. Finally, I said, 'How else will I find someone? I don't want to be alone for the rest of my life.'

'Maybe your person is thinking exactly the same thing, maybe they're not in a nine to five job either, have you thought of that? Maybe they're out travelling and you're not going to find them putting on a suit every day. I hate to say this, Em, but maybe you're not even meant to be in Sydney.'

Her words shocked me. 'You think?'

'Are you happy?'

Happy. I hadn't stopped to think about that for a while. It had been weeks of long nights, and little sleep, and focusing at work – but was I happy?

'I don't know,' I admitted.

'OK, tell me three good things about working at Maker.'

'OK!' I said confidently. 'One, it pays the bills. And ... two, I'm learning new things. And three ... um ... three ...' I struggled to think of a third one. 'Um, three ...'

'Well, I think that says it all, doesn't it? I feel bad giving you the Maker details to begin with.'

'No, don't. I just thought I'd grown up, that's all. That I was ready for this.'

'But you *are* grown up. That doesn't necessarily mean you're going to want what me and Maggie have.'

'It doesn't?'

'No, silly. There are more than just two ways of living. It's not just backpacking travel or settling down in a city. There are so many other things you could do. Have you thought about that at all?'

I hadn't.

'I mean, we love having you here, but you've never liked big cities since as long as I can remember. You've always been trying to escape them. And working in PR – is that really what you think you should be doing?'

'I'm not sure,' I said slowly. 'I thought since I had The Plan ...' I trailed off.

'Maybe that life isn't ever going to be your plan.' In true best-friend fashion, she always knew how to cut to the chase.

'When did you get so wise?'

She laughed. 'Am I? I don't feel wise. Today I put the car keys in the freezer and it took me over an hour to find them.

And I only found them because I was having such a bad day, I wanted a spoonful of ice cream.'

We chatted about her kids and busy schedule for a few more minutes, then she had to go because Brie had woken up. When I put the phone down, I wondered if what she said was true. *Maybe that life isn't ever going to be your plan.*

Then I thought about the last few weeks, and everything that had happened with my bad Sydney dates, and Nick and Honey and Macabre. The more I thought about it, the more I realised I was exhausted all the time. I lived in a shoebox; I had sore feet from high heels; I couldn't sleep well at night and had started taking sleeping tablets, I was a professional babysitter, and I was lonely. And the one guy I thought I felt a connection with didn't like me like that, at all. And now I was at his house, and trying to chat casually, as if we were just friends.

I knocked on Nick's door. He answered it. 'Emma. Third time tonight.'

'Sorry, locked myself out,' I said sheepishly.

He let me in. 'How's the phone battery?'

'Actually I think I need a bit more, almost down to zero.' The phone call with Tansy was making my mind race. My head was reeling. Was I ready to give up Maker? To leave? And if I was, where the hell would I go?

'Emma, are you OK?'

I wasn't sure.

'Emma,' he said quietly, and reached for my cheek with his hand. He brushed back a strand of my hair. I looked up at him. 'Emma,' he said again. His fingers curved around my jaw, as his other arm slipped round my waist. Inside my stomach flipped. I got goosebumps. He pulled me into him and I didn't resist it. I lay my head on his shoulder and felt the warmth of his body through the fine cotton of his shirt for a few seconds. It felt as if my head belonged there; I couldn't move. I wanted to press pause for a second, and just enjoy how he felt. He leaned back and was staring at me. 'You looked like you needed a hug.'

So that was all it was. A friendly, you-look-miserable kind of hug. I tried to swallow back down the feelings that were fluttering – like giant butterflies – in my stomach.

'I should go,' I said, leaning back from the safety of his hug, because I knew if I stayed I'd do something or say something I would definitely regret.

Before I could move away, he reached both hands onto my cheeks, cupping my face.

Somewhere in my mind I knew he was going to kiss me. I didn't move. He leaned over, until there was a space between us only a thin sheet of paper could slip between; his breath was warm and smoky like whisky. I sensed if I moved at all we'd touch. We stayed like that for a few seconds and then, sensing I wasn't backing away, he leaned over, and touched his lips to mine. Just quickly grazing them with his, before pulling back.

I could barely breathe. He leaned towards me again. This time he kissed me softly, tenderly. Then urgently, and deeply, as it flared into something more passionate. There were fireworks going off in my chest, warmth exploded into heat. It made me shiver. My boss had just kissed me. What the hell was he doing? But he'd kissed me, and I'd felt – I'd felt *everything*.

'I didn't mean to do that,' Nick whispered, breaking away. 'We can't.'

'Can't,' I repeated, my head swirling.

'Shouldn't,' he murmured.

'Agreed.' I looked up at him – God, I loved how tall he was.

But then he stared at me again, with those delicious eyes, and said, 'But I want to. Badly.'

'What about Honey?' I asked.

'Honey?' Confusion crossed his face. 'Our child? I think she's fine in her hotel room.'

'But aren't you guys, a thing?' I said.

Nick laughed and brushed away more of my hair. 'No, wherever did you get that idea?'

But I couldn't think of anything now, except being in Nick's arms. And if he wasn't with Honey, and he was kissing me, well, that told me everything I needed to know. 'It doesn't matter.'

'Good,' Nick said. 'Let's just focus on us, together.

'Together,' I murmured.

'Together,' he said, brushing his lips against mine.

And that was all he needed to say, because I fell into him, and he lifted me up – like actually carried me, as if I were weightless – into his room.

He laid me down on the bed, gently, and leaned in and kissed me. At first, he was slow, tender, but then he was moving more urgently, pulling up my silk blouse, yanking my tuxedo pants off me, as if he couldn't wait to put his hot lips on my skin. When he did, using little flicks of his tongue on my stomach, and trailing a line of kisses down my legs, and then up my chest, I broke out in goosebumps.

He pushed down my bra cups to free my breasts, which he kissed softly, letting his teeth graze the tops of my nipples. Every hair on my body stood to attention. He stood, staring at me as he took off his shirt, and pants, until he was standing there naked, with his perfect body, staring at mine. He undid a condom and rolled it on, slowly. Then he lay on top of me and then embraced me, so we were skin against skin. And then he was kissing me, on the mouth, hot and passionate, and then down my body, my neck, my breasts, as though I was something to be devoured.

He couldn't wait, and neither could I. 'I want you,' I said, and I meant on top of me, inside me, every part of him, and every part of me, together.

Excited, he pushed my lacy knickers to the right side, not even bothering to take them off. I was wet and so ready for him. He moaned as he entered me with one big thrust. 'God, Emma.'

I felt as if something flashed across my entire body. I couldn't stop my body moving, writhing under his. I clasped at his shoulders, my nails digging in, making lines down his back, unaware if it would hurt, because everything now just felt good, so good.

I lifted myself up, wrapped my arms around his neck, and pulled him into me, kissing him. 'I want to do this forever,' I said, lost to the moment.

'We can,' he said, stopping for a moment, and looking into my eyes. This was something else, something way more than the Medusa effect. The way he looked at me – with such a mixture of desire and care – undid me.

I writhed below his body, wanting more and more of him. He groaned. 'Come, baby,' I whispered. 'You feel so good inside me.' I could feel the rise of my own orgasm, flitting at the edges. 'Oh, God, come, baby,' I moaned into his ear.

My body was wracked with absolute desire; I wanted every inch of him, everywhere. Our pace quickened. I gripped his body with my legs, my arms, attached to him in every possible way. 'Fuck, Emma,' he groaned as we increased in pace, as he thrust even deeper into me. My hands were running wild down his back, through his hair. Every second sent us closer together. He gripped me, the back of my neck, as if he wanted to hold me forever. We were moving together like mad, as if it was never going to be enough, as if we were insatiable.

'Oh, God,' I moaned as the orgasm took over. I let out a high-pitched scream of ecstasy, at the same time that he let out a groan, and his body shuddered as we climaxed together. My entire body stretched out into bliss for what felt like an indefinite eternity.

He looked down at me and kissed me, a last passionate, caring kiss. Then he collapsed on my chest and lay there for what could have been ten minutes or ten hours. Time had no bearing on us. I slipped my hands around his neck and kissed his sweaty head. He looked up at me and kissed my nose. Then brushed away my hair as he rolled onto his back and then scooped me up, so I lay on his smooth chest. It felt as if this was exactly where I belonged.

This wasn't hot Fiji sex; this felt like something else. I didn't want to say it, but it felt a lot like love.

I woke up with a smile on my face.

Nick and Emma. Nemma. Enick. We'd need to work on that. Perhaps our middle names were a better match? But it didn't matter, because I hadn't imagined it: this whole time there *had* been a connection.

I rolled over in bed; the clock read 7 a.m. Seven! I had to get up; so much to do today, in the final countdown for Macabre. But first, I wanted to lie in bed with Nick a little. I rolled over to say good morning, and reached out for his warm, beautiful body, but my hands found only empty, cool sheet. I lifted myself up on my elbows. Nick wasn't there, and he wasn't in the room either. He must have already got up.

I stretched and yawned. I bet he was busy in the kitchen, making us coffee, or on an early morning shop run, getting us bagels. I smiled as I thought about the night, and how amazing it had felt to finally kiss him. Our clothes from last night were still strewn across the floor – discarded in the heat of the moment. And, God, what a *moment*.

'Yeeeeeeee!' I whispered excitedly. Did this mean the girl got the guy? I think it did. With adrenaline pumping through my veins, I thought, *I'm going to get up and see what's going on in the kitchen, and where this gorgeous man is.*

I threw on an old shirt of Nick's I found hanging over

his brown leather chair, which was so long it ended mid-thigh. It was perfect for the sexy morning-after look, because who knew, we had enough time to go back to bed, for a little while.

I padded out of the bedroom, and down to the corridor to the lounge. The sun was already bright and streaming in, and it took a few seconds for my eyes to adjust. I expected to see Nick fussing over the kettle, the toaster, the stove top with eggs and bacon, but the kitchen was entirely empty. I ducked back down the hall to the bathroom, to check if he was in there, because I hadn't heard any signs that he was. But the bathroom was empty, and clean, as if no one had been in there at all.

OK, he was doing a bagel run. I shrugged, and thought I'd take the time to freshen up and have a quick shower. I turned the water on hot, and stepped under the large rainwater showerhead, the water pummelling down onto my shoulders, kneading out any knots in my muscles. Twenty minutes later I emerged, fresh and clean, with newly washed hair smelling of Nick's green-apple shampoo.

I walked to his room in the towel, expecting to smell the beautiful wafts of breakfast, but there was still nothing. 'Nick?' I called out into the bedroom. No answer.

'Nick?' I padded back out into the lounge and kitchen. But it was empty, still. I picked up my phone, but there were no texts or voicemails. I even checked my personal email and my work one, but there was nothing.

How strange.

In the bedroom I tried to think about where else Nick

could be. Maybe there'd been a work thing, but then he would have left a note.

I called his work mobile but it went straight to voicemail. I didn't leave a message. And I didn't have any other number for him. For the next five minutes I scoured the bedroom and kitchen for a note, but there was absolutely nothing. He kept his minimalist urban-whatever-chic flat super clean, and all the benches were spotless and empty.

It's not like he's done a runner, I thought, amused, walking back into the bathroom, *not from his own apartment.* But it was becoming stranger and stranger that he wasn't there. I checked the clock, and it was almost eight, and I was going to be late for work if I hung around here any longer. I still had to go home and get a change of clothes, before my day of finalising the menus, and confirming all the media spots, then getting ready for the designer decorations to be shipped into The Westin Hotel and setting up for the big event.

I poked my head out of the front door, but the hallway was empty. I even gingerly looked through Brett's door, because I knew he was out of town for the week, but his bed was perfectly made up. An hour had gone by; surely if he was picking up bagels, he'd be here by now.

I called Nick's mobile again, and left a quick voicemail in a slightly shaky voice. 'Where are you?' Because suddenly I was getting worried. Had something happened to him?

Somewhere a phone buzzed and it wasn't mine. Curious, I followed the sound to the lounge. On a small glass table propped against the wall was a charger cord and phone. I leaned over, wondering if it was Nick's. The phone buzzed again and the screen lit up with several text messages.

And there it was. The reason he wasn't there. My mouth went dry. Oh, God.

The first was from Honey, around midnight: *Hey you, when are you coming over? x*

The next two were from Chloe, the first at 5 a.m.: *Answer your phone. Need to speak asap xx*

And then at 5.25 a.m.: *Where are you? On your way? Need you here with me right now. Love you xxx*

I ran to the toilet and only just managed to make it before throwing up. I washed my face with cold water, my hands shaking. I looked white and cold and drained in the reflection. I stood there, with only his old white T-shirt on, feeling totally exposed and vulnerable.

Chloe. Honey. Their names felt cold and hard in my mouth like a piece of ice.

My mouth burned. I rinsed it once, twice with water, then toothpaste. I couldn't process it, them, what had happened with Nick ... *anything*.

Nick *was* with Honey. He'd lied. To my face. In shock, I walked back into the bedroom, feeling as if I weren't even in my body. Last night was nothing. It hadn't felt like nothing, but then, that was what players did, made it seem like things were real, when they weren't. He was playing us all, wasn't he? He had to be. God, I felt like such an *idiot*.

I was grabbing my clothes, sliding on my pants, whilst hopping around the room. 'Where's my shirt?' I was picking up items of clothes off the floor. His jeans. His belt buckle. His jumper. 'WHERE'S MY SHIRT?'

Tears burnt at the corners of my eyes; my throat had a massive lump in it. There was a stabbing and pulling in my chest, in my heart. And that was the only reason I knew I was still breathing. I found my shirt under the bed, and pulled it on, and left his apartment.

I went home and got straight into bed, sending a quick email in the cab to Glenn: *Sorry can't make it in today, really sick.* Before switching my phone off, and crying softly until I fell asleep.

When I woke up a few hours later, the same sentences were playing out in my head.

When are you coming over?

Need you here with me right now xxx

Their words kept haunting me.

I switched my phone on just after midday, expecting Nick to have contacted me – but nothing came through. I looked at my texts, my emails, my missed calls. Nothing from Nick. Nothing. That was how little he cared about me?

My head was a mess. I kept thinking about how he'd kissed me, as if he liked me, no – as if he almost *loved* me. I'd let him in last night, really let him in. I'd been completely vulnerable, because I'd thought he felt as I did. As if we had a connection, as if it was *special*.

The truth was, I was one of several girls. Who knew how many? I felt like throwing up again and ran into the bathroom, hanging my head over the toilet, but I only managed to spit out some saliva. In the bathroom mirror I looked dreadful, tired and drawn, dark and puffy circles under my eyes.

I curled back up in my bed, and turned my phone back off again. What had last night meant to him? Clearly nothing. The lump in my stomach hardened. Who slept with someone when they were seeing other people? Nick did.

I just felt like staying in my studio apartment forever. I couldn't even bring myself to tell Tansy or Maggie; it felt too raw, too painful. And if anyone had reached out to comfort me, I felt as if I'd start crying and never stop.

Suddenly, I did that terrible thing that girls who had been dumped or ghosted did. I started thinking, what could I do to *get him back*? I thought about a thousand texts I could send: the hurt texts, the 'do you care?' texts, the 'Where the fuck are you!?' texts. I even thought about the nonchalant texts, 'Hey where did you go mister?' texts, just to get a reaction. A response. *Anything*.

I pulled out my phone and switched it on, tempted to craft the perfect message. But what was that message? I started to type out a few beginnings ...

Hey is everything OK? Where are you? I'm worried. (Too bland and *way* too nice.)

WHERE THE HELL ARE YOU? (Too much.)

So I woke up this morning, and you were gone. Smiley face. I'm a big girl, and managed to get home OK, but I missed you. Where did you go? (Way too much of a pushover.)

Hey, a heads up. What you did was so uncool. Don't ever do this to other girls. Think about your actions. (Too teachery. That was the thing about guys who cheated: they didn't care in the first place. Trying to appeal to their heart or conscience and *force* them to care would never work.)

I saw the texts Nick. I saw them. Chloe. Honey. Who else? Who else are you screwing over? FUCKING JERK. (Too ... something.)

That was what Old Emma would have done. Old Emma would have sent a text. She would have sent many texts – probably all of them. Old Emma who thought everything was her fault.

I wrote each one, and then deleted them. I didn't see why Nick got to leave, and then *I* was the one chasing *him*. Besides, what if I sent a message, and he *still* didn't respond? Then I'd become fixed to my phone, obsessed to see if my message had been delivered. If he'd read it. Looking for those three dots that suggested he was writing back. There was nothing worse than waiting for someone else, when they might never respond. It was the horrible unknown, the mystery of not knowing what the hell was going on.

I knew texting him and waiting obsessively for a response wouldn't help me at all. Using all my willpower, I put my phone down.

The lump formed again in my throat. Nick was a cheater and a player. Nick, who was also my *boss*. Oh, God. My stomach sank and I felt sick. I couldn't go back to work. Maybe ever. I'd be reminded of him every morning, his office, his couch. The way his aftershave made our team area smell of leather and mint and the woods. I'd be reminded of him everywhere. I wouldn't be able to go into a meeting with him without feeling sick. Or wanting to hurl a chair at his awfully good-looking head. I'd never be able to go near Hyde Park again. His apartment.

I could see exactly what life would be like – avoiding Nick, more projects, more deadlines, more babysitting, more working round the clock, then coming back to a damp studio apartment. More spending money I didn't have. More lonely singles walks. More long weekends with not much to do. I'd feel empty. I'd feel as if everyone was getting on with their lives – with kids and marriages and house renovations – and I would be stuck.

A wash of panic came over me. I had to leave Maker. I couldn't stay. But I couldn't just quit, could I? Not without another job. I had bills to pay. Rent. And even though Maker paid a mere pittance, it was better than nothing.

All at once, this feeling felt all too familiar. This one had snuck up on me, and pulled the rug out from underneath. But it felt like The White Horror all over again. Failing at something. Miserably. And then being left alone, to pick up the pieces.

I grabbed a bottle of sav blanc and a large glass and I flicked on the TV, and what did you know? Bridget Jones was on. I thought, *Is that me?* Single. Living in pajamas. Eating cereal straight from a box. Drinking straight from a bottle of wine. Terrible luck in love. Because it was true, no matter what I wore, or how I did my hair, perhaps I'd never be as cool or gorgeous as Donna or Sadie or Honey. Perhaps it was time to accept I was just plain old Bridget Jones.

Before she got Mr Darcy. And maybe there wasn't even a Darcy for me.

I grabbed a handful of cereal clusters from the box and shoved them into my mouth. For a second last night, I had thought Nick could be my Darcy, but the truth was clear: Nick was my boss. And it seemed as if he was also into other women. Nick was very clearly my Daniel Cleaver.

Suddenly my phone beeped with a text. I lunged at it, sure it would be Nick. But it was Glenn.

PR mixer tonight. Take a Tylenol. You need to represent Maker.

Chapter 24

The PR mixer function was already buzzing when I arrived. It was a monthly get-together of everyone in the industry and it reeked of style. All around me, women in slinky black jumpsuits and Alexander McQueen scarves were carrying Champagne as if it were a life source. Botoxed to the hilt, no one made any expression, so you had to listen very carefully to their voices, which was the only way you knew if they were angry or ecstatic.

Young twenty- and thirty-something men in tight pants, and open-necked, lumberjack, red and blue plaid shirts looked as though they'd just come in from chopping logs to chat about artisanal bread and microbrewerys, some with man buns, and all of them with perfect man hands – which made me swoon. And the older men were all pocket hankerchiefs and perfect navy three-piece suits. Also swoon.

I felt completely out of place in my black A-line dress, with capped sleeves, a blue snakeskin belt and ankle boots. The dress had become a little, um, tight, after too many nights wolfing down mac and cheese when I was too tired to cook. It was especially restrictive under my arms, like a squeezing boa constrictor, so I had to lift them up at intervals to keep the blood flowing. Plus, I'd had to heap a pile of make-up on, and a lifetime of concealer under my eyes, just to look as though I hadn't been crying all day.

As Glenn had suggested, I had dosed up a little, not on Tylenol, but Panadeine Forte. It was meant for really bad pain, like migraines, or being left alone in apartments. Just one tiny tablet. But already, it had helped to take the edge off, so at least I wasn't feeling as anxious as I had been an hour ago; in fact, I felt a bit warm and light-headed and floaty.

I was proud that I'd managed to put my phone away in my bag and not think about Nick, Daniel Cleavering his way around the office. Well, not much. I had even managed to stop looking at the entrance to the PR mixer, seeing if Nick was going to walk in. I didn't know what I'd do if he did. I didn't want to create a scene, but maybe I could throw a Champagne or the entire food table at him and call him a jerk.

I repositioned my badge, looked around, and smiled half-heartedly at some glitzy woman who totally blanked me, as if I were just empty space.

Some people had nightmares about turning up to school naked. Some people about being eaten alive by rats. I had a recurring nightmare about having to make small talk with business people, and, even worse, perfectly glitzy, very cool people, and never knowing what to say. For me, a party in full swing where nobody noticed I was there was perfect, just like this one. That way I just hung about the food table, where, thankfully, because this was a PR gathering, it was completely untouched.

'You're Emma, right?'

'Yes.' I turned around to see who was asking. A tall guy smiled. He was cute. Spiky dark hair, strong jawline, a little stubble on his face – not too much or too little, in fact on a Goldilocks' scale it was just right. He was at least a head taller than me and he had piercing green eyes. But I hated men right now, especially gorgeous ones, so he could just get lost.

'Trent,' he said, offering his hand. 'Enjoying the night?'

'The free food,' I said, refusing to shake his hand, instead picking up another falafel from the table and shoving it in my mouth. *Please go away.*

He leaned over to me, and, slightly touching his hand on my lower back, whispered, 'Little known fact but the bruschetta here is out of this world. They do something sinful to true Italians and put avocado on it and then tomato, garlic and buffalo mozzarella. To die for.'

'Noted,' I said, stepping away from his hand, leaning over to grab three small toasted sourdough bruschettas. I piled them into my mouth at the same time, hoping this would disgust him. Unfortunately, it didn't. He stood there staring at me in awe, or almost, it seemed, admiration.

'You're with Maker,' he said, still sounding full of awe.

'Who are you here with?' I said, looking for his name tag. 'Let me guess, a bunch of Botoxed women and over-compensating men. Possibly also Botoxed.'

He let out a laugh. 'Wow, you hold nothing back, do you?'

I responded by grabbing another bruschetta and shoving it in my mouth.

Trent continued. 'I'm here with the usual gang. We're a small boutique PR firm. Hunters. Have you heard of it? We get the entrails of the deals you guys at Maker decline. Then Cromwells decline it. Then Red Hot. Then maybe it reaches us.' He laughed. 'So basically, I'm trying to get the world excited about new local medical equipment currently. They're not.'

That made me smile a little, even though I tried not to. Which unfortunately seemed to encourage him to keep talking.

'What are you working on?' he asked casually, leaning over to get another bruschetta. 'Told you these were genius.'

'It's top secret.' I shoved another falafel in my mouth so I didn't have to say any more.

'Who am I going to tell? The large gathering of orthopaedic surgeons I meet each Monday?'

I shrugged. 'I'm sworn to secrecy.' I made a pretend blood oath pact. And he laughed.

'Oh, to be involved in something that has a bit of secrecy about it. That's the dream. Can I get you another Champagne? Wine? Whisky?'

Whisky. I thought about the last time I'd had whisky. Nick. Ugh. He flew into my thoughts before I could even stop myself. Just like that a surge of sadness filled my stomach. I needed not to think about him at all. I looked down; my glass was half empty. 'Sure, why not? Champagne.'

Trent nodded the waiter over and handed me a Champagne. 'For the beautiful lady.'

I laughed bitterly. 'Beautiful? Is that your standard pick-up line? Think you can do better than that. I mean, you are in PR.'

'OK,' he said thoughtfully, mulling it over for a few seconds. 'How about this? Emma of the Maker Clan. Wearer of tight black dresses. Holder of amazing green eyes. Sporting a Kim Kardashian booty – not that I'm looking; I'm a gentleman. OK, I looked a bit.' He smiled sheepishly. 'Eater of Falafels. Taster of Bruschetta. Someone I'd like to meet again.'

'Well, now we know one thing. You're an absolute *Game of Thrones* geek,' I said, taking a sip of Champagne. His joking was having a softening effect on me, or was that the Panadeine Forte kicking up a notch?

'How about we take a walk out into the gardens here? They're quite magical. No dragons, I'm afraid.' He offered up his arm. 'Then I promise we can come back for food replenishments.'

I thought about Nick again, and gave the room a quick glance, but he still wasn't there. Not that I needed him to see that I was fine. Although, it couldn't have hurt to see me on the arm of some other gorgeous man.

'OK, then.' But I didn't take his arm, instead I strode out in front, through the large ballroom and out into the gardens. Trent wasn't lying; it was magical. A landscaped garden with a fountain in the middle led into a large hedge maze that made me feel I was lost in a labyrinth. Tiny fairy lights dotted the sky, strung like pearls, the only light besides the almost-full moon.

'I didn't know anything like this existed in the city,' I said, running my fingers along the perfectly cut tree walls, thinking this could be a good place to hide from the people at the mixer, or from my life.

'Haven't been to one of these functions before?'

'No, I'm new back in the city and new to these PR functions,' I said distractedly, still staring around at the hedge, which was almost as tall as my head. I could just see over it, and manage to get my way in and out – should I ever need to become lost, this could be great place.

'Well, what you need to know is this – no one eats, so feel free to tuck up the food in napkins and take them home with you. Everyone drinks. Call everyone darling because no one can remember names, and the name tags are useless because everyone is too sloshed to read, so no one wears them.'

I looked down at mine. 'No one, huh?'

'Well, except newbies.' Trent led the way out of the maze and stopped at a large plant that had been shaped into a tall skyscraper. 'Oh, and you can't forget the phallic trees. They're everywhere, just to remind you it's a man's world,' he teased.

'Great, another chauvinist.' I rolled my eyes. 'Just what the world needs. How refreshing.'

'I'm open to be proven wrong,' he said cockily.

I couldn't believe how he was acting like a grade A idiot, but I had a point to prove now, on behalf of my entire gender. And after Nick, I was ready for a battle. 'I'll have you know I'm heading up my own project. And it's not about medical bits and pieces.'

'Ouch,' he joked, grabbing his heart. 'She hits where it hurts.'

'You're an idiot. And that was an idiot statement and you know it,' I pointed out.

'Possibly true.' He smiled genuinely. 'But how did you go from travelling in London to coming back here and heading up a project?'

I stopped in my tracks. 'How did you know I lived in London?' Had he done research on me?

'Oh, an old friend told me. Nick. You know him? He mentioned that you guys now worked together and dropped in that you used to live in London, because I lived in Clapham for a few years. He also told me about your ...' his fingers air quoted '... top-secret event.'

Just hearing Nick's name made me feel like throwing up. I wasn't sure why Nick had told him about the hush-hush event, when he'd sworn me to secrecy, from even telling Phil. But then Nick was turning out to be a complete liar about *every-thing*. I managed to spit out, 'You're friends with Nick?'

He nodded. 'I am. We go back years,' he said flippantly. 'And by the way, I love the event theme.'

I narrowed my eyes. 'You love it?'

'I do. But I wanted to hear a female take on it. Rather than Nick's. He's always going on about how it feels a little off track and how it could be improved.'

'What?' I stopped walking and stared at Trent in disbelief. 'Nick doesn't like what I'm doing?' I was shocked. What could you even say to something like that?

'I think he said he would have done it differently.' Trent shrugged apologetically.

I felt extremely bothered by that comment, and could feel

the anger inside me building. What *exactly* had Nick been saying?

'Don't worry.' He leaned down and whispered into my ear. 'I know you are more than capable, no matter what he says, and I'm sure you're doing a brilliant job. Now, should we head inside to grab another bruschetta?'

I nodded, because I couldn't risk just exploding here in the middle of the mixer, could I? It wasn't Trent's fault that Nick was saying these things. No, it was Nick that needed to be yelled at, not poor, awkward Trent. Who the hell did Nick think he was? Sleeping with me and multiple other women was one thing, but telling people about the event? And that I was terrible at my job? At the job I'd dedicated my entire life to recently, running about doing everything for everybody.

Inside, Trent got me another Champagne, which I took gratefully. I could feel the lightness of Champagne bubbles swirl around my head. It felt nice to not be thinking so much, especially round and round in circles, as I had all day. He joked that he was happy just to be at the PR function and was lucky he'd even been invited this time. 'What about you put your number in my phone? That way when your event gets too much, or you need to blow off any steam, you can call me.'

'That sounds like a booty call,' I said suspiciously.

'Does it? Oh, boy, I need to work on my game, then! I just meant we can go for coffee, chat – it's good to know someone in the business you can be open with.'

He handed me his phone and I was about to put in my

number when Trent stepped backwards and into the waiter with a full tray of Champagne. 'Idiot!' Trent exclaimed, looking down at his wet shirt. 'This is Prada!' The red-faced waiter started trying to mop up the shirt, but Trent shook him off and stalked off to the bathroom.

Left with his phone, I entered my number and wrote Emma, then changed it to Em, then back to Emma and, as an afterthought, added Maker. While I was calling my phone number so I could save his details, a message popped up on his screen:

Call now. Belview spillage is worse than first thought.

A few seconds later a quick call came through, then another text.

SOS, stop anyone finding out.

As Trent was walking back a third text came through, which read:

CALL NOW.

I didn't want him to think I'd been snooping so I handed back the phone as someone was calling again and said, 'My number's in there and I called my number from yours.'

'So now we're official.' He laughed. 'What a night. Lovely spending time with you. I have to go sort out this wet shirt.' He was wearing his jacket buttoned up and his white shirt was wet and folded in his hand. 'Until next time.' He waved and disappeared out of the front door.

I took out my phone and texted Honey, because it was still my job to babysit Nick's extra-young mistress (God, what was my life?). *Where are you?*

She wrote back, *Silly, I'm in the VIP section of this ultra boring PR mixer!* Of course, except there wasn't a VIP section at a PR mixer, because all PR people assumed they *were* the VIPs of their industry. Then I saw a small roped-off area in the corner, and, behind the rope, Honey's hair. Her delicate hands were moving about as if she was animatedly chatting about something, pausing only to lift a glass of Champagne. I could see the leg of a perfectly creased black trouser next to her. Was it him? From the looks of it, it was. My stomach sank. I didn't want to look and see if she was with Nick; I bet she was. I didn't want to see him. I wasn't ready – would I ever be?

Feeling exhausted, I took this as the perfect moment to leave. On the way home, in the back of an Uber, I couldn't shake off the night. Firstly, PR mixers were an entire waste of time. Secondly, Honey was with Nick and maybe he'd been with her all day. Or maybe he'd been with Chloe. Either way, he'd clearly not thought about contacting me. How about a sorry? How about something? God – how did I keep choosing men so badly? And thirdly, Nick thought I wasn't doing my job well at all. And instead of telling me, he'd told Trent. I wondered if they laughed about it, laughed about me.

I felt a rush of frustration through my body. I'd been busting my butt, working longer hours than most people, living, sleeping and eating work. I hadn't even had time to do anything else and they paid me a pittance in return. My stomach churned and my face flamed red with anger. I was seething.

I wanted to call Nick and give him a piece of my mind. I wanted to yell every swear word under the sun at him. But he'd probably see it was me calling and not even answer. Coward, I thought bitterly. Either that, or he'd fire me. And despite disliking my job, I still needed it. Which made me feel even more like a prisoner.

Suddenly the last thing I wanted was to go home alone and sit in my studio apartment. I asked the Uber driver to stop at the next pub on the corner, but it was closed. And the next one too. Locked and dark inside.

I gave up and went home, opened my bottle of Lagavulin and poured a double nip. Sitting on the couch, I suddenly felt really alone. I had tried so hard to make things work, to make them right. But things just kept on going wrong. I needed to talk to someone who would understand. I couldn't help myself – I opened my phone and dialled Trent.

'Yes.' He sounded annoyed.

'Hey, it's Emma. From tonight.'

'Oh, Emma. Hi.' His voice immediately shifted gears. 'What's wrong? You OK?'

'Actually no.' I sniffed a bit. 'I've had a rotten night, and I can't stop thinking about what Nick said.'

'What Nick said?' Trent sounded distant.

'That he would have managed the project differently.'

'Oh, yeah. It's a shame when a manager doesn't see talent

standing right in front of him. I think he mentioned he wasn't sure if you were up to the task.'

I couldn't keep it in any longer. 'I'd like to see what Nick would have done. When you have a theme like Macabre Nights, what else are you going to do? I mean, mixing African kids and orphanages with a dance of the dead murderous theme – who chooses that idea? God only knows. Turning it into a magical death celebration night, well, at least that gives it a hint of something glamorous. The executives thought it was quite ingenious, so God knows what Nick would have done.'

'Could spell PR nightmare really,' Trent said soothingly. 'I think you've done so well, Emma. Really.'

'You think so?'

'I really do.'

'Thank you.' I sniffed. 'It was good chatting to you, Trent.'

After speaking with him I felt so much better. He was right: it was good to have friends in the industry. People who I could trust. And who needed Nick?

Chapter 25

'Oh, my God,' Phil said, almost dropping his phone.

'What?' I looked up from my email and mega-take-away cup of coffee, which wasn't doing anything to make me feel awake this morning. I'd hardly slept a wink last night; my brain had been teeming with everything that had happened over the last forty-eight hours. Sleeping with Nick. Being alone in his apartment. The text messages. And to top that off, now I was bad at my job. Urgh. What a nightmare.

I couldn't even be bothered getting dressed up for work or being Professional Emma. I had barely a speck of make-up on, my hair was pulled back into a ponytail, and I was wearing a blue dress that I hadn't washed (again), and I didn't care. At all. I'd even refused to put on my heels, opting instead for small white ballet flats that were a little shabby on the end, with a streak of dirt. And I kind of liked it. It was my way of rebelling against the fashion-obsessed here at Faker.

I wasn't ready to see Nick at all. When I'd woken up this morning and looked at my phone, he'd left me three voicemails, and two texts. But it was too little, too late.

In an angry rush I'd deleted them all. Ten minutes later, in a moment of weakness, I'd wondered what they'd said, but then I'd replayed the image of me walking around his apartment alone, and that had made me angry all over again. And I'd realised I didn't care what he wanted to say; I didn't want to hear it.

Thank goodness, when I'd arrived at work, later than usual at just before 9 a.m., he was in his office and his door was closed. Sitting at my desk, though, I felt miserable, and horrible, and I was thinking of ways to feign sickness again and go home. The only place I wanted to be was my bed. Could I pretend I had tonsillitis? Maybe measles? Something that was awfully contagious and would make Glenn want to send me home, rather than telling me to just take a Tylenol. I was wondering how hard it was to feign a case of necrotising fasciitis, and was about to search for symptoms, but Phil was getting in the way, flapping his arms up and down like a cockatoo over something.

'Holy shit. Have you seen this? Holy *shit*.'

I heard Nick wrench his door open. 'We have a problem.' He was staring directly at me.

Yes, we do, I thought. *You're a wanker. But it's not 'our' problem, that's very much yours.*

'I'm a little busy,' I said, looking at my computer, scrolling through the latest media alerts.

'Emma, we need to talk in my office.' Nick's face was white.

Shut up, Daniel Cleaver, I thought. *What do you have to be angry about? I'm the one who gets that right.*

'Emma, honey, it's ... it's bad. Really bad,' Phil whispered and continued his weird flapping.

I thought about grabbing my bag and leaving. I considered

ignoring Nick, but some of the other employees from other teams had heard his tone and were looking at me. I didn't want to cause a scene, so I stood, and walked into his office, wondering what the hell he was worked up about.

'I don't really want to talk to you,' I said bluntly, sitting on the couch and not looking at him. 'About anything. Especially *personal.*' I could feel my voice was shaking and I tried to gain control, but being around him still made me feel strange – part of me still liked him, my body wanted him, the other part wanted to never see him for as long as I lived.

'We can talk about personal things later,' Nick said, looking slightly distressed.

Fat chance, I thought. *That won't be happening.*

'Have you seen this?' He swivelled his screen around to show me the *Mail News*. 'Front page news.'

PR Firm Maker Makes Fun of Children Being Murdered by Hosting a Star-Filled Death Night.

I gasped. Then he flicked to *The SydneySider*, which said, *Maker Is the Real Faker: Lead PR Rep Has Zero Experience.*

I felt sick; waves of nausea were permeating my entire body. I stammered, 'I- I don't understand.'

'The theme was top secret. So top secret not even our execs knew about it. How the hell did it get out, Emma?' Nick started pacing up and down his office.

My mind was racing. 'I don't know ...' I faltered. I could feel myself getting weak, as if I was about to faint. Or throw up. Or both.

Nick ran a hand through his hair. 'Think, Emma. Did you let any proprietary information slip?'

I shook my head.

'No one had access to your phone?'

'No one,' I promised.

'Did you tell anyone, speak to anyone?' He had his fingers pressed against his temples as if a migraine was coming.

The smell of Nick's breakfast on his desk – egg and tomato roll drizzled with garlic sauce – started to smell rancid and off, as if it had been sitting out in the sun for days. I gulped down the bile I felt rising.

'Not anyone that didn't already know. Just you and Donna and your friend Trent.'

'Trent?'

'From Hunters PR – you know, he looks after medical supplies.'

Nick looked confused. 'I don't know anyone called Trent.'

'You don't?' I asked in a small voice. 'He said he was your friend.'

'Oh, and because he said that you believed him? Jesus, Emma.'

My stomach dropped and my mind was a blur trying to work out why Trent had said they were friends, and remember exactly what I had said to him on the phone.

Nick stopped pacing and stared at me. 'Where did you meet this guy?'

I bit my lip. 'He was at the PR function.'

'Great, so you spilled our secrets to someone in our industry, someone who's a *competitor*.' He shook his head in disbelief. 'Wait, not the blond guy you were talking to at the food table?'

'You saw us?' So Nick *had* been there. With Honey. I should have known.

'Yes,' he snapped. He typed quickly into his computer and swivelled the screen around again. 'That him?'

I looked up into the piercing green eyes of Trent, in a smart suit, a headshot. The title read Lachlan Groves to Inherit the Hive PR Firm and Media Empire.

'Lachlan Groves, son of the CEO of Hive. Nice work, Emma.'

My mouth fell open. I felt a rush of panic, and then shock, and shame. 'God, I didn't know. I'm so sorry.' I looked up at Nick, who was refusing to look at me. 'So sorry.'

'I don't need to be the one to tell you this is bad, Emma. This is worse than bad.' He shook his head. 'I'm really struggling to understand ...' He paused. 'I don't want to ask this question, but I have to. I need to,' he said pointedly, 'as your *boss*.'

I braced myself.

'Is what they say true? Have you ever actually worked in PR, before Maker? If I called through to the companies on your CV, what would they say?'

A look of dread showed on my face. And I knew the timing couldn't be worse, but I had to tell Nick. *Everything.*

I felt as if I was shaking, about to faint. I could feel my head pounding. Sweat dripping down my back. When I started talking, the voice that came out was squeaky, and didn't sound at all like me. 'You know, I was travelling for a while, around the world. And when I was in the UK, it was hard to get a job, any job.' I licked my lips. 'So I took the only thing I could get.'

'A job in PR.' Nick nodded.

'Actually ...' I squeezed my eyes shut '... I worked in a Mexican restaurant.'

'In PR? How did that work?'

'No, as a waitress. I took orders and ...' I saw the look on his face.

'And before that?' He looked worried.

'Before that I worked for a PR company in London.'

'Oh,' he sighed with relief. 'As a PR executive?'

I shook my head.

'This isn't even funny, Emma,' he warned, looking as if he expected me to suddenly yell, *Surprise, it's a joke!*

'I uh ... received press releases, and did a bit of filing, and made teas, and set up meeting rooms.' I cringed as I heard what I was saying aloud. I knew it didn't sound good.

He made a face. 'So, you have no idea what you're doing. God. I should have known.' He slid a hand through his hair.

I looked at him nervously, my head still reeling from what had happened. 'I mean, I did a PR course and I passed with the top mark. And I've been making sure I'm doing everything right, by uh, um using Google to double check things, and for best in practice approaches.'

His face looked stormy. 'Thank you, Emma, for that concise How to Be a Liar speech.'

That was rich coming from him. I snorted. 'Ha! If we're talking about liars, I think this conversation goes both ways, don't you, Nick?'

He looked at me, confused, before saying, 'Emma, you *lied* on your *CV*. And the worst thing is, now you've made me complicit in your lie. And Phil. And Glenn. And everyone who works here at Maker. We're front page news, Emma. Everywhere.'

I swallowed heavily as the weight of what had happened sank in. He was right: it was worse than I thought.

Nick took a breath and stepped away, sitting back down in his chair. I could tell he was angry, because a vein was throbbing in his neck. 'I can't take you off the project now, this far in, but how is that going to look to everyone here? Someone working on a lead PR project, when they've never done one day's work of PR in their life. Someone who lies about everything.'

'Everything?' I said hotly, because that was a bit much coming from someone who had been banging a thousand women around town.

'A lot of things,' Nick said, trying to hold back, but I could sense he wanted to let loose. As if he couldn't hold it in any longer, he suddenly said, 'Apparently you're a free spirit. Meant to be in Alaska. A true traveller. But look who's working at Maker. In a nine to five job, dressed like every other corporate ladder-climbing person. For all I know, everything out of your mouth is a lie. You probably lied the entire time we were together in Fiji for all I know.'

'I can explain.' My mind was reeling across all the lies I had told to keep my new life afloat. Lies to Nick. To Maker. To the press. About Honey. About everything. It was all one big gigantic lie, and I wanted then to just come clean, about it all. That was the only way it felt I could cleanse myself from this ... *mess.*

'No need.' He stood as if to say the meeting was over and I felt a flash of irritation run through me. Why *did* I have to explain myself to Nick? About Fiji and being a free spirit. I'd known him for one night. On a holiday somewhere. On an island, and God knows what happens on islands should stay on islands. And besides, he was the one who was sleeping with everyone and keeping that a big secret.

I stood and said, with a touch of frustration in my voice, 'I was figuring out who I was, Nick. Or aren't people allowed to do that?' I felt annoyed that this was even a topic of discussion. It felt personal, not about work. 'Besides, I didn't realise I had to give you an entire thesis on my life including my likes and dislikes before we kissed,' I said through clenched teeth.

'Slept together,' Nick corrected.

'Or slept with multiple people!' I said hotly and watched Nick's eyebrows rise almost to the roof. 'But if you're so keen for an entire list of my likes and dislikes, here we go.'

I put my hands up, ticking off things. 'Likes: dogs, eating pasta with cheese, flat shoes, travelling.' I looked pointedly at him. 'Dislikes: cheating, arrogant high-powered suits, people who are judgemental, people who go hot and cold and can't just choose a lane and stick with it, people who leave me to look after Honey whilst they go gallivanting around town, and everything about Daniel Cleaver!'

He leaned over his desk. 'Well, here's mine. Dislikes: People who lie. All liars. People who pretend to be free spirits but are really corporate queens.'

'I'll have you know I am not a corporate *queen*.' My voice

was getting louder and my body was shaking. 'I am a corporate ...' I searched frantically for a word before landing on one that was just as terrible '... princess!'

We were almost nose to nose, close enough I could see the flash of something in his eyes. His smooth lips, his perfect teeth.

Suddenly someone knocked on the door. 'Nick?' It was Glenn and he sounded furious. My stomach dropped. He knew.

'Yes, mate, just on a VIP call. I'll come up there in a second,' Nick said quickly.

'Make it quick. I'm fucking fuming.' And we heard his footsteps storm away, even on the carpet.

'You can go now,' Nick said without looking at me.

I realised I'd just made everything a lot worse, by yelling at Nick.

'I feel like you're going to fire me,' I said in a small voice, feeling as though my entire life was falling down around me.

'Good, then you won't be surprised if maybe I do.'

At his desk, Phil looked horrified.

'Did you hear that?' I whispered to him.

He shook his head. 'Just yelling.'

I nodded, feeling dizzy and light-headed. I sat at my desk.

'Did you spill about our event?' Phil asked. 'To our competitors?'

'I didn't mean to.' I felt a pang of deep shame and guilt.

He looked shocked.

'What do I do?' I fidgeted on my chair. 'I'll do anything.'

'Yes.' He stared at me as if we'd never been friends. 'You will. Because if you don't, Emma, you'll be going down with this ship. You'll never work in PR again. You'll never work in Sydney again.'

Would that be so bad? I thought. Truthfully, it didn't matter if my career was over; maybe it was a Godsend, maybe it was a message from the Gods of Jobs or Future Lives, trying to get me back on track. But it did matter if I took Maker down with me. That wasn't fair to all these other people. That could *not* happen.

At my desk I tried to keep breathing deeply. But my head was spinning. My life was a mess. Nick. Honey. Chloe. Sex. And now Trent or Lachlan, or whatever his name was. God. What could I do? How could you spin this around? I had spun stories before – my own CV; that time in the Mexican dive bar when a group of people had got food poisoning and I had been coerced by staff to make it go away, and had convinced most of the patrons they had been breathing in the air conditioning on the local bus, and it was known for being a perfect carrier of viruses. And that had worked, kind of. But this was front page news. Flashed across everything. It needed massive damage control.

I ran a search on our database for crisis plans, praying there was one. Luckily, I found one from another team from a year ago, but it had nothing in there about competitors luring information from you and then selling it to the papers.

My phone was flashing with voicemails from our media and corporate affairs departments and others I assumed were the media. I didn't know what to say. I'd single-handedly screwed up not just my project, but the entire company's reputation. I *had* to fix this. My mind was in overdrive. How had Trent/Lachlan found out about me? He must have done some digging. He must have sensed when he spoke about London how I froze for a second; he went looking for lies, and he found them. That was exactly it. And that's what I needed to do too.

Taking a deep breath, I remembered something from last night that could possibly help. It was a hunch, and a last-ditch effort. I tried to remember what Lachlan's phone message had said. Belrose? No, Belview. I typed it in. And after doing a bit of Internet research, I knew I was onto something.

Then I picked up the phone and made a call. Not to save my career – I knew that was well and truly over – but to save Maker.

'Phones down for this, please,' Nick said seriously, later that day during a hastily arranged Friday afternoon staff meeting.

Everyone exchanged looks and put their phones on the boardroom table. We were all stuffed in there, about fifty of us, from Media, Corporate Affairs, Creatives, Marketing and Events and PR.

'We have an issue. A serious one. With Macabre,' Nick began. 'The aftermath is as bad as you've heard and seen splashed over the pages. I want to make one thing clear: we will not go down, and we will fight this thing. We have crisis plans and emergency plans but they don't cover exactly what's happened.

'What we do have is one possible save. Emma.'

Everyone turned to look at me. I felt my face flame red. I looked around the room and cleared my throat. 'Yes, I've written another press release to refocus the headlines. I've called it: *Death Is Happening – Why Aren't We Doing Anything?* It focuses on the fact that premature death is happening across the countries of Africa, particularly children, and that we are bringing this to people's minds, rather than covering it up. We've got a few quotes, and Honey has agreed to do another press conference with IAH about, um, what is really happening in Africa.'

People looked at each other as if they weren't buying it. I took a breath and continued.

'The thing about Maker is we're different from Hive. We don't cover things up at Maker, like Hive did in their most recent campaign on Belview Health.'

Some people looked confused. Others shared glances that said 'what-is-this-girl-on-about?' I cleared my throat again. 'Hive publicised how they were helping the community with new medical supplies, and they hid the fact that Belview had been dumping medical waste illegally in the Hawkesbury river.'

'How do you know this?' Kara, the marketing advisor, asked suspiciously.

'I spent some time with Lachlan Groves.'

A collective gasp went around the table. 'Lachlan Groves from Hive?'

I nodded and looked at my lap. People were staring at me as if I'd just confessed to murdering their mother.

'So you're the one who spilled it in the first place?' That was Sadie.

Nick stepped in. 'You'll see the breaking story about Hive come out in the next few hours. We've had Legal look over this and they're guiding us through the next steps. Obviously, this opens up the playing field for Hive to retaliate, so I want you all to be on your game and keep things confidential.'

Nick looked back at me. 'But we are certain the headlines will be focused on Hive from now on, and not on Maker.'

Everyone stared at me. 'I'm sorry,' I said quickly but no one said, 'That's all right,' or, 'It's OK.' They just picked up their phones and left the meeting room. I felt like a pariah. Even Phil couldn't look at me, and when I walked out of the meeting, I saw he was having a coffee with Sadie in the kitchen. And that pretty much told me where I was currently sitting in the Most-Hated pile.

I left work early that afternoon, just after the meeting ended at three. I couldn't sit there and feel everyone's eyes on me as if I was some massive traitor. I'd done what I could do to try and fix this, but it was possible no one would ever forgive me.

On the train, I tried not to cry. But I felt the tears burn at the edges of my eyes, and when I realised I'd stuffed up so badly, the barrier broke, and I started crying about *everything*. About the life I'd created that I really disliked. About Nick sleeping with me, and Chloe and Honey. About my small flat. About trying to settle down. About being a general fuck-up, because it was true, I was. I didn't want what everyone else wanted – I didn't want that life at all. And I couldn't even pretend to make it work. What was wrong with me?

Thankfully I got off at the next stop, because I thought people were actually considering calling the guard. I wished they had. Then maybe they'd have taken me off in a cell for a while, where no one could find me, and I could have a sleep and pretend this wasn't my life.

I got home and curled up in bed. From where I was lying, I could see The Plan hanging on my wall, as if it were mocking me. Well, I thought, that entire thing was useless. When I couldn't take it any more, I jumped off the bed, grabbed the piece of paper and the silly vision board I'd painstakingly made, and, with a sudden force, I threw them on the floor. God, that felt good.

I picked it up and threw it again, so the board cracked. The third time I picked it up, I ripped up the stupid images of couples I'd stuck on there with hope. Of girls that were slim in designer corporate fashion. Of perfect houses. And perfect people. It was all so silly. How did I ever think I wanted this?

I trudged outside in my sweatpants with the ripped-up images and half-broken vision board and stuffed them in the garbage bin.

When I let myself back into my apartment, I saw my phone vibrating on the bedside table. I looked at the number, which said Unknown, and I decided to leave it. But then a bunch of messages came in from Phil.

Have you seen it? Check this out now. He'd sent a link.

I opened it up. My media contact had come through. Breaking news was in and it wasn't good for Lachlan. Hive and Belview were all over the news. The headlines read: *Toxic*

Outburst and Belview's Blunder – Hive Has Burst. I breathed
a sigh of relief.

My phone started vibrating, again an unknown number,
this time I answered.

'Emma. What the fuck?'

'Oh, hello, Trent,' I said chirpily. 'Or is that Lachlan? It's so
hard to keep up these days.'

'What have you done, you little bitch?' he snarled down
the phone.

'Now, now, now,' I said. 'I thought PR people were a group,
a team, that got together to blow off steam, help in any way.
I was helping you guys out, with your number one corporate
strategy. I believe that's transparency?'

'You've made yourself a solid enemy, Emma.'

'Well, that's fine, Lachlan, because I don't work in PR any
more. Now be careful when you walk down the street, especially if you're wearing Prada!' I laughed then hung up the
phone. For the first time in a long time, I felt as though I
could breathe.

When I woke up on Saturday morning, it took me a while
to remember what had happened. Then the last few days
quickly flashed through my mind. I thought about Lachlan
and laughed. Then I thought about Chloe and Honey, and
me wandering around Nick's apartment wearing his stupid
shirt, and that made me angry. But then I thought about Nick
and what he'd said about me being a liar, because it was kind
of true, and I suddenly felt really empty and sad.

I got up and made toast and coffee, thinking I just needed

some food, since I'd forgotten to eat dinner the night before. But it didn't work; my mind was stuck on repeat – Lachlan, then Nick, then Honey – going over and over the same things.

The same question replayed in my mind – *what am I going to do now?*

My career was over. I had no savings and wouldn't be able to afford my rent. I'd lose my flat. I'd have to move back home with Mum and Dad. I'd be thirty-four, no, thirty-five, in a few weeks, unemployed and living with my parents. And that was even worse than Bridget Jones.

Even though it felt as if my entire life was imploding, I still couldn't bring myself to call Tansy or Maggie or Mum and tell them what had happened. They'd be so disappointed that I just couldn't make it work. And I couldn't handle disappointing anyone any more than I already had.

Suddenly the world felt really, really big. But I couldn't spend the rest of the day in my small unit, I'd go crazy. So out of sheer desperation I took a long bus and train ride over the bridge, and found myself heading to the aqua centre, to hang out with my elderly petal-capped friends – by *choice*.

I slid into the pool next to Betty and Lena, and did the eggbeater, and the noodle, and the whirlpool sprint. After the class, Betty waved and called me over, 'Emma! Where has my little petal been these past few months? We've missed you.'

And because she was so lovely and kind, and I was feeling rather sad, I simply burst into tears.

As she towelled off and put on her long floral dress in the change room, she said, 'Right, let's get a tea and you can tell me everything.'

Over tea, I told her the whole story, including Nick, Fiji, the naked shower, and then the Maker disaster.

'You've been busy.' She took a sip of her Earl Grey tea, then laughed.

'Yes.' I nodded, sniffling. 'It feels like everything that I had is slipping away – my job, my flat. What do I have? Tansy has her husband and three beautiful children. Maggie has her lovely family. Amy is getting married. And Nick has Chloe *and* Honey, because one is clearly not enough.'

'And what about you?'

I looked up at her. 'What about me?'

'Well, those things you mentioned are all other people. Forget about what they have. What do you want?'

'A country cottage. Chickens,' I said, blowing my snotty nose.

She laughed again, and put her wrinkled hand over mine; it felt warm and nice, like a giant hug. 'This doesn't look much like either of those things.' She looked outside the café window to the busy highway.

I shook my head. 'It doesn't.'

'Then why are you here?' she asked softly.

As if on autopilot, I tilted my head up to tell her about The Plan. It had been my go-to spiel for so long, the three steps to being happy, before I had realised none of those steps had made me happy at all. Deep down, perhaps I'd always known I didn't want to be here, trying to settle down. 'I don't know. And I keep getting things wrong.'

She patted my hand. 'Well, at least you're not a well-behaved woman.'

'But I can be!' Thinking she meant I was horrible for the things I'd got up to … Maybe she was right, maybe I wasn't very nice at all.

She tutted. 'You shouldn't want to be. A well-behaved woman ends up married to someone she doesn't like, having kids before she's ready, passing her days in an office doing a job she may not like. She buys stocks because that's a good decision. She gets low-fat yoghurt because she's worried about her hips. She stares at herself in the mirror and prays for thinner thighs. A well-behaved woman has a list of "to-do's" and "should-do's" that are longer than any list should be. But for what?'

I sat in silence.

'Who is she trying to please?' Betty took a large bite of carrot cake, before answering her own question. 'Everyone but herself.'

'Are you a well-behaved woman?' I asked, sniffling into my tissue.

Betty snorted. 'No. Never. My parents wanted me to be a secretary. And I did for a year. It was soul destroying. They all wanted me to marry Lance, a nice wholesome farmer that lived down the road. It could have been so easy to have fallen into that life.'

'But?' I prompted. 'What happened?'

'I got on the next ship leaving Sydney and I went to America. Over there, I went to art school. I travelled along the west coast of California with a group of, I suppose you could call them hippies. I went to Woodstock.'

'You went to Woodstock?' My mouth hung open.

She smiled proudly. 'I did. I met Ray there. We moved to a small house in upstate New York. I painted during the day. We drank whisky at night and talked about life. We had sex on the rug, sex on the grass outside, we even got caught by the postman once!' She laughed loudly.

'Then I left Ray and New York five years later, and went to London. I painted there. And went to musicals and theatre and operas. I travelled to Paris. I was like you, Emma, exploring. I lived on a farm in France, and then the south coast down by the sea.' She nodded. 'I had an affair with a Frenchman, and it was intoxicating. We spent days in bed, he wrote poetry and read it out loud to me.' She laughed again.

'I was bolder and more adventurous over in Europe,' I admitted. 'I danced on a tabletop once. OK, more than once.'

Betty laughed and banged the table with both arthritic, soft-papered hands. 'Damn right you did!'

I took a sip of my tea. The more I thought about it, the more I realised there were two types of people in this world. Some people were trees, they liked to put down roots, to stay. Tansy. Maggie. Murray was the biggest, oldest oak tree of them all. Never moving – and that made him completely happy. Trees were very good at having long-term permanent jobs and buying houses and having mortgages.

And it turned out some other people were birds, that liked to flit about, to roost for a while, then move, to keep changing with the seasons. They were flexible and adaptable and seekers of the *out there* (wherever that was). Like *me*.

Trees often thought birds should grow up to be a tree, when they matured, because being a bird was confused with being immature. Surely, the trees collectively thought, a bird will some day want what a tree has. But it wasn't true! Would you ever look out of the window and hope that one day that beautiful dove or mischievous magpie would turn into a birch tree? Um, no.

Neither was wrong, or right, they were just *different*.

I roosted with Murray for a while – but in the end it wasn't for me. I wanted to move, and he never did. What I really needed was another bird to fly around with.

Nick had been a bird too, a very terrible bird (maybe a vulture?) but a bird all the same.

I was a bird. A free-flying, move-when-the-seasons-change, non-well-behaved bird.

'I'm a *bird*!' I said to Betty, explaining my theory.

'Yes! And I'm a bird too!' She laughed. 'I'm planning a trip to the Dolomites next year, because all these tree people around us ...' she waved her hand around '... can stifle a bird after a while.'

'I don't want to be a well-behaved woman,' I admitted. 'And I'm really rather bad at it. I turn up to work with chips in my hair. I drink too much on dates. I have showers with naked men I don't know. I slept with my boss.'

'Amen!' she said. 'That's right. Have stories, not chores. Have joy, not "must-do's". Your worth isn't based on matching up to anyone else's expectations or approval. And if people don't like what you're doing, they're not your people.'

She took another bite of cake.

'So what do I do now?' I asked her. 'Get a new job? Move? I don't know.'

'Ah, my girl, you don't need a house or a job to complete you. You just need you.'

'I just need me.' I said letting her words sink in. 'I. Just. Need. Me.' I swallowed the thought of what that meant.

She looked at me. 'Get really quiet, and ask yourself: what do you want?'

I looked at her and laughed. 'Is it really that simple?'

'Yes. It is.'

'Well, I think I've always known that. Deep down.' I thought about travelling, about the country cottage, about being in the wild. Which was everything opposite to settling down in an office, and wearing white silk shirts and nude high heels. 'I want to go to Alaska. And live in a cottage. With chickens.'

Betty laughed. 'Did you say Alaska?'

I nodded. 'Does it sound silly?'

'Not at all. I'm laughing because this is perfect. In fact, I have a proposition for you.'

I sat up in my chair. 'I'm listening.'

'My sister Ruth lives over there. She's also not a well-behaved woman and is full of great stories of travelling around India and Africa. But she's getting on. She's two years older than me. And she needs some help around the house, the garden. You'd be paid, of course. And you'll get free accommodation, in a small cottage on the property – it's lovely really. She did it up when she first moved there twenty years ago with a fireplace and two rooms, and a little breakfast nook that looks over the gardens. She has an apple orchard that needs picking and tending. And a large veggie garden, herbs too. Chickens. She sometimes fosters wolves that need rehabilitation, and dogs. She's a bit dog mad. But really, she's too old to do every-thing herself. And she's been trying to find someone, a good fit, for ages, but she can't. You'd be doing me and her a favour if you considered it. But there's a lot of time too, for you to get another part-time job if you want extra money ...'

'Or paint,' I said breathlessly, feeling as if my entire dream had just landed with a '*plonk!*' in my lap.

'Yes! What a wonderful idea! Paint! Do you paint?'

I looked her straight in the eye and said, 'Yes, I do. Landscapes.' It was the second time I'd confidently admitted it, and it felt rather wonderful.

Betty called the waitress over.

'Another tea, madam?'

'No, two glasses of Champagne.'

The waitress looked surprised. It was ten-thirty in the morning. I laughed as she scuttled off and we heard the POP! of a cork out the back.

When she returned with two glasses of perfect fizz, Betty held hers high. 'I want you to remember this moment, Emma. To being anything but a well-behaved woman! And to Alaska!'

We said cheers, and when I took a sip the bubbles went up my nose and made me laugh.

On the way home, my phone beeped. It was a message from Betty – that little devil even had a mobile phone.

Ruth said to say, Welcome to Alaska. P.s. bring your paints and your wellies!

Chapter 26

On Monday I wore something different to work, something from deep within the Emma closet. Harnessing the essence of not being a well-behaved woman, there were no high heels. No black dress. No cinched in waist. Today I felt like wearing gladiator sandals, a floating floral-print dress, long feather earrings (bird status!) and my fingers were covered in small silver and turquoise rings.

I didn't think about being suited and booted any more. I didn't think about being like Donna Allbright. Professional Emma had left the building. It was just me, Emma Londstown, 'EL' from now on.

Sadie gave me a weird look up and down as I entered the atrium for the Monday morning event debrief. She was in a short red dress, tight with matching red lacquered heels.

'Is this ...' she waved her hand across my outfit, looking confused '... ironic?'

'Sure, Sadie, let's go with that.'

'Hey, Woodstock.' Phil came up from behind me. 'How is time travel?'

'This is what I wear, Phil. In real life.'

'Yes, well, Faker is hardly real life, is it?' he whispered.

Strangely, it seemed people had forgiven and forgotten what happened last week. Last week I'd been a traitor, and today it was as though everything was back to normal. All it had taken was Hive being splashed on the front page of the news, and two days' reprieve. It was entirely strange that, just three days ago, these people would have come at me with a blunt pencil to the jugular if they'd had the chance.

I purposely did not look out for Nick; he could be there, or not be there, it didn't matter. I was not a well-behaved woman and, truthfully, I didn't give an actual hoo-ha where that evil bird man was. It would be suitable should I never have to look at him, see him, talk to him again.

Glenn murmured on in a monotone voice about Maker's overall quarterly results and profits and new projects and I zoned out, watching Sadie's hair instead and noticing how crisp it was from all the hairspray. Surely, she'd combust if her blonde curls got anywhere near a match?

'Folks. As you know this week is the Macabre event at The Westin, the team led by Nick Taylor and Emma Londstown. Wonderful reports all round that we have already managed to raise the IAH PR profile up fifty per cent, and the charity has already raised over one million dollars.' The division erupted in applause. 'Thanks, Emma and Nick.' Absolutely zero mention of what had happened last week. Nothing about Hive or Lachlan Groves. Or how the entire event had almost been a bust. It was as if, if they didn't talk about it, then maybe it never happened. I looked around to see if anyone else noticed how absurd this was, but everyone was just smiling and nodding and pretending to eat quiche. It was as if all was well in the PR world again.

At the end of the meeting I walked purposefully over to Glenn and said I needed to talk to him.

'Now?' He seemed in a rush, as always.

'Yes, right now.' I smiled with confidence.

In his office, he turned to me and said, 'This isn't about Macabre, is it? Another fuck-up?'

I shook my head.

'So?' Glenn raised his eyebrows as if to say, 'What are you doing in my office?'

'Everything is on track,' I assured him. 'We've got—'

'I wanted to fire you, you know,' Glenn interrupted, pausing for effect. 'In fact, I was going to.'

He sat at his desk. 'What you did, Emma, could have ended so many of our partnerships. Could have almost ended our *company*. Do you realise that?'

I nodded and kept silent.

'I was this close, this close ...' he held up his pointer finger and thumb, showing less than an inch gap '... to letting you go. But then Nick called a meeting, with the senior executives and the board, and told us you'd done some good work.' He paused. 'Some really good work.'

I lifted up my head, shocked. 'He did?'

'He did.' Glenn leaned back in his chair. 'He said you'd single-handedly delivered us a wonderful event, and that you'd done it all without any experience. Which shocked me, Emma. It really did. You lied on your CV. But Nick had a point – with no experience you did a wonderful job. Magnificent, really.'

'I did?'

'You did. Plus, you'd talked to a new catering company who are launching a new business arm, using them for Macabre and the Foragers account, and they needed PR representation. A deal which Sadie closed yesterday.'

'Oh, wow, that's amaz—'

He interrupted me again. 'So thankfully for you – you're staying. But pull another stunt like that and you're out.'

'Well, firstly I want to reassure you everything really is on track for this week. Honey's speech is ready to go. The press releases are out. The photographers lined up. Media coverage is massive off the back of the Hive, uh, situation. Catering, decorations, guests – all confirmed.'

'So, Emma, if everything is fine, why the hell are you in my office?' He leaned back in his large black chair, staring at me intently.

'Macabre is all ready to go, Glenn.' Then I took a deep breath and said, 'But I won't be there.'

Chapter 27

I called my mum and dad and shakily said, 'I'm going to Alaska!'

'On a holiday?' Mum asked.

'No, Mum, I'm going to live there.'

She paused and I could hear her breathing down the phone. 'I ... I ...'

'Mum, are you OK?'

'Oh Emma. Just imagine how lonely you'll be. Stuck in the middle of nowhere.'

Before I would have agreed with her, or argued with her because deep down I wanted to please her. I wanted her to be proud of me. But now, I knew more than anything, I needed to please myself. 'No Mum, I think you're imagining how lonely *you* would be.'

'Oh ... am I?' She paused and seemed to be thinking about that.

'Mum, I love the mountains, I've always dreamed of living in the middle of woods, with chickens, a cottage. The snow. Painting. This couldn't be more perfect for me. In fact, it feels like I place I could stay for a while.'

'*Does* it?' She sounded unsure.

'I think this is my version of settling down Mum. I know it's not what you imagined, it's not a city, a stable job, a three-bedroom house. But this is what it looks like for me.'

'But Emma, if it's in the middle of nowhere ... how will you meet someone?'

'Maybe that's just not in my future.' I shrugged. 'And that's OK, as long as I'm happy, I think that's OK.'

I could tell she didn't know how to answer that, because the next thing she said was, 'OK well good. Did you hear your cousin is going to compete in a triathlon? He's starting training for it next week. Isn't that exciting?'

After I finished talking to Mum, I texted all the girls saying, *I'm moving to Alaska!*

Calls flooded in. Tansy. Bec. Maggie. All screaming, 'WHAT?'

I said the same thing over and over, *Yes, I'm moving to Alaska. To paint. And live in a country cottage.* And even then, it hadn't really sunk in. And still didn't feel real. I'd been even more surprised when Ruth had emailed me (and even offered to call me on Skype!) with the details of the arrangement, including the pay. She must have been pretty wealthy, because my new salary was slightly more than Maker had paid, and far fewer hours. Plus, I'd never have to wear high heels again, thank the Lord. But the best thing was – all the things I was about to do, excited me, deeply excited me. I wasn't doing this for anyone, but me.

'What about *him*?' Tansy asked on the phone, after I finally told the girls everything that had happened with Nick. I expected them to be absolutely livid – as I'd been – but instead they seemed almost sad. 'Maybe you should answer his texts? Or at least read them?'

'No, absolutely not,' I declined. 'I don't want to think about him ever again.'

'But maybe he got worried because he liked you and—'

'I'm just going to stop you there,' I interrupted her. 'He called me out for being a liar, and yet he was lying the entire time.'

'Well, um,' she said tentatively, 'technically, he didn't lie. You weren't exclusively dating. He didn't actually say he wasn't seeing other people, he just omitted it. A little.'

'Tansy! I can't believe you said that. He slept with me and then left me at his house and thought that was OK! Maybe that's how he thinks he can treat people,' I mused aloud. 'Besides, whose side are you on? You sound very much like Switzerland, and I don't want that, you need to pick a side. How about you pick America? Yes, be America since that's where I'll be.'

That afternoon, Phil demanded I go for a celebratory drink. And as he asked me I could see Nick hovering in his doorway. We hadn't exchanged more than an obligatory hello that morning in the corridor, and I'd only done that since Glenn had been standing next to him.

Nick had tried texting, and leaving voicemails, and when that hadn't worked he'd tried emailing my work email, asking if we could talk, but I'd deleted them all. Which I felt very proud about.

Besides, what could he say that would change anything?

He was staying in Sydney, and I was going to Alaska, and we'd be on separate continents, with thankfully one of the coldest seas dividing us – just in case he thought about skinny dipping. Plus, I was sure Chloe or Honey could keep him warm at night. Ugh.

'No drinks, I have to get rid of all the heels and silk shirts I bought. And find all my old travel clothes!' I laughed. 'And I need to pack!'

At home, I collected bags of my clothes and gave some to Tansy and Maggie for kids' dress-ups, some to charity and some to Mum to keep, because she made me promise not to throw everything out.

'Just in case,' Mum said, 'you come home, and get your job back, at Maker. That was a very good job, Emma.'

She picked up a soft peach shirt. 'I'm sad about these lovely clothes being given away. Do you think you should keep them, just in case?'

I laughed. 'In case I decide to settle down, get a city office job and a large mortgage and pop out a few kids?'

She nodded sadly.

'Mum, I'm not coming back. At least, not to that job.'

She looked a bit crestfallen.

I smiled at her. 'You can come and visit me and see the Northern Lights! Besides, I don't need them any more. I need thermals and snow boots.' I'd picked up a pair of amazing snow boots that looked like yetis' feet. The best thing was I wouldn't need to keep them pristine and clean – they'd be full of dirt soon, as I trekked through mountains, snow and ice. I'd be out in the wind and the water and surrounded by nature. Best of all, I would finally get my country cottage.

I held up a windproof jacket. 'I need this kind of stuff for my wild wandering and travel. This kind of stuff makes me happy.'

Over the next few days, I was barely in the office except for a few hours, attending meetings to wrap everything up and hand it over to Phil.

I noticed Nick's office door was closed, and the lights were off. Someone said it was because he was planning for Macabre. But I didn't care. I was too busy planning for my Non Well-Behaved Woman Life, and I felt relieved that we wouldn't have to keep avoiding each other.

I didn't hang around at work that much, off at five on the dot every day. I was busy cleaning out my unit, and packing my life up, and trying to fit everything into boxes, as well as filling in forms for permanent visas and temporary visitor visas and going off to the American consulate for an interview to see if I could get into their country. Thankfully, I passed.

On Wednesday, my third last day at Maker, Glenn's EA Kerry brought me down some flowers and a generous gift card to say thank you and goodbye. It was almost as much as my weekly salary.

At the shops, I bought a new long coat that was thick and wool and would be perfect on a chilly autumn day. I used the rest of the gift card to buy sensible waterproof shoes and pants, a new fry pan for Mum – the one she'd been banging on about – some boardshorts for Dad (no budgie smugglers, please), and finally, I bought an expensive bottle of Champagne and a card with a naked cartoon woman. Inside I wrote, *Dear Betty, I'm leaving to do what we wild women do best – explore and adventure. Here's to being us. So much love, Emma.*

On Thursday, Nick was back at work. And he was glowing. Glowing as if he had been having one of those oxygen facials every day, or on a clean-eating detox (who did that to themselves?), or – most likely – he'd been sleeping with Honey or Chloe, or both together, and planning a new polygamy sect.

'Emma, can I have a word?' he called from his office door. It was the first sentence he'd uttered to me in days.

I called back, 'Sorry, Nick, I'm really pushed for time.'

An hour later, he saw me chatting with Phil in the kitchen, and smiled warmly at us both. 'Emma, congratulations, I, um, heard about your move. I'm not sure I said it before. I really need to talk to you before you go.'

I looked up at him. 'I've already sent you a list of all the handover items, where everything is up to. The hit rates. The market saturation. The customer feedback on the new logo. Social media hashtags around the new collaboration. IAH's feedback. Everything. If you need anything else just shoot me an email.' I smiled. Untouchable.

Phil looked at me wide-eyed. Then at Nick, as if he were watching a game of tennis.

Nick said, 'OK,' but didn't sound convinced and left the kitchen.

'What is going on?' Phil demanded. 'Why are you being so mean to McDreamy?'

'I can't tell you.'

'Oooohhhh!' he squealed, clapping his hands together. 'I smell gossip.'

'No, it's not that.' I shook my head. 'Just some people have another side, and when you see that, well, then you find it hard to see the good in them at all.'

He leaned forward on his hand. 'I'm intrigued. Spill.'

I ruffled his hair. 'Not this time, champ.'

On Thursday night Nick left two voicemails, asking if I would *please* call him back. I didn't.

Friday was Macabre day, and also my last day in the office. I packed up the last of my things, gave back my keys to cupboards I didn't think I'd ever opened and endured a cringy farewell party with the entire team, where they all said they thought I was amazing. (Glenn failed to admit he'd thought I was the coffee girl and couldn't remember my name for the first few weeks.)

'I'm kinda glad you're going, coffee girl – the coffee you made was always crap!' Phil teased.

I rolled my eyes. 'Yeah, yeah, I get it. You'll miss me. And on the plus side you're getting my job! More work and hardly a skerrick more pay!' I laughed.

'Yes, get out, whilst the real star takes over.' But his face got serious. 'I'll miss you.'

He reached out and gave me a big hug.

'Don't worry, you always have the copy boy Kevin to hug if you get sad.'

'Ear wax,' I mouthed. Phil looked as if he was going to vomit.

Bunches of flowers – too many to carry – lined my desk. A stack of balloons and a card. People really went to such an effort even for someone they'd never spoken to. At 4 p.m. I left, trying to juggle all the cards and flowers down to my Uber waiting below.

Beth and Bel both came out from Reception to help me pop them in the boot. On account of their kindness I snuck them both the smaller bouquets and said, 'Enjoy.'

'Thank you,' they twittered like loving little birds, waving before heading back into the building, just as Nick rushed out of the elevator.

'Emma!' he called loudly, opening the foyer door and spilling out into the street.

He ran over to me. 'Did you get my voicemails?'

'I saw some missed calls,' I said not looking at him as I put the last bouqet in the boot.

'You didn't call me back?'

'No, I didn't.' I closed the boot.

Nick was standing there staring at me, like some puppy-faced Daniel Cleaver. But I'd seen Bridget Jones enough to know apologies meant nothing. It was a waste of time to even listen to whatever excuses he had. 'I really need to speak to you.'

'About?'

'About us.'

I laughed hollowly. 'I think I'll take a pass.'

'But you don't understand—'

I put my hand up. 'There is no us. You made that really, really clear. There's a you and – well, who knows, really? And now there's a me and Alaska. That's it.'

320

'But, Em—'

'No, Nick. You don't get to talk to me now.'

I felt giddy. Who was this take-charge girl who didn't want a partner? Scratch out Step 3. Screw being well behaved, or doing what everyone else expected me to do. And I didn't need him to say he was sorry about us – blah, blah, blah. I got into the backseat of the taxi before he could say anything else, closing the door.

As I did I looked up at his face, which genuinely looked concerned, and I felt a twinge of sadness for a second that it hadn't worked out between us. Because we had had a wonderful connection. Better than anything I'd ever experienced. Suddenly, I didn't trust myself to hear what he had to say, and didn't trust what I'd do. I could feel him still standing there, as if he was going to open the door and get in after me. So, I locked it. And before he could say another thing, I leaned forward and, just as they did in the movies, I said to the driver, 'Drive. Quickly.'

Chapter 28

The business-class lounge was decadent – thank you frequent flyer points from all those years of travelling. I'd been offered a glass of Champagne as soon as I entered, and was now nibbling on some grapes and a slice of Brie by the window, staring out on Sydney and her lights glowing in the early evening.

My parents had dropped me at the airport – and how different it had felt from when I'd left the last time, seven years ago. How different I felt now, from just last week, when I was still another Maker clone.

Today, instead of wearing a white silk singlet, and black cigarette pants – my uniform the last few months – I was in an old vintage Ralph Lauren red knit jumper I'd managed to find at the bottom of a box in my cupboard, tight blue jeans and white tennis flats.

Due to finally giving up my chip, wine and mac and cheese late-night-snack habit, now that I was actually *happy*, the weight had literally dropped off me in the last week. I somehow managed to fit into my size twelve jeans with almost absolute perfection. No tightness. No circulation being cut off. My hair was piled up into a messy bun and I had on zero make-up. Not a bit.

I sighed happily. I was going. *Leaving*. To go to my dream life. For real.

Everything about it had seemed so rushed, so quick, I hadn't stopped to catch my breath. Until now. I checked my watch: 7 p.m. The Macabre event would just about be starting. The red carpet would be filling up with all the guests, the caterers would be running around like crazy, pots and pans clattering in a steamy kitchen, the giant multicoloured skulls would be hanging from the ceiling, with candles in their eyes, and I felt relieved that I wasn't there. That scene had never been me. Too glamorous. Too stuffy. Too fake.

I sipped some more Champagne. What a relief it would be when I got on that plane, stretched out in business class, watched *Bridget Jones's Baby* twice, and drooled as much as I wanted, without having to worry that someone like Nick or Honey was going to pop out of their perfection pod and discuss the plain girl with the big (now medium-sized) bum. In fact, I could walk around without worrying about bumping into him on the streets. Or at work functions. Or awkwardly avoiding him in the office. In fact, I never had to think about him ever again.

'Emma.' I was thinking about Nick so much I could actually hear his voice in my head, saying my name.

'Emma.'

I shook my head. I could *not* go loopy just hours before Alaska.

'Emma.'

Someone touched my right shoulder and I jumped a little. Turning around, I was startled to find myself facing Nick.

My mouth fell open. 'What. On. Earth. Are. You. Doing. Here?'

He was wearing tight dark blue jeans, a white shirt, blue blazer, brown loafers and a dark grey scarf tied around his neck. His dark blond hair was styled in a windswept way. I could see the girls on nearby couches turning around to get a better look. I caught a whiff of his smell – leather, coconut and minty man soap. At his feet was a large duffel bag, with an airport tag on it. He was clearly on his way somewhere, and what were the actual chances our planes were leaving on the same day, at around the same time? Thanks, fate. Thanks a lot.

'I needed to talk to you.'

'Couldn't you have just emailed me?' I drummed my fingers on the table in front of me. I couldn't believe he was there. He was the last person I wanted to see.

'No.'

'Why?' My mind started racing. What was so important he needed to see me? Had I stuffed something up? Did I forget something with Macabre?

'I needed to ask something.'

'Which is why you could have used email. It's a trusty little technological solution for when the other person doesn't want to talk to you.' I held up my phone to show him how easy it was. 'Besides, shouldn't you be at Macabre?' I said pointedly.

'Yes. Probably. Well, no.' He looked nervous. 'Can I sit?' He motioned to the chair opposite me.

Kate Mathieson

'No.'

He cleared his throat and kept standing, which was slightly annoying, because he was very tall, and that meant I had to look up at him. I don't think I remembered him being this tall. 'Well, firstly, I wanted to apologise for yelling at you. I was stressed and frustrated when I found out about everything, but that's no excuse. I'm sorry, Emma.'

I scoffed and took a sip of my Champagne. '*That's* what you want to apologise for?'

He stood there awkwardly for a second, shifting on his heels, before he said, 'Emma, I've been trying to tell you this for a while now.'

He paused and rubbed his hands together.

'Spit it out,' I said without looking at him.

'I like you.' He cleared his throat. 'I really like you. I always have.'

I stared out of the window. 'I think it's a little late for this, Nick.'

'I hope not.'

I spun back around towards him. 'Well, actually, Nick, there are many reasons why it's a little late. Firstly, this is my trip to Alaska, and you can't spoil it by turning up and making this about you. Secondly, you had a chance with me, in fact several times, but you blew it. And thirdly, you think I'm a liar, about *everything*,' I said, throwing his own words back at him.

He looked extremely uncomfortable, which, I had to admit, I was quite enjoying. 'Actually, Emma, there's a bit more to that story, some gaps, that we've never really discussed. And I wanted a chance to fill them.'

I looked down at my watch. 'Well, you have twenty minutes until I board. And you can take no more than five of them. I have Champagne that needs to be drunk, and some emails to send.'

He nodded. 'OK, well, I came to just say something that I've been trying to tell you since I saw you in the foyer of Maker that first day. I liked you when we met in Fiji. When I saw you at the bar that first time, I couldn't help noticing you ...' he hesitated.

I shook my head. 'I'm not the kind of girl that gets noticed in a bar, so don't give me that story. Like you think this is some *rom-com*.' I dropped the last bit in there so he'd realise how silly he sounded.

'You were to me.' He leaned forward slightly to emphasise his point. I could see the pulse in his throat. 'There was something about you. And then I saw you at the bar downing whiskies. You were hilarious. Sassy. You told me you wore a Goddamn pink swimming cap doing aqua aerobics with people three times your age. You didn't care at all what anyone thought about you. That your mum was trying to fix you up with men in the pool that you didn't want a bit of.'

'Well, they tried to drown me,' I said huffily.

'Yes, sassy then and sassy now. But also lovely.' He looked at me. 'So lovely.'

I was lovely?

'And we had the best night. Didn't we? Do you remember that swim at the beach?'

'Naked crazy swim,' I mumbled, shaking my head.

'Yes, that naked crazy swim on the beach. Do you remember everything we spoke about that night?'

I shook my head. I could, but I didn't want to admit it.

'We spoke about life, Emma. About the universe. You said your favourite planet was Saturn because you were sure it rained diamonds.'

I tried not to smile. 'I did say that, didn't I?'

'You did. You said you love dogs, but you couldn't get another one, because when your retriever died it crushed you for years. You said that you write in a journal. That you dream of living in a cottage ...'

'With chickens and a veggie patch,' I said haughtily. 'So you've made your point – you have a good memory.'

'Emma ... I ...'

I stared at him, and could tell he was nervous. His voice started wavering a little. I was enjoying it a little – actually, a lot.

He continued, 'I really liked you, and I wanted it to be something real, not just a one-night thing. But you left the next morning after I made you breakfast. I wanted to take you for a walk to the beach, have a seafood lunch. Get to know you more.'

Was he about to go over everything in our past with a fine-tooth comb? Because that was going to take a long time. Could we speed it up? I had a flight to catch. I really needed another Champagne, or perhaps something stronger to get me through this very strange and weird moment. I mean, what boss in their right mind found their ex-employee at the airport and started talking about their one night in Fiji?

And the more he talked about how lovely I was, the harder it was to forget how it felt when he kissed me. When he held me. *Right, that's it, Emma*, I chided myself, *you will not let him Daniel Cleaver his way back into your life or your pants.*

'You had my mobile number and I didn't have yours.' He paused. 'And you never called.'

'I called.' I said. 'I texted and I called, and I sat at a restaurant done up like a trussed-up turkey at Thanksgiving.'

'I didn't get a call?' He looked bewildered, astonished.

'Because you can't write. Your ones and sevens. You have horrible chicken scrawl.' I said with disdain.

'You called.' He smiled then, not a nervous smile, but a large genuine one. 'You liked me too.'

'Oh, stop looking so smug. I liked you for a bit. Sure. But that was then, and this is now.'

'I hoped you'd call me, when we got back to Sydney, but when I didn't hear from you, I thought you didn't like me. Even though I couldn't stop thinking about you. The feeling on the beach wasn't something I'd had before. I felt like I'd found someone I could be myself with.' He paused.

I remembered that feeling he was talking about, but that was before he decided to sleep with me and then *leave*. And before I'd found out about Honey and Chloe. Where the *hell* was that waiter?

He shrugged. 'Then I got a new job, and when I walked in and saw you there, I couldn't believe it. I was going to tell you that it seemed like the universe was putting us in one spot, for some reason—'

I held up my hand. 'But if you liked me *so* much,' I said, feeling great that I was catching him in his own lie, 'why did you completely shut me down and talk about seating charts?'

He looked slightly hurt. 'You told me you regretted saying you wanted to be with me.'

Oh, yes. I had done that. But it was because I had been trying not to fall for him, not because I hadn't wanted to be with him.

He continued, 'And I just agreed, because I felt I'd misread the entire situation. Sure, we had banter, and a connection, but I didn't know how to read it. And when I heard you planning dates with Phil, I thought you didn't consider me like that.'

'I didn't,' I said stubbornly.

'You didn't?' he said softly. 'It seemed to me like maybe you did. When we hugged at the cemetery.'

'You hugged me,' I stated plainly.

'Yes, but you leaned into me, and, and ... didn't you feel that too?'

I didn't answer.

'Then things got confusing, yes, we hugged, but I didn't know if you were still dating other guys, or if you liked Lachlan Groves.'

'Lachlan Groves,' I practically spat. 'Disgusting.' Then I added honestly, 'Well, I didn't know if you were dating Honey or—'

'Honey!' he exclaimed. 'Where did you get that idea?'

'Let me see, there was the dinner at Oil and Salt. Oh, the doggy date at the park, apparently about "work" when Honey was supposed to be at the spa, the way she looked at you, when you were together—'

Nick interrupted. 'Emma, for the record, I wasn't with Honey. I've never been with Honey. And I don't want to be with Honey. The reason I went to dinner with her is because Glenn told us to give her everything she wanted. Yes, she was flirting a little with me, but she did it with everyone. I even saw her do it with you, Emma. She'd give you the wide-eyed look, and ask sweetly for something. Same as she did with me. I want you to know, it was work – and nothing more. And the park was because Tom had taken photos of her being in a rather messy state when she met some marketing guy, who'd taken her out and got her drunk, and she had begged me to help her fix it, without telling anyone. She found me at the park that day. I was there with Sherlock, and then suddenly she was talking to me about photos and dancing on bar tops and kissing someone, and asking all these questions about who Sherlock was, and then suddenly you were there. Nothing else.'

Oh, the marketing guy. I did remember something like that. I'd thought she meant Nick. Oops. 'Well, what about a little text message I happened to see? "*When are you coming over?*" sent to you at MIDNIGHT.'

'Emma, how many times has Honey sent you that text message, when she's bored?'

I sat back and realised he was right. She'd sent me that text at all times during the day and night, including the kiss after it. God, it was a copy and paste. 'But she sent it to your personal phone,' I pointed out.

'Yes, as you know, Honey has a habit of getting what she wants, including my personal number courtesy of Glenn and HR. You wouldn't know anything about that though, would you?' he said with a cheeky smile, which then faded. 'How do you know about Honey's text?'

'Well, she's not the only one I know about, Nick. What about *Chloe?*' *There, explain your way out of this one,* I thought.

'Chloe? Chloe?' he spluttered. 'Chloe's my sister!'

'Your sister?' My entire body went numb.

'Yes, Emma, my sister.' He fumbled in his pocket and grabbed his phone, scrolling through it and then holding it up. 'See, there's a photo of her with me, and her husband, and her two children. Here's another one of her with my mum.' They did look rather alike, blonde hair, gorgeous, the same eyes.

Nick continued. 'And I left that morning because I got a call that Mum was in hospital and Chloe needed me to get there asap. I didn't have time to tell you, or let you know, or leave a note. I should have and I'm sorry – but I had other things on my mind. And then my phone ran out of battery at the hospital and I didn't even get to charge it until the next day. I'm sorry, I was an absolute jerk for leaving you alone. I admit that. Hands up. I want you to know this, if this is the only thing you take with you.'

'Your *sister,*' I repeated numbly.

'Yes, my sister. Do you want to call her and ask?' He offered his phone to me.

I shook my head, not able to say a word, feeling extremely ... *guilty*. Was this true? Had I been totally off base? Was Nick really a lovely guy, who looked after sick people's dogs, and his mum in hospital, rather than a cheating chauvinist?

'Is your mum OK?' I asked, trying to let everything he'd said sink in.

'Yes.' He smiled. 'Thank you, she's fine now. On blood pressure medication and thankfully everything is fine.'

Then his smile faded. 'Wait a second. How do you know about Honey's text? And Chloe's texts?'

'I saw your personal phone,' I said sheepishly. 'But in my defence, it was the day you left me all alone in your apartment and you left your phone. I heard something was buzzing. And there it was.'

'Stalker,' he teased.

'Leaver,' I retorted.

'Well, I didn't leave for long. That night I went straight to the mixer because I knew you were going, my phone had died, the Uber driver didn't have a charger so I couldn't call you, and I wanted so badly to see you.'

Nick cleared his throat and kept talking. 'I felt that there was always something between us, but I just didn't know where you stood. After our night together, I thought it was pretty clear for both of us. But as soon as I walked in, I saw you with Lachlan at the food table. It looked like he was feeding you, then you were laughing with him and going outside. It got me pretty riled up. To make matters worse, he walked out of there without his shirt on, and I could only imagine what you guys had been doing.'

'He tried to feed me – and failed. Then I laughed at how

lame he was. Finally, a waiter crashed into him with some Champagne, hence the no-shirt thing,' I explained.

'I thought you'd realised you'd made a huge mistake at my house. And you didn't want to be with me. And then the next morning, that huge stuff up with Hive happened. I got so mad, and, well, I was angry at you for liking Lachlan, and it all just came out at once. And I'm truly sorry for yelling at you. For the record, I don't think you're a corporate queen.' He smiled ruefully.

I was trying not to look at his eyes, because they would suck me in, because he was beautiful, because he was standing here, apologising and undoing all the horrible things I'd ever thought about him.

There were a thousand thoughts in my head, and my body felt flushed. Besides, I wasn't sure how I felt now – how did I feel? Still angry? Hurt? Even a bit ... *excited*. Oh, no. But I'd been excited about Nick before, and look where that had got me. And now, we had two different lives: he was staying in Sydney, and I was about to live in an icy igloo (well, probably a warm insulated house, but still) and there would be thousands of miles between us.

I licked my lips and went to say something, then thought better of it. Finally, Nick said, 'Spit it out, Emma.'

I took a deep breath. 'I ... uh ... I don't want to sound rude or selfish here, but couldn't you have just texted my mobile that morning, letting me know where you were? Or left a voicemail. Or a quick little note that said, "Urgent – had to go, talk soon". I know you were thinking of your mum, but, Nick, I woke up in my boss' house. Alone. After we'd had sex, and not talked about it. And then you went AWOL. And I felt so ... so ... horrible and used.'

'You're right, I should have. I'm sorry.' He looked down at his shoes as though he was really unsure. It was the first time I'd seen that in him. 'Honestly, Emma, that night with you scared me. I felt feelings I really hadn't in a long time, maybe not at all, *ever*.'

I nodded, because I'd felt that too.

Nick continued, 'I did want to be with you. Being with you that night was amazing. Too amazing. All those feelings rushed back, of being cheated on, being lied to, being left, and they scared the hell out of me. Maybe that's also a bit of the reason I didn't text you earlier that morning.' He paused. 'I felt vulnerable, and I didn't want to get hurt again.'

'So you decided to hurt someone else?'

He looked shocked, as if it was finally registering. 'I did. I'm so sorry, Emma.' He paused. 'Maybe we were both just scared.'

'You were scared, Nick. *You*,' I said with a frown on my face. 'I was willing to go for it.'

'Oh, were you?' he challenged me. 'When you went on dates with other people that were clearly very wrong for you, when you gave me an entire spiel about being left at the altar and how terrible vanilla people were. You may as well have had a big "I'm scared" sign on your forehead.'

Was he right? I thought about it quickly, and realised with surprise that he was. I *had* stepped back from him. And I'd thought it was because he was my boss, but now I realised it was because I liked him so much. I was scared. Petrified. 'I'm sorry Nick.'

'Maybe we understand each other because of what we had both been through,' he admitted honestly. 'And I think we've both lied to each other enough, don't you?'

I nodded and found myself feeling a little disappointed that he'd be getting on a plane to ... to wherever he was going soon.

I looked up at the departure screen, then at my watch. A call came over the lounge PA, announcing final boarding for Sydney to LA.

'Well, that's me,' I said, feeling as if I was unable to tear myself away from where I was sitting, stand and leave. 'Looks like you used up more than five minutes.' I smiled. 'But I'm glad you did. I'm glad we talked, and are leaving on a good note. And I'm glad that we can now be ... civil.' I was going to say friends, but I didn't know if he wanted that, and the thought of only being his friend made me feel sad. It wasn't what I really wanted.

I stood and picked up my bag. And since there really wasn't anything else to say, I added, 'And I hope you have a safe flight, wherever you're headed.'

He paused, grabbed the rest of my Champagne and took a large gulp. 'Wait. Before you go, I have to say this.' He cleared his throat. 'When I found out you were going to Alaska, I knew I couldn't lose you again. It kicked me into gear over the last few days. I had to do something, and, well, here I am.'

I held up my hand as if to say 'wait a second' and said

336

jokingly, 'Are you going to say something like I'm just a boy, standing here in front of a girl, asking her to love him?'

He laughed. 'Actually, I am.'

My stomach dropped. 'What?'

He took a step closer to me. 'It was you from the start, Emma Londstown. I just didn't know you felt the same. And I wanted to make sure everything was perfect, before I did actually ask you out on a date. And things haven't been perfect. But that's how life is.'

He looked around nervously. 'So I came here to tell you that I like you. Really like you. Perhaps, maybe, even, love you.'

'Oh,' I said faintly, losing my ability to speak.

'I can't stop thinking about you. I never could. And I know this might come late, too late, because I've used up my five-minute quota, but, Emma, would you go on a date with me?'

I could feel my cheeks burning up. My knees felt a bit wobbly. I wasn't sure I trusted my voice not to squeak when I spoke.

'Well, Mr Taylor, I'd like to tell you it's highly unprofessional for a manager to ask out an employee, because today's my last day, so technically, I still work at Maker until midnight. Also, that date would have to be in Alaska, seeing as I am going to be living there very shortly.'

'It's a good thing that I'm not your boss any more. In fact, as of ...' he looked down at his watch '... two hours ago, I don't work at Maker.'

'*What?*'

'Emma, I'd do anything for a date with you.'

'So where are you going?' I pointed to his carry-on duffel bag, feeling all my resistance drop away.

'I was kinda hoping to live somewhere outside the city. Like, a country cottage. In the cold and the snow. With a veggie patch and—'

'Chickens,' I said breathlessly.

'And hopefully my most favourite person.' We locked eyes. 'That's you, by the way.'

He stepped towards me ever so slightly, lifted his hand, and gently pushed some hair out of my eyes, his fingertips stroking my cheek.

'Wait.' I held up my hand, stopping him from moving any closer and taking a step back. 'What will you *do* in Alaska?' I was *not* going to be some sugar momma, particularly because I couldn't, not on my salary.

'I hear some of the towns need some help with the local marketing and events for a spring festival, and I think I have a bit of experience with that.'

'But you'll have to live on a measly salary. Not in a penthouse.'

'Possibly on baked beans.' He smiled.

I nodded. 'And old, stale bread.'

'I think I can handle it. We'll have a toaster, right? They have those there?' he teased. 'Or else we could sell the penthouse, and the Fijian timeshare, and build something kinda wonderful, you know, ourselves.'

He went to step forward again.

'Wait!' I said to him again, stopping him from getting any closer.

'Something else you should know – I'm a bird, not a tree!'
He looked very confused. 'I'll explain that later. And I'm not
a well-behaved woman. And I don't ever want to be one,' I
said defiantly. 'I get chips in my hair. I drink too much on
dates. I wear Ugg boots. I drool in my sleep. I want to have a
country cottage, where I grow old. But I also want to pack it
all in and travel the world if I feel like it. And live in small
huts without electricity. I want to do handstands on the beach
under the moonlight. And aqua aerobics in pink petal caps.
And I want to swim with whales. Who don't wear pink petal
caps. Or maybe they do. I don't like wearing high heels. Or
silk shirts. I'm not like Donna or Sadie or—'

'I know. I know all of that, Emma,' he said, looking at me
and stroking my cheek with his finger. 'You're not a Maker
clone. Thank goodness. You're bold. You're a bit nuts. You're
you.' He grinned. 'That's what I love most about you.'

'You love me?' My heart fluttered.

'With all my heart, Emma Londstown. I tried my hardest
not to. But I couldn't help it. There was someone who once
told me, when you know you know. Even if it's only been a
week.'

I grinned. 'That person sounds very wise.'

I felt the intensity of his eyes staring at me. I let his fingers
trail down my neck.

'Now will you please stop telling me to wait, and let me
kiss you?'

He pulled me close, so our bodies pressed together. I felt
the firmness of his chest beneath his shirt. His breath on my
neck, warm and smelling of Champagne. And when I couldn't

wait any longer, he leaned slightly forward, both hands on my cheeks, holding my face. My breath caught. Our lips met. When he kissed me I forgot to breathe. Every part of my body, our bodies, melted into each other.

When we finally pulled away, my heart beating so loudly, I thought my ribs would break. He smiled at me and whispered, 'Shall we go to Alaska?'

I nodded. 'Yes, let's.'

THE END

Acknowledgements

To my tireless and wonderful mum and dad, who slightly inspired Lorna and Ted, but are much kinder, calmer versions of them, thank you for supporting me in every weird and wacky adventure I have embarked upon, including the times I quit work, travelled the world and wanted to call myself a writer. Without your love and support (and the use of your second bedroom), I'd be lost. I love you mum and dad.

Thank you Charlotte my wonderful publisher, Emily my amazing editor, and the team at One More Chapter – you've been a delight to work with. Thank you for helping me craft Emma and Nick so well that I almost think they are real, and could bump into them on the streets of Sydney (or Alaska).

To Jane and Spot, for the many laughs at Kyushu's and reminding me that a relationship over 20 years can still be full of humour and love.

To Jean, and the Flix Chix girls, our monthly wine and movie nights (and sordid tellings of the things we've done in our lives), have given me plenty of ideas for the next book. You guys are one in a million.

To my closest friend Tara, who I've known since I was 3,

30, and hopefully 90. We have our own soul language and there's a special bond that can never be broken. P.s. Shall we take that trip to New York now?

In all the vastness of the world, and all the billions of people you can meet, it was a sheer delight that I happened to meet Sean. Thank you, Sean, for your everyday chats, and for supporting this wild heart who can't be tamed. If there was one person I had to be stuck in hell with – it would be him; he'd protect me, make me laugh, hold my hand, figure out a plan to get us elsewhere, and demand coffee. Finger hugs, Sean. I like you just the way you are.